Sandra's phone buzz

It was a text from Ma

**No sign of Ellie but her car is still in the parking lot. Either she left on foot or she is still somewhere in the building.**

Sandra took Lucas by the hand. "Come on, you can help me look for her."

They checked all the classrooms, the teachers' lounge, the remaining restrooms, even the administration offices, to no avail. Finally, after a thorough search of the premises, Sandra was about to give up when she noticed at the far end of the hall, a door slightly ajar.

"What's that?" Sandra asked.

"A supply closet. It's usually locked. Only the teachers and janitorial staff have keys."

Sandra's heart pounded as they slowly approached.

She gripped the door handle and swung it open.

"Whoa!" Lucas cried.

Sandra threw a hand to her mouth, suppressing a scream.

Lying on the floor in a heap was the crumpled-up body of Ellie Duncan.

And the despised spelling bee coordinator was most definitely dead . . .

# Murder at the Spelling Bee

*Lee Hollis*

Kensington Publishing Corp.
www.kensingtonbooks.com

# Murder at the
# Spelling Bee

# Chapter 1

"Someone is threatening my son," Eugenio Fanelli said with a pained expression, squeezing the hand of his wife, Lucia, as they sat close together on the couch in the private detective offices of Maya Kendrick and Sandra Wallage.

Maya leaned back in her chair behind the desk. "How so?"

Eugenio glanced at his wife, who appeared to be near tears, and squeezed her hand before turning back to the two detectives. "There was a note left in his locker. He didn't want us to know about it. But Lucia found it when she was picking up laundry in Rocco's bedroom."

Sandra, who was perched on top of the edge of Maya's desk, leaned forward, clasping her hands in front of her. "What did the note say?"

Eugenio reached into his coat pocket and extracted a folded-up piece of paper, which he handed over to Sandra. She opened it to read the words *Drop out or die* scribbled in red ink.

Sandra raised her eyes, confused. "Drop out of what?"

Eugenio paused and took a deep breath before answering. "The South Portland Middle School Spelling Bee."

Maya, who had just taken a sip from her mug of coffee, practically spat it out. "This is about a *spelling bee?*"

Eugenio nodded. "Yes. Last year Rocco placed second in the state competition, and this year he has been crushing his competition in all the early practice sessions. He is pretty much the odds-on favorite to go on to nationals."

"I had no idea spelling bees were so cutthroat," Sandra marveled.

"You have *no* idea," Lucia mumbled, sniffing.

Sandra had never met the Fanelli family. Her own two sons were much older than Rocco, so their paths had never crossed at PTA meetings or any other school functions. Eugenio and Lucia were both compact-size people with dark hair and olive skin. Although Eugenio was born in Chicago and Lucia in Worcester, Massachusetts, before they met at college in Poughkeepsie and got married, both their grandparents had emigrated from Italy, and they shared a true, authentic Sicilian background. Sandra could easily detect the deep bond they shared, holding hands, eyeing the other before speaking.

"We had no idea about Rocco's talent for spelling. He came so close last year but tripped up on 'Chihuahua.' The poor kid was devastated. To make matters worse, it was one of his practice words. He knew how to spell it. But he got so excited when he heard it, he raced through it too quickly and missed one of the *h*s. It did such a number on his confidence, but we eventually got him back on track, and now he's been on a big winning streak."

"You must be very proud of him," Sandra said, smiling.

They both nodded. "Before me and Lucia, no one in our family had ever even gone to college. We both come from a long line of butchers and bakers, very working class, back in Italy. When our grandparents first moved here, they broke their backs working to give their children a better life and our parents did the same. When Rocco was born the whole family pinned a lot of hopes and dreams on him, and he has exceeded all our expectations. He's a true miracle. A real intellect. Mark my words, this kid is going places."

"He sounds like an amazing boy," Sandra remarked.

Lucia sat up. "He is. But I'm afraid this threat is going to destroy his confidence again, and he might drop out. That would be such a shame because he has worked so hard to get to this point."

Eugenio nodded in agreement. "He's been so excited about the spelling bee this year . . . until he received that note. And now he's been acting quiet and withdrawn. We're both very worried about him."

"So you want to hire us to find out who wrote the note and left it in Rocco's locker?" Maya asked.

"Yes. What if this person decides to step up his

efforts, perhaps even stage some kind of physical attack?" Lucia asked, shuddering at the prospect.

"You know, pull a Tonya Harding," Eugenio added. "We can't just stand by doing nothing and risk that happening."

Both Maya and Sandra were keenly aware of the historical reference. Back in 1994, Olympic ice skater Tonya Harding's trashy husband contracted his dimwit buddy to literally knee-cap the competition by whacking rival skater Nancy Kerrigan in the thigh with an expandable baton after a practice session, although Harding consistently denied any knowledge of the attack.

Sandra studied the note. The writing looked as if a five-year-old child had scribbled it. But she knew an adult would most likely try to disguise his or her handwriting with this kind of obvious chicken scratch.

"Why don't we bring Rocco in now?" Maya said.

Eugenio and Lucia had parked their son outside in the hallway with his phone to play games while the adults discussed this very serious situation.

Sandra hopped down from the edge of the desk and crossed to the door, opening it. "Rocco, would you mind joining us now?"

An adorable twelve-year-old boy with a mop of curly black hair, thick dark glasses, and olive skin similar to his parents, shuffled in, head down as he clutched his phone, staring at the small screen.

"What are you playing?" Sandra asked.

"Wordle," the boy mumbled.

"Why don't you have a seat on the couch with your mom and dad," Sandra suggested.

Without looking up from his phone, Rocco plopped down on the couch between his mother and father. His fingers tapped the screen at incredible speed.

"Put that away now, okay, slugger?" Eugenio said firmly.

The boy ignored him.

Finally, Eugenio reached over and plucked the phone out of his son's hand, pocketing it. Rocco was left with no choice but to finally acknowledge Maya and Sandra.

"We hear you are a pretty impressive speller," Maya said.

Rocco shrugged. "I'm okay."

"You must be better than okay. You've been slaying the competition," Sandra chirped.

He shrugged again. "Just in the practice sessions. It'll just get harder at county and then the state contest, if I even make it that far."

His parents were right.

His confidence was wavering.

A sobering development for any prospective champion.

Confidence was always key to winning.

Sandra circled around the desk next to Maya and opened a desk drawer. She pulled out a Tupperware container and walked back over to the Fanelli family, unsealing the top. "I baked some chocolate chip cookies this morning before I came in. Care to try one?"

Maya rolled her eyes, chuckling. Of course Sandra was up at the crack of dawn baking cookies, while Maya kept slapping the palm of her hand down on the Snooze button of her old-fashioned alarm clock while still buried underneath her heavy goose-down comforter.

Rocco studied the cookies, then picked the biggest one, taking a huge bite. Sandra then offered one to Eugenio and Lucia, who both politely declined.

Rocco chomped loud enough that his mother gently squeezed his arm and whispered in his ear, "Don't chew so loud. It's not polite."

Rocco swallowed, then took another bite of the cookie, this time trying to munch more quietly.

"Rocco, your parents tell us someone left a note in your locker at school," Maya said. "Do you have any idea who that person might have been?"

The boy stopped chewing as if he was trying to figure out the best way to respond. Then he abruptly shook his head. "Nope." He let out a deep, heartfelt sigh, his shoulders slumping. "But it was no big deal. I don't know why we're even here."

"He's embarrassed. He doesn't like to be the center of attention or get any kind of special treatment. It makes him very self-conscious," Eugenio explained. "But it's the exact opposite when he's spelling. It's like he's in his own world, very focused; he tends to tune out the rest of the world."

Rocco sighed, annoyed, and turned to his father. "Why do you have to talk like I'm not even in the room?"

"Your parents are just worried, Rocco," Sandra said soothingly. "The person who slipped that note in your locker did a very bad thing. We all just want to make sure you stay safe."

"I know," Rocco grumbled, kicking the base of

the couch with the heels of his sneakers. Then he sighed again and turned to his father. "Can I have my phone back? I just thought of a word with a lot of vowels."

His Wordle game.

That was his top priority right now.

His father gave up, reached into his pocket, and tossed his son the phone. Rocco was immediately glued to the screen and already tuning them out.

"So, will you take the case?" Eugenio asked expectantly. "Will you find the person who wrote that note?"

Maya could tell the Fanellis were not a family of means, and if they were going to take on this case, they would probably have to give them some kind of a discount on their services. It was no secret their relatively new PI firm needed more high-paying clients to cover all their bills and overhead, and they were in no position to take on any pro bono cases like all the fancy law firms in downtown Portland, but maybe they could make an exception just this one time. . . .

"Yes, we'll take the case," Sandra announced brightly.

"We can pay the upfront retainer fee," Eugenio said warily. "But as for the rest of it, maybe we can work out an installment plan?"

Sandra waved them off. "Don't worry about that. We can discuss all that later."

Maya smiled at their new clients. "You go home and we will be in touch once we have something."

Maya knew she did not have much of a choice now that Sandra, who was independently wealthy and never had to worry about paying any gas or heating bills, had made the decision to accept this case for them. But this was one instance where they would not have to argue about money because it was obvious to both Maya and Sandra that they shared a burning need to know what kind of person would stoop so low as to threaten the life of a twelve-year-old kid.

# Chapter 2

Lucas Cavill's handsome face lit up at the sight of Sandra sashaying through the door to his office in the athletic department of South Portland High School. He jumped to his feet, quickly circled around his desk, and grabbed Sandra by the hips with his large hands, pulling her in close for a sweet, romantic kiss. Sandra stiffened, signaling him with her eyes that she was not there alone. That was when Maya followed her in through the door with a knowing smirk. But Lucas could not resist even with a witness on hand. He leaned in, his pursed lips landing on Sandra's with a loud smack.

"Well, how did I get so lucky today?" Lucas cooed. It was obvious he was infatuated with Sandra.

She politely wriggled from his grasp, glancing back at Maya, who was enjoying her discomfort at such a public display of affection, especially in her son's high school, where Sandra once presided as PTA president.

"We're here on business," Sandra said hurriedly.

"I'm intrigued," Lucas said with a flirtatious wink.

Sandra had been dating the young athletic director for some months now. At first she had resisted his efforts to take her out on a date because she was going through a divorce from her husband of over twenty years, Senator Stephen Wallage. But Lucas finally had worn her down with his charm and innate kindness and overall enthusiasm. There was a big age difference between them, one Sandra described as a "chasm," but Lucas was relentless in his determination not to allow that to be an issue between them. He self-admittedly always had preferred the company of more mature women and kept reminding Sandra of that fact every time he saw her. Still, Sandra was over forty and Lucas was still in his late twenties, so she was hyperaware what people must be thinking when they were out in public together. Someone had called her a "cougar" once, a term she despised, finding it demeaning. But Lucas had just shrugged and advised her to simply ignore the naysayers.

"Do you still coach softball over at the middle school on Saturdays?" Sandra asked.

Lucas nodded. "Yes. But as things have gotten busier over here at the high school with baseball season, I've been considering pulling back on my other commitments, including the softball team, though I'd hate to disappoint the kids. They're awesome."

"So you must know people in the administration who would have access to any security footage," Sandra said.

"Sure. I mean, I'm not certain they would just hand something like that over to a part-time employee, but yeah, I could at least give it a shot and put in a request."

Sandra knew instinctively Lucas would come through for them. All he had to do was turn on that boyish charm, flash that winning smile with his perfect white teeth, give a wink with one of his ocean-blue eyes, and he could probably get his hands on just about anything, including nuclear secrets.

And she wasn't wrong.

By late that afternoon, Lucas called Sandra to let her know the principal, Birdie Munn, had agreed to allow her and Maya to review the footage from the day Rocco Fanelli had found the threatening note in his locker on one of the computers in the school library.

There were a handful of students reading books and writing essays and exchanging notes under the watchful eye of the stern, stone-faced librarian as Maya and Sandra, both standing out like sore thumbs among the prepubescent set, crowded each other in a small cubicle, eyes fixed on the outdated desktop computer screen.

Maya fast-forwarded through a throng of students filling up the hallway after getting dropped off by the school buses, chattering and laughing and chasing one another before the bell rang and they scattered, disappearing inside the classrooms, until the hallway was empty. Sandra had spotted Rocco at his locker, alone with no one nearby. He put his sack lunch inside, grabbed a textbook, slammed the locker shut, and then headed off, disappearing out of frame. Sandra tapped the fast-forward button once more, speeding up until the bell rang again and all the kids filed back into the hallway from the classrooms. They identified Rocco ambling back to his locker, but this time he was not alone. Another boy, taller and stockier, hovered behind him, stopping and loitering, his eyes peering over Rocco's shoulder as he spun the lock.

Sandra excitedly pointed at the screen. "Look, that kid's watching Rocco open his locker. He's memorizing the combination! Quick, fast-forward, let's see if he comes back."

The librarian behind the desk about ten feet away hissed, "Shhh!"

Sandra flipped around and mouthed the words, *I'm sorry.*

But the librarian was unmoved. She just bristled and focused a harsh gaze on Sandra, as if to say, *At your age, you should know better than to talk so loud in a library.*

Mortified, Sandra pivoted on her foot back toward the screen, where Maya had sped through more footage, landing on the end of the school day, when most kids were grabbing their knapsacks and heading outside to board the school buses for home. Rocco was stuffing his L.L.Bean Explorer backpack with a few heavy textbooks before slamming his locker shut and slipping his arms through the straps. A few moments later, the boy they had seen earlier reappeared. He took a swift look around to make sure no one was in the vicinity watching him, and then he input the combination, swung the locker door open, and surreptitiously dropped the folded note inside before shutting it again and hustling off before anyone noticed.

"We should show this to Principal Munn and find out who this kid is," Maya suggested.

"Shhh!"

Another warning from behind the library desk.

Sandra snickered and whispered, "Let's get out of here before we're sent to detention."

The two women downloaded the footage onto a thumb drive and went straight to Birdie Munn's office, where the principal took one look at the kid on the security cam and said, "Hunter Hamlin."

"Who is Hunter Hamlin?" Maya asked.

"A real troublemaker. He's been known to bully a few of the smaller kids in his class," Birdie explained. "We've been dealing with his behavioral issues for some time now. I thought we were making progress. It turns out Hunter is a very good speller, so we've been encouraging him to take part in the spelling bee, and he's been doing surprisingly well in all the practice rounds. His parents even called to thank me for giving their son a purpose, something to focus on besides video games and violent graphic novels. But obviously he's starting to revert back to his old ways."

"It looks as if he's nervous about the competition and wants to even the playing field by scaring off his top rival, Rocco," Maya surmised.

Birdie tapped some keys on her computer.

"Let's find out, shall we?" She stood up and crossed over to a speaker system, leaning in close to the microphone and pressing a button. "Hunter Hamlin, please report to Principal Munn's office. Repeat, Hunter Hamlin to the principal's office immediately." She released the button and rotated back toward Maya and Sandra. "That will no doubt put the fear of God in him. It's not the first time I've had to make that announcement."

Less than five minutes later, an uneasy, anxious Hunter Hamlin was escorted into the office and told to sit down in an empty chair in front of Principal Munn's desk. He apprehensively looked at Maya and Sandra, who stood off to the side, quietly observing.

Before he could ask who they were, Birdie clasped her hands together and leaned forward. "Hunter, I would like you to meet Mrs. Kendrick and Mrs. Wallage." She paused for dramatic effect. "They're private detectives."

This news seemed to startle Hunter. "Really?"

"Yes, we're investigating a crime here at the school," Maya said, staring at him impassively.

"A-A c-crime?" Hunter stammered.

"Someone left a threatening note in a student's locker," Sandra said, extracting the note from her bag and reading it aloud. " 'Drop out or die.' "

Hunter silently squirmed in his seat.

"Does that sound familiar to you?"

Hunter vigorously shook his head. "No."

Sandra cocked an eyebrow. "It doesn't?"

Hunter gazed guiltily straight ahead. "I said no!"

Birdie emitted a heavy sigh. "Come here, Hunter. I want to show you something."

Hunter hesitated, remaining planted in his seat.

"Hunter, if you refuse to cooperate, I can always call your parents and have them come down here right now," Birdie warned.

That did the trick.

Hunter was out of the chair like a shot and rounded the desk until he was in front of the desktop computer screen. He watched the footage of himself putting the folded-up piece of paper in Rocco Fanelli's locker.

Out of self-preservation, Hunter shouted, "That's not me!"

Birdie shook her head, disappointed. "Hunter, if you can't tell us the truth, I'm going to have to suspend you until you do. That is clearly you in the video."

"It must be some kind of deep fake!" His eyes shot back and forth between the principal and Maya and Sandra. He knew he had been caught red-handed. Finally, realizing he was out of options, he croaked, "Okay, it was me. I put the note in Rocco's locker. Please don't disqualify me from the spelling bee. My parents will kill me."

"Were you afraid of losing to Rocco? Is that why you threatened him?" Maya pressed.

Hunter's eyes widened. "What? No. I didn't write the note. I didn't even know what it said until just now."

"How is that possible?" Sandra asked skeptically.

"Someone put me up to it," Hunter murmured.

"Who?" Birdie demanded to know.

Hunter shrugged. "I don't know who it was, I swear. I was in history class the other day and I opened my book because we were reviewing the freedoms in the Bill of Rights and I found a twenty-dollar bill with instructions to leave a note inside Rocco's locker."

"Why didn't you just keep the twenty dollars and not do it?" Maya asked.

"Because the person said I would get another twenty-dollar bill once the job was done, so I went ahead and did it. I didn't know I was doing anything wrong."

"Do you honestly expect us to believe you didn't take a quick peek at the note before you slipped it in Rocco's locker?" Maya pressed.

"No! I thought maybe some girl in our class had a crush on him and it was some gooey love note! I didn't care! I just wanted the money! I've been saving for the new Super Smash Bros. game!" He nervously scanned the room, looking at them, hoping they believed him.

Sandra's gut told her the kid was telling them the truth.

Especially when he admitted that Rocco was helping him during the practice sessions with flash cards, which was supernice of him because Hunter had been known to bully Rocco in the past. The two were slowly starting to become actual friends.

As they listened to him, it became more obvious to Maya and Sandra that, despite Hunter being Rocco's rival in the spelling bee, he did not appear to have the drive to win at all costs; he just seemed happy to be participating. Which meant there had to be a third party determined to scare off Rocco with that death threat.

And the perpetrator was smart enough to know how to avoid the school's security cameras and remain anonymous.

They were back to square one.

# Chapter 3

As Sandra walked through the front door of her nineteenth-century New England Colonial–style, two-story home and kicked off her shoes, exhausted after a long day, she heard voices coming from the living room and a Dua Lipa song playing softly in the background. Her seventeen-year-old son Ryan was home and was no doubt canoodling with his girlfriend, Vanessa, who also happened to be Maya's teenage daughter. They had met independently from the friendship between their mothers, two years earlier as sophomores, and had been an item ever since. Although Sandra adored Vanessa, she suspected the romance might cool down once the two of them headed off to separate colleges in the fall. She paused in the foyer before going in to say hello.

Sandra suddenly felt a twinge of apprehension in the pit of her stomach. Ryan was going to graduate this year and move out. He had already been accepted to New York University in the Tisch School of the Arts program for acting, with a minor in political science as a nod to his father, the US senator from Maine. Her older son, Jack, was going to be in his second year at Boston College. Her soon-to-be ex-husband, Stephen, was now living full time in Washington, DC. She would be facing the empty nest syndrome in a matter of weeks, living all alone in this big, drafty house with the exception of the holidays and a handful of weekends, when her sons might pop in for a brief stay.

She wasn't sure how she was going to handle it. She had never been alone for any long period of time in her entire life. It was going to be a huge adjustment. She made a pact that when the time came she would throw herself into her work with Maya and just plow ahead, and maybe see where her relationship with Lucas might lead, although she was insisting to herself and others that she was a very long way from any kind of serious commitment.

As Sandra rounded the corner into the living room, she instantly sensed something was wrong. Ryan and Vanessa were huddled together on the couch. Vanessa had her arm around Ryan's shoulders. His face was flushed with anger, his eyes downcast. He was obviously in some kind of funk.

"Hey," Sandra said tentatively.

Vanessa looked up and offered her a wan smile. "Hey, Mrs. Wallage."

"What's going on?"

Ryan remained silent as Vanessa rubbed his back and spoke softly in his ear. "You should probably tell her."

Sandra's ears suddenly perked up. "Tell me what?"

Ryan folded his arms defiantly. "Never mind. It's my problem. I will take care of it."

Sandra could tell Vanessa really wanted him to confide whatever was bothering him to his mother, but he was being his usual stubborn self. Something he had no doubt picked up from his father.

Sandra was not about to give up. "Did something happen at school?"

Ryan kept his eyes fixed on the floor.

Vanessa silently nodded to Sandra. "Come on, Ryan," she coaxed. "Maybe your mom can help."

Ryan pursed his lips and wagged his head.

There was a long moment of silence.

Finally, Vanessa could not take it anymore. "He's failing a class and he might have to retake it over the summer, which means he won't be able to march down the aisle with his classmates at the graduation ceremony."

Sandra's heart leapt into her throat. "*What?*"

Ryan flashed Vanessa a peeved look. "Vanessa!"

"I'm sorry, but she's going to find out eventually. You might as well tell her now."

Sandra was utterly confused. Ryan had always been a capable and conscientious student, with mostly A's and B's. "What class?"

"Geography," Ryan grumbled.

Sandra's eyes widened. "Geography? But that's always been one of your favorite subjects!"

"I know! The teacher has it out for me!" Ryan spat out.

Sandra instantly knew to whom he was referring. "Ellie Duncan?"

Ryan nodded, pouting.

Sandra had heard about Ellie Duncan but had never actually met her. She had started teaching at South Portland High only last year, and had quickly built up a reputation for being exacting and intractable, a real demanding, hard-nosed dictator in the classroom. Still, Ryan had a passion for travel, and Sandra often found him spinning the globe in his bedroom, picking out places around the world he wanted to visit one day. She found it incredibly difficult to believe her son was actually flunking geography, of all classes.

"Ryan's a whiz at geography, he aces all the tests and pop quizzes," Vanessa said, coming to his defense.

"Then I don't understand. What happened?"

Ryan picked up his laptop from the coffee table in front of him and punched a few keys, bringing up an essay. He turned the screen around so his mother could see it.

"We had to write a paper on one of the Seven Wonders of the World. I chose Machu Picchu in Peru. She gave me an F!"

Sandra bent down to read the essay. After a few paragraphs she sprang up again. "This makes no sense. It sounds good to me."

"That's the problem. It sounds *too* good. Ms. Duncan is convinced I plagiarized the whole thing and she's out to punish me for it by sabotaging my graduation!"

This was ridiculous.

Ryan had always been an excellent writer from

the moment he was ten and started writing plays based on his favorite movies and TV shows and staging them in the backyard or at fifth grade recess.

"Did you try to explain that you've been writing for years, that you're a natural, and that none of your other teachers would ever question the veracity of this assignment?"

Ryan rolled his eyes. "Of course I did, Mom! But she refused to listen. I even emailed her all my notes and source materials, but I have a feeling she never even bothered to look at them. She just hates me for some reason."

"I'm going to go see her first thing tomorrow morning," Sandra announced.

Ryan jumped to his feet. "Mom, no! Please. I don't want you fighting my battles. Give me a little more time. I'm working on it."

"He's got an appointment with Principal Williams next week to discuss the matter," Vanessa said. "I'm sure the whole mess will get resolved by then."

"I'm sorry, Ryan, but this is way too important to wait another week. We need to get out in front of this."

Spoken like the true wife of a politician.

"But I've already been accepted to NYU. Even if she ends up failing me, it won't affect me in the long run," Ryan argued. "I'll still be going to college in the fall as long as I make up the class over the summer."

"That's not necessarily true," Sandra warned. "I'm sure NYU reserves the right to rescind their acceptance offer if a student starts failing his classes."

"It's an acting program, Mom. They want me to play Hamlet, not write an essay on Portugal's gross domestic product."

"What about us Instagramming selfies together in our caps and gowns on graduation day like we planned?" Vanessa asked, disheartened.

"I will be there regardless; you can count on it, even if I can't march down the aisle with you," Ryan said.

Sandra knew she should allow her son to try to fix this problem on his own. But she also did not want to risk him failing a subject for no reason and having his whole senior year marred by an unfair grade.

No, she was going to have to get involved.

And as she prepared dinner for Ryan and Vanessa, she was confident that she could reason with Ellie Duncan, just show her that she had simply jumped to the wrong conclusion. This would be settled by midmorning.

How wrong she was.

# Chapter 4

It was glaringly apparent from the sour expression on Ellie Duncan's face that she was not at all pleased to see Sandra slipping into her classroom after the last of her students had filed out, heading to their next class.

Despite the cold reception, Sandra nevertheless donned a cheerful grin. "Hello, Ellie! How've you been?"

"Fine," she growled, gathering up some papers and stuffing them into her briefcase.

"I was hoping to catch you between classes so we could have a little chat."

"I'm late for a staff meeting so now's not really a good time," Ellie said before snapping her briefcase shut.

"This will only take a minute, I promise," Sandra pressed.

Ellie clutched her briefcase and vented a sigh of weariness. "I assume this is about Ryan."

Sandra nodded. "His report on Peru."

"You mean the one he plagiarized?" Ellie said, dripping with disdain.

"I don't believe that's the case," Sandra insisted.

Ellie snickered. "No, I suppose you wouldn't. But it is my professional opinion that he cheated."

"Okay. So where is your proof? Do you have the text he supposedly passed off as his own? How can you accuse him without any hard evidence?"

"This is not a courtroom. There is no jury of his peers. There is only me, and I believe that in this particular situation I am right. Ryan deserved the grade I gave him."

"But Ryan has always been a very good writer. I am sure if I gave his paper to his English teacher, Joyce Higgins, she would agree that he did indeed write this report on his own and never stole some-one else's words or ideas."

"Of course Joyce Higgins would take your side. She's hopelessly enthralled with your whole family. Well, I refuse to be swayed by the mighty power of the great Wallage dynasty."

Sandra stopped suddenly. "Wait, what does our family have to do with Ryan's grade?"

Ellie's bottom lip quivered as her whole face flushed with anger. "You think because of your sta-tus and position, you can just wave a magic wand and make a bad grade on a report card go away. Well, you're wrong. I am not one of your hus-band's fawning constituents. I will never bow down to pressure from him or any other reckless politi-cian who voted to cut federal resources for educa-tion!"

Sandra took a step back, utterly confused. "I have no idea what you're talking about, Ellie."

"He is trying to break the teacher's union with his hardball tactics down in Washington!"

Something suddenly dawned on Sandra. "That was an amendment in a much larger bill critical to continuing funding the government. Stephen has always been a huge supporter of increasing the budget for public education. But why are we even discussing this? That has nothing to do with Ryan's grade."

"I wholeheartedly agree. Your son single-handedly created the mess he's in. My political views had nothing to do with it."

Sandra suddenly knew that this was hardly the case.

Ellie Duncan had a beef with the entire Wallage family, especially its patriarch, a US Senator who had riled her up with one particularly odious but necessary vote two years before.

No, politics had everything to do with it.

Sandra steeled herself. "I am afraid I cannot let this stand, Ellie. I'm going to have to go to Principal Williams and let her know what's happening here."

"You go right ahead," Ellie sniffed.

"You clearly have strong negative feelings about my husband . . ." She did not bother clarifying that he was about to be her ex-husband. "And it's grossly unfair that you're taking those feelings out on my son."

"You are welcome to think whatever you want, Mrs. Wallage, but the fact remains, I am the teacher and Ryan is my student, and I can give him any grade I see fit. And as much as you might try, you will never be able to change that."

She had thrown down the gauntlet.

Ellie Duncan was hell-bent on flunking Ryan.

And it was going to cost him the cherished memory of walking down the aisle with his classmates on graduation day.

Sandra did an about-face and stormed out of the classroom as Ellie called after her with a sarcastic sneer, "See you at the next parent-teacher conference!"

Sandra fumed, desperately trying to keep her emotions in check. As she marched down the hall toward the exit, she knew one thing for certain.

This was far from over.

# Chapter 5

Sandra's eyes fluttered open and she stared at the ceiling, the bedcovers pulled up to her neck. She blinked a couple of times to get her bearings before realizing someone was holding her from behind. She lowered the covers to see a man's forearm with fine blond hairs spread across it locked around her waist.

She smiled.

It was Lucas.

After a quiet dinner for two with a couple of bottles of wine at Sandra's house the previous evening, the amorous pair, their hormones racing from the alcohol and romantic candlelight, had decided it wise that Lucas should not risk driving home under the influence and spend the night at the Wallage home. It had been a calculated move on his part. Lucas had been angling for a date night with Sandra when her sons were out of the house and they could spend some private time together, just the two of them. So he was not going to blow this opportunity by heading back to his house before midnight.

Friday was perfect. Ryan had taken the train down to Boston after school to join his brother at his dorm room at Boston College, and the two of them then planned on hopping on a plane to Washington, DC from Logan Airport early Saturday morning so they could spend the better part of the weekend with their father. Ryan would be gone until late Sunday night.

Lucas snuggled Sandra tighter, murmuring something in his sleep that was unintelligible. After a moment he began snoring softly. Sandra knew she was not going to be able to fall back to sleep. It was already going on ten in the morning. They had stayed up talking until well after one before the kissing and cuddling started, which led them to retreat upstairs to Sandra's bedroom.

Sandra gently wriggled herself free from Lucas's grasp, planted her bare feet on the warm, plush white carpet, and hauled herself up, yawning. She slid into some cushy slippers and threw on a pale green silk robe, tying it around her waist, and quietly left Lucas sleeping soundly as she withdrew from the room and padded down the hardwood staircase to the kitchen, where she could smell the coffee already brewing in the pot, which was set off by the timer. She took two cups out of the cupboard and began preparing a tray for herself and Lucas with coffee, cream, and some sugar cubes when she was startled by the sound of the front door slam open and loud voices.

It took her a moment to register who it was because their presence was so unexpected. But sure enough, it was her sons, Jack and Ryan, who were supposed to be in DC with their father by now. Sandra dropped what she was doing and hurried out to the foyer, where she found the boys shedding their coats and chattering with each other about some kid in Jack's dorm who was partying too much and underperforming in his classes and was on the verge of losing his scholarship money.

"W-what are you two doing here?" Sandra sputtered, tightening her robe and staring numbly at the two boys.

"Nice to see you too, Mom," Jack cracked. "You're always getting after me about never coming home on weekends, so voilà! Here I am!"

"But you're supposed to be with your father down in DC," Sandra said, a sense of dread building up inside her as her eyes flicked up the stairs to the second floor, where Lucas, she hoped, was still sleeping.

"We never made it out of Boston," Ryan explained. "Dad called us last night. Apparently, the Senate majority leader recruited him for some last-minute, top-secret trip he couldn't tell us about, but it's all over the news this morning. He's on a congressional delegation to Ukraine. They flew through the night and are already there, meeting with the president and military leaders."

"Oh, I see," Sandra muttered in a daze, unable to erase the vision of the boys discovering Coach Cavill in the California King bed she had once shared with their father.

Her obvious, painstaking discomfort was not lost on her sons.

"Mom, is anything wrong?" Jack asked.

"No, nothing," Sandra said too quickly. "I—I just wasn't expecting to see you here this morning."

"We can always walk out and come back in so it's less of a surprise," Jack joked.

The brothers eyed each other suspiciously, wondering why their mother was acting so strange.

It did not take long for them to get their answer.

Their eyes drifted past her and up to the top of the staircase where Lucas, shirtless and in boxer shorts, rubbed his eyes as he walked barefoot down the steps toward them, yawning.

The boys stared slack-jawed as they recognized the young, half-naked, relatively new athletic director from their high school nonchalantly descending the stairs.

Sandra opened her mouth to alert Lucas that they were not alone, but when he finished rubbing his eyes with his two forefingers and opened them again, he was able to see for himself. He stopped halfway down, open-mouthed and astonished. "I thought I heard voices, but I thought you had the TV on."

"No, we're really here," Jack said, giving him the once-over.

Sandra, dying of embarrassment, kept tightening her robe, wishing she was anywhere else at this moment. "Um, boys, you, uh, you know . . ."

"Uh, yeah, Mom, I know Coach Cavill," Ryan sneered. "I see him every day in fourth-period phys ed class."

"Nice to see you again, Coach," Jack gushed, loving every minute of this. "All of you."

Suddenly feeling self-conscious, Lucas spun

around and clambered back up the stairs. "I'm just going to go put a shirt on."

Once he was gone, Sandra locked eyes with her sons. "I can explain."

Jack shrugged. "Mom, there's nothing to explain. We get it. You and Coach Cavill thought you had the place to yourselves and then we showed up out of the blue. It happens."

"Am I the only one weirded out by our mother dating one of my *teachers*?" Ryan whined.

"Get over it," Jack scoffed. "Mom's a free agent now. She can join any team she wants."

"You make me sound like an NFL draft pick," Sandra moaned.

Jack smirked, then turned to his younger brother. "Why are you so freaked out? It's no secret that Mom's been seeing the coach. Everyone in town knows by now."

"Yeah, but it's one thing to just hear about it and a whole other thing to actually witness it up close."

Jack ignored him. "I say good for you, Mom. He's a nice guy, not to mention superhot!"

Sandra hardly felt better with a nod of approval from her gay son. This situation felt wrong on so many different levels.

"You know, if you do the math, Coach Cavill is closer in age to you, Ryan, than he is to Mom," Jack observed.

He was enjoying this way too much.

"Okay, Jack, that's enough," Sandra warned.

At that moment, a sheepish Lucas came fumbling back down the stairs, this time fully dressed in a half-buttoned-up, collared shirt and blue jeans.

He carried a pair of sneakers in his hand. When he reached the bottom, he plopped down on the bottom step to put on his shoes.

"I'd better get going," he whispered.

"What's the hurry?" Jack asked. "Why don't you stay for breakfast? Mom's an awesome cook. But I bet you know that already."

"Jack!" Sandra snapped.

Jack snickered before turning to Sandra. "Come on, Mom, we're all adults here. There's no reason to shield us from the man in your life." He then whipped his head around to Lucas. "Do you like blueberry pancakes?"

Lucas nodded warily as he finished with his sneakers and popped back up to his feet to continue buttoning his shirt.

"Then it's settled," Jack said, taking in Lucas's red eyes and tousled hair. "Come with me. It looks like you could use some caffeine and I smell coffee." He guided Lucas by the arm and they tottered off into the kitchen.

Sandra shot Ryan a perturbed look.

"What? This is all Jack's doing! The last thing I want to do is spend Saturday morning with my gym teacher," Ryan snarled before heaving a sigh and following Jack and Lucas into the kitchen.

Sandra hung back, queasy about what was to come.

But she need not have worried.

As she set about making breakfast, pouring blueberries into the pancake batter, squeezing fresh orange juice, and filling a dispenser with maple syrup, she was amazed at how fast Lucas was bonding with the boys, talking sports with Jack and

local politics with the more community-minded
Ryan. She could tell he was winning them over
with his easy sense of humor and keen under-
standing of what interested them. By the time
Lucas was helping clear the dishes and loading the
washer, Sandra knew Jack and Ryan approved of
him, which meant everything to her. There would
still be some awkward moments, especially with
the local gossip mill already on overdrive, but at
least on the home front there would be no storm
clouds.

Ryan was feeling so comfortable around Lucas,
he even brought up the topic of his geography
class travails and how it was going to affect graduation.

Lucas listened to him, incredulous. "That doesn't
sound right. She ought to give you the benefit of
the doubt. If you swore you wrote the report yourself, she should accept that unless she has the evidence to prove you wrong."

"Which she doesn't because I definitely wrote
it," Ryan growled. "She just hates me."

Lucas shifted in his chair toward Sandra, who
was pouring herself another cup of coffee from
the pot. "Did you go to Williams about this yet?"

Sandra shook her head. "Not yet. I was hoping
Ellie Duncan would see the error of her ways before I had to go over her head, but it looks like
that's never going to happen."

"Why is she targeting Ryan?" Lucas asked. "He's
a good student."

Sandra explained Ellie Duncan's antipathy toward Ryan's father and his brand of politics.

"That's messed up," Lucas exhaled.

"What about you? Have you had any run-ins with her?" Sandra asked.

"Our paths don't cross much except at faculty meetings, but I'm not a fan. Not by a long shot," Lucas said. "I see her causing problems all the time. It's like she goes out of her way to upset her students and even their parents, and she also seems to enjoy fighting with her fellow teachers. It's as if she thrives on conflict. I've made it my mission to steer clear of her. Luckily, there's very little connection between geography and sports."

"I had her my senior year," Jack said. "She was a horrible sourpuss back then too. She'll never change. The school would be a better place without her. Maybe someone should just take her out."

"Jack, do not even joke about something like that!" Sandra scolded.

"I meant they should *fire* her," Jack quickly clarified. "But she'd better watch out if she's not careful. If she keeps ticking people off, someone might just decide to take it to the next level."

Sandra could not imagine things going that far.

And yet time would prove just how prescient her older son was when it came to how much people despised Ellie Duncan, herself included.

# Chapter 6

"Pneumatic," Annabelle Chastain-Wheeler pronounced before running the word through her head and spelling it out. "P-n-e-u-m-a-t-i-c. Pneumatic." She twisted her head around to judge the faces of her two fathers, Doug and Noah Chastain-Wheeler. As Doug checked the flash card in his hand, Noah nodded approvingly.

"Correct. Next word," Doug said, flipping over to the next card. "Embryonic."

"Embryonic," Annabelle repeated. "E-m-b-r-y-o-n-i-c. Embryonic."

Noah turned to his husband expectantly.

"Correct. She's got this in the bag!" Doug gushed.

"But she misspelled protoplasm earlier, and that worries me because it's an easy lay-up. We practiced that word last week and she knew it then. I'm afraid her nerves might get the best of her when she's actually up there on the stage," Noah lamented.

"She will be *fine*," Doug assured him before turning to Annabelle. "Right, honey?"

Annabelle gave her fathers a strained smile. "Yes, Daddy."

Sandra, who had been watching the scene, felt sorry for the twelve-year-old girl. She appeared to be under an enormous amount of pressure, as did several of the other children competing in the local middle school spelling bee that was being held today in the school auditorium.

Maya and Sandra had shown up to observe the kids and their parents, which included their clients, the Fanellis, and their son, Rocco, hoping to suss out any clue that might point them in the direction of the person who'd had Hunter Hamlin leave that threatening note in Rocco's locker.

The first family Sandra had focused on were Doug and Noah Chastain-Wheeler, transplants from New York City who had recently moved up to Maine with their adopted daughter, Annabelle, when Doug was hired as the chief financial officer for a health care company's clinical divisions and related entities after a long, successful run at Goldman Sachs on Wall Street. His partner of fifteen years, Doug, was a house husband who gave up a promising career as a chef at a Greenwich Village restaurant to raise their daughter. Both men were in their late thirties, slender, handsome, and whose lives now seemed squarely centered on Annabelle, a pert, precocious, pretty little blonde who exuded a palpable intensity not often seen in someone her age.

Sandra had never met the Chastain-Wheelers but had heard all about them. They were well-liked in the community and tried to engage with other families on occasion. But they were mostly wrapped up in Annabelle's promising future, which would only be bolstered by her winning the county spelling bee, and then, hopefully, going on to sweep the state and national competitions.

As Sandra looked around at the other helicopter parents frantically testing their kids with flash cards minutes before the contest was scheduled to begin, she realized that Doug and Noah were not at all unique. A lot of hard work went into the training of these kids, a lot of money spent on personal tutors and advanced computer programs. It had to take a toll on the kids themselves with the profound pressure put upon them. Any one of these parents—or kids, for that matter—could have snapped at any time and resorted to extreme measures to clear the field of the most worrisome competitors for an easier path to victory.

Sandra spotted Maya talking with Hunter Hamlin's parents, who were both gesticulating wildly, no doubt defending their son, who had been allowed to remain in the competition after the principal, Birdie Munn, concluded that she believed him when he claimed he had never read the note and was just doing it for the money, like a job for TaskRabbit. The other parents who had heard about the story immediately protested, not out of any sense of moral outrage but mostly out of a keen desire to see one less kid in the spelling bee who might knock their own child out of the competition.

But Birdie Munn had stuck to her guns. Although Hunter had a history of being a troublemaker, she had seen firsthand how his talent for spelling had boosted his self-esteem and put him on a better path, and she certainly did not want to destroy that progress over one bad decision on his part. Sandra admired Birdie putting a child's welfare above school politics. And in her gut, Sandra felt Hunter had been honest with them about what he knew.

Which basically was nothing.

"Sandra Wallage, where have you been hiding?" a man's voice called out from behind her.

Sandra whipped around to see Don Talbot beaming at her as he approached. Don was tall, imposing, and distinguished, with a full head of graying hair. He wore an expensive-looking Brooks Brothers suit and stood out from the rest of the more informally dressed parents. He was a wealthy businessman, owner of an asset management company, whose older son, Cooper, was in Ryan's class. His youngest, Phoebe, was competing in the spelling bee, Sandra guessed.

"Don, lovely to see you," she said as he leaned in and gave her a peck on the cheek.

"I just got another fundraising email from your husband. He's not up for reelection for another two years. Does he ever stop campaigning?"

Sandra resisted the urge to correct him.

Stephen was now her ex-husband.

At least he would be in a few weeks, when the divorce papers were finally signed and filed with the state.

"You'll have to ask him," Sandra replied, hoping to dodge any further discussion regarding Stephen. "I heard Phoebe is the one to beat today."

"That girl's a regular phenom. I have no idea the meaning of half the words she can spell off the top of her head. I'm so proud of her," Don said, nervously checking his watch. "I'm feeling pretty good about her taking first prize if she stays focused. I just pray that Fanelli kid trips up at some point. As far as I'm concerned, he's Phoebe's stiffest competition."

Sandra's ears perked up at the mention of Rocco Fanelli.

Don Talbot was acutely aware of Rocco's formidable spelling talent, which could cost his daughter in the final round.

Don sighed irritably. "Are they going to start this thing soon? I have an important meeting I need to get to." He looked around the auditorium, annoyed that no one was working to get the spelling bee underway. He then returned his gaze to Sandra. "Who are you here to cheer on?"

"I'm not here to choose any favorites. I'm here on official business," Sandra said.

"As president of the PTA?" Don asked with a raised eyebrow.

"No, Don, I stepped down from that position years ago."

A light bulb seemed to pop on in Don's head. "Yes! Right. I heard a rumor you were dabbling in crime solving these days."

He could not have sounded more condescending if he had tried.

"Yes, Don. I work as a private investigator now," Sandra said coldly.

"It's always nice to have a side hobby," Don chuckled, checking his watch again and tapping his foot impatiently.

"It's more than just a hobby," Sandra insisted, even though he was barely listening to her.

"So what are you investigating today? Someone pilfer paintbrushes from the art supply closet?"

"We have to respect the confidentiality of our clients, so obviously I can't discuss any case I'm working on—"

Don appeared bored with her answer and began swiveling his head around. "Come on, come on, what's the holdup? Why can't they get this thing underway? At this rate, I'm not even going to be able to stick around to see Phoebe crush the competition."

"I'd love to stay and talk, Don, but I need to—"

He held up a hand in front of her face, beating her to the punch. "Excuse me, I'm going to see why these people can't get their act together."

He hustled off, leaving Sandra embarrassed for feeling the need to explain herself to a jerk like Don Talbot.

Maya was suddenly at her side. "I've engaged in conversations with most of the parents here, and in my honest opinion, any one of them could be guilty. They're all merciless, fiercely determined that their own kids win."

"Have you seen Rocco? How's he doing?"

"Better than Eugenio and Lucia. Rocco appears relatively calm, but his poor parents keep looking over their shoulders, waiting for someone to strike at any moment."

"Excuse me, would you mind explaining what you two are doing here?" Ellie Duncan barked as she charged up to Maya and Sandra.

Fearing she might explode and say something she would regret to the odious geography teacher, Sandra took a small step back to allow Maya to take the lead.

"It's a public school," Maya said, dripping with disdain. "Are we not allowed to watch the spelling bee?"

Ellie eyed them suspiciously. "I suppose so. I just find it odd that you two are here when your kids are in high school and not even competing."

"What can I say? We're big bee fans," Maya cracked sarcastically.

They had no intention of revealing to Ellie the real reason they were there.

"We could ask you the same thing," Maya said. "You don't teach at this school."

Unlike Maya and Sandra, Ellie had no compunction about explaining why she was attending the spelling bee that day. "I volunteer every year as the coordinator for the school at the local, county, and state competitions, all the way up to the nationals in the event any of our students make it that far. I am not sure if you're aware, but back in the day, when I was twelve years old, I was a state spelling bee champ."

"I had no idea," Maya marveled.

"Yes, I was. I lost to some kid from Indiana at nationals, however. What a terrible day that was," Ellie sadly reminisced, frowning at the memory.

Sandra could not resist finally speaking up. She had to know. "What word did you misspell?"

"Nauseous," she answered without missing a beat. "I forgot the *e*. I was so mad at myself. Believe me, that word has stuck with me for years because it's exactly how I feel whenever I think back to that day."

There was a long pause as Ellie apparently once again replayed that horrible moment in her life in her mind. Then she returned her attention to Maya and Sandra, her eyes narrowing. "Are you really interested in watching the spelling bee or are you two here looking into some kind of case? Everyone in town knows you work together as detectives."

Unlike Sandra, Maya was far more amenable to discussing their investigations. Most likely to see if she could shake up Ellie, Sandra suspected.

"Someone left a disturbing note in Rocco Fanelli's locker, threatening to kill him if he didn't drop out," Maya said flatly, studying Ellie's face for her reaction.

She appeared genuinely surprised. "*What?*" Then her shock gave way to anger. "Why wasn't I told about this?"

"Because we want to keep this on the down-low while we talk to the students and their parents and try to figure out who might be behind it, so we would appreciate your discretion," Maya said pointedly.

"Of course," Ellie sniffed. "And I expect the same

from you. The last thing I need is for two gung-ho detectives running around upsetting the parents and scaring the kids and spoiling everything. Do you understand me?"

Maya nodded, biting her tongue.

Sandra could tell it was taking every last ounce of self-restraint for Maya not to lay into this annoying, obnoxious, off-putting woman.

Ellie then stalked off, clearly rattled by this revelation but determined to keep her precious spelling bee on track.

She had no idea at the time how soon her efforts would spectacularly unravel.

# Chapter 7

When the first round of the local spelling bee got underway in the middle school auditorium, where five students from the community would eventually advance to the county competition, Phoebe Talbot stood apprehensively in front of the small podium with a standing microphone in the glaring spotlight, ready to receive her word. Seated at the table in the front row were three sober-faced judges. On stage with the children, relishing her moment in charge, was former champ and self-appointed host of the event, Ellie Duncan.

One of the judges, a hefty, balding man in his late forties, read from a card. "Malfeasance."

Phoebe started to sweat under the glaring lights. "Could you repeat the word, please?"

The judge nodded. "Malfeasance."

Sandra could see Annabelle, seated in a chair behind Phoebe, with a knowing smirk on her face.

Sandra guessed that she was already spelling the word correctly in her head.

Phoebe nervously cleared her throat. "Could you use the word in a sentence, please?"

The judge cleared his throat. "Two officials were dismissed by the bank for malfeasance."

Phoebe stood frozen, worried she was going to make a mistake. Behind her, Annabelle's lips were moving as she spelled the word silently to herself. Rocco and Hunter sat a few chairs down the row of contestants, both of them staring out at the packed audience.

"M-a-l-f-e . . ." Phoebe stopped suddenly, a panicked look on her face.

The crowd was silent.

Phoebe's head bobbed up and down as she spelled the word in her head and then picked up where she had left off. ". . . a-s-a-n-c-e. Malfeasance."

The judge glanced up from his card and smiled. "Correct."

There was wild applause from the audience as Phoebe emitted a heavy sigh of relief and took her seat. Annabelle was up next, and she practically danced over to the podium, brimming with self-confidence.

Sandra scanned the audience to get a glimpse of Phoebe's proud father only to see him bounding out of the auditorium in a huff, his phone clamped to his ear. Sandra, who was seated on the aisle, got up from her seat and followed him out as Annabelle received a word from the next judge, Dory Baumgarten, a middle-school math teacher who used to work at the high school when Sandra was PTA president. "Demitasse."

Annabelle's face lit up. "I know that one!" She waved at her two fathers, sitting in the front row, on the edge of their seats. "I practiced this one the other night with my dads!" Then, chin up, she spoke into the microphone so loudly there was some earsplitting feedback, causing some in the audience to cover their ears. "Demitasse." Before spelling the word, she cranked her head back in Phoebe's direction. "And I don't need to hear it in a sentence. D-e-m-i-t-a-s-s-e. Demitasse."

Dory nodded. "Correct."

More applause as Sandra walked out the doors to the auditorium to find a livid Don Talbot screaming at someone over the phone. "I want it filed today! Do you hear me? This woman is a nightmare and needs to be punished for the way she's been targeting my kids!"

Sensing someone behind him, Don whirled around to see Sandra eavesdropping. "Larry, I'll call you later, but make this happen, do you hear me? Great. Keep in touch." He stuffed his phone back in his coat pocket. "Sandra, what did I miss?"

"Phoebe spelled her word correctly."

"I saw that. What about that spoiled brat Annabelle; did she blow it like I prayed she would?"

Sandra shook her head. "Um, no, Annabelle spelled her word correctly as well."

"Damn it!" Don roared, yanking a white handkerchief from his breast pocket and dabbing the perspiration from his face.

"Is everything all right, Don?"

"Not by a long shot. I left to take a call from my lawyer. I'm suing Ellie Duncan for defamation."

Sandra's mouth dropped open, floored. "Why? What happened?"

Don tried to compose himself with very little success. He appeared as if his whole head was about to explode. "I went backstage to wish Phoebe luck and that witch Ellie was hanging around and I distinctly heard her say under her breath, but loud enough for me and Phoebe to hear, 'Cheater'! She actually accused my kid of cheating!"

"On what grounds? Why would she say such a thing?"

Don was breathing so heavily, his face so full of rage, Sandra feared he might have a heart attack at any moment. "When Phoebe showed promise as a speller, I decided to invest in a tutor for her. I'm a busy guy, a single dad, I don't have time to coach her myself . . ."

Don's wife, Gwyneth, tragically, had died of cancer a few years earlier.

The doors to the auditorium flew open and people began filing out for a fifteen-minute break.

Don plowed ahead, even more apoplectic, but lowered his voice so those milling around them could not overhear their conversation. "So I hired this grad student and she got remarkable results. In just a few months, she turned Phoebe into a champ, a force to be reckoned with, but then Ellie Duncan got wind of it and threatened to disqualify Phoebe for having an unfair advantage. Can you believe that?"

"Was there a rule about not hiring outside help?"

"No! There was nothing! Ellie was just trying to make trouble. Well, I wasn't going to stand for it. I took it all the way to the school board, which, not surprisingly, sided with *me*! Phoebe was given the go-ahead to compete. Ellie was furious, but there was nothing she could do. So what does she do? She started taking her frustration out on my older boy, Cooper. Suddenly, out of the blue, he starts failing geography, and take one guess who teaches that class!"

Sandra did not have to guess.

She was going through the same thing with Ryan.

"I went to complain to Principal Williams at the high school about Ellie unfairly targeting certain students, and yeah, Williams made noises about looking into it, but nothing ever got done about it. That horrible woman is still at the school teaching," Don lamented.

They heard a shrill voice behind them. "Maybe I still have a job because the problem isn't me. The problem is Cooper and his astounding lack of motivation."

They both turned to see Ellie Duncan standing directly behind them, having emerged from the auditorium with the rest of the crowd. She had obviously stopped for a drink at the nearby water fountain and had overheard them talking about her.

"I understand how so many entitled students feel they should be able to just skate through school with little effort because their rich parents are going to buy their way into a good college with a large donation, muscling out the less-advantaged students who have to work twice as hard to get accepted and then may not even be able to afford the tuition without a scholarship," Ellie sneered. "But do you honestly feel that's fair?"

"It's a false equivalency, Ellie!" Don wailed. "Cooper is a good student."

Ellie chortled. "If you believe that, you haven't been paying attention. Talk to his other teachers. Hear what they have to say. I'm not saying he's some dumb jock party animal, but maybe you should try to read the room. He's not Ivy League material by any stretch and the sooner you accept that, the more time you'll have to formulate a more realistic alternative plan for Cooper's future."

Sandra automatically took a step back, waiting for Don to literally detonate into a mushroom cloud. She was keenly aware of Don's strong hopes for his son's future despite Cooper's own lackadaisical attitude toward academics. But Don had already made up his mind about Cooper one day ruling the world, and he was not going to allow one peevish, annoying high school geography teacher to stand in his way.

"You will be hearing from my lawyer," Don threatened.

"Oh goody. Is he going to ask me out on a date? Because I happen to be free this weekend," Ellie joked, reveling in Don Talbot's meltdown, which only managed to provoke him even more.

"I'm suing you for defamation. You called my daughter a cheater!" Don screamed.

The corners of her mouth crept up into a self-satisfied smile. "I honestly don't remember saying that, but you can't win a defamation lawsuit when someone simply speaks the truth."

Sandra feared Don was about to lunge at Ellie and take a roundhouse swing, so she forcefully gripped his arm. "Don, I think it would be best for you, for Phoebe, and for Cooper, if you just stopped talking and walked away."

Don's feet remained planted in place and he was now breathing through his nose.

"No need," Ellie said, checking the wall clock. "I need to get back to the stage for round two. I wish your little Phoebe all the luck in the world." Then she turned on her heel and breezily glided off.

Don took a step forward, about to run after her, but Sandra kept a tight grip on his arm. "Don, let it go. She *wants* you to cause a scene. It will just strengthen her case."

Don covered his face with his hands. "I can't believe I lost it like that. She's just going to take my outburst out on my kids. She'll flunk Cooper no matter what he does and she's going to find some insidious way to punish Phoebe to ensure she doesn't make it to the county competition."

"We won't let that happen, Don," Sandra promised, although she had no idea how she was going to do it.

But, luckily, they did not have to because by the end of the local middle school spelling bee competition, Phoebe was advancing to the county contest after spelling the especially challenging word "crustaceology" correctly, which Sandra had to explain to Don meant the study of crabs and shrimp. Annabelle and Hunter were also winners, as well as Maya and Sandra's client, Rocco, who nailed "milquetoast" to thunderous applause, especially from his elated parents, who celebrated by jumping up and down in the aisle of the auditorium.

But despite Phoebe's success, Don was more determined than ever to somehow bring Ellie Duncan down, and Sandra had a queasy feeling that the situation with the power mad geography teacher and spelling bee coordinator was about to get a whole lot worse.

# Chapter 8

Maya and Sandra arrived at their office, located on the second floor of a drab, two-story brick building on the outskirts of downtown Portland, early the following morning to discuss the Fanelli case and the frustrating lack of progress. Sandra had just made a fresh pot of coffee and served Maya her usual onion bagel smeared with cream cheese, which she had picked up at a bakery down the street, when there was a loud knock on the door.

Maya had just taken a bite of her bagel and quickly swallowed it, catching some falling cream cheese with her napkin. "Are we expecting a client this morning?"

"No, I have nothing on the books," Sandra said, jumping up and answering the door. A six-foot-two, slender, handsome man with a full head of red hair and a scruffy, ginger beard, stood before her. He was wearing an open-collared shirt, jeans, and a casual blazer.

Sandra offered him a tentative smile. "Ewan, what a pleasant surprise."

"Pleasant" was being generous because Sandra knew this man and was not particularly fond of him. Ewan Murphy was the president of the school board, and despite his good looks and easy smile, he had proven himself to be an egotistical and aggressive official with whom she'd had to deal constantly during her tenure as the PTA president. Sandra had noticed immediately upon meeting him that he had a deep love for the sound of his own voice when he droned on endlessly at school board meetings, not to mention an irritating propensity to half listen to anyone trying to discuss an important matter with him. He would raise a hand and listlessly ask the person to repeat his or her last thought because his mind had obviously wandered to other, more pressing topics. Ewan Murphy much preferred being the one who was doing all the talking.

"Sandra, you're looking lovely as always," he said with a leering gaze. "I hope I'm not here at a bad time. I apologize for dropping by without an appointment."

She eyed him warily, wondering if he was here to hire them for a case, which she deemed unlikely. If Ewan Murphy wanted to hire a private detective, odds were he would find a man to get the job done.

"No, please, come in," Sandra said, stepping aside and welcoming him. "Our first client meeting isn't until ten."

It was a fib. They had no scheduled appointments at all this morning. She just wanted to make the infuriatingly sexist Ewan Murphy think they did.

Sandra gestured toward Maya, who was taking another bite of her bagel. "Have you met my partner, Maya Kendrick?"

Ewan strode over, extending a hand, which Maya politely shook after hastily wiping her hands clean with her napkin. "I haven't had the pleasure, although I certainly know her daughter, Vanessa. I hear she will be delivering the valedictory speech at this year's high school graduation."

"Yes," Maya said, beaming. "We're very proud of her."

Sandra resisted the urge to bring up her own son's trouble with his discriminating and vindictive geography teacher that might prevent him from even attending the graduation ceremonies, but she did not feel that now was an appropriate time to discuss the matter. Little did she know, however, that that particular subject was the entire reason Ewan Murphy had shown up at their office today.

"I'll come right to the point about why I'm here," Ewan said with a stern look as he pivoted back toward Sandra. "There has been a complaint lodged against you."

Sandra reeled back, stunned. "*Me?*"

"Yes. Apparently Ellie Duncan has filed a grievance claiming she has been the victim of a harassment campaign orchestrated by you personally."

Sandra scoffed. "That's the most ridiculous thing I have ever heard. It's true I went to speak to her about my son's grade because I thought she was being unfair, falsely accusing him of plagiarism. I was very concerned, and yes, maybe a little angry, but mostly because I believed, and still believe, that she is being grossly unjust and needlessly stubborn."

"You can't strong-arm a teacher into giving your son a better grade," Ewan scolded.

Sandra could feel her cheeks burning. He had not listened to one word she had just said. He was automatically taking Ellie Duncan's side.

"Maybe I did not make myself clear just now—"

Ewan did not allow her to finish. "Ms. Duncan went to speak to Principal Williams initially, hoping to resolve the matter by scheduling a sit-down with you, Ryan, and the principal, but unfortunately, Williams apparently bulldozed over that suggestion by pressuring her into giving Ryan a passing grade and strongly hinting that she should forget about the whole thing. I know you and Caroline Williams are very close."

Stung, Sandra took a deep breath. "We worked together when I was PTA president, but I would not exactly call us close. Just what are you implying here, Ewan?"

"All I'm saying is that Ellie did not feel supported, so she had no choice but to go above Caroline's head, which is why she contacted me with her complaint, hoping something might get done now."

Maya, who had been listening silently while chewing on her bagel, could not keep silent anymore. She rose to her feet. "I find it incredibly insulting that you would waltz in here and insinuate

Sandra Wallage would dare use her position and personal relationships to persecute and bully one of her son's teachers. That's not who she is, and if you know anything about her, you would agree."

Sandra appreciated Maya rushing to her defense, but she felt it was only making the situation worse. The more she pressed, the more ganged up on and defensive Ewan would no doubt feel.

"So what's next? A hearing?" Maya barked.

Ewan's eyes widened. "What? No! The last thing I want is a public spectacle, not with school board elections coming up in the fall. I just want this whole problem to go away."

Sandra folded her arms. "And how do you propose we make that happen?"

"Just keep your distance from Ellie from here on in, that's all I ask," Ewan begged, keeping one eye on Maya, who he feared might pounce on him at any moment like a predatory leopard.

"I am happy to do that," Sandra assured him. "The last thing I want is to have any contact with that woman ever again."

Ewan smiled, relieved. "Thank you."

Sandra took a step forward. "But . . ."

The relief in Ewan's face slowly washed away. "But what?"

"We still need to deal with Ryan's failing grade on his essay. I believe, and his English teacher, Miss Higgins, is happy to attest to the fact, that Ryan did not plagiarize his assignment. He just has a talent for prose, and obviously Ellie Duncan doesn't have the capacity to recognize a good writer when she sees one. She just assumes they must be cheating."

Ewan rubbed his eyes. "Let me talk to Ellie. Maybe she'll be open to allowing Ryan to redo the assignment."

"Not good enough," Sandra persisted. "He's already completed the assignment honestly and with integrity. Ellie Duncan needs to just admit she was wrong."

Ewan dropped his head, defeated. "Let me talk to her, okay? I'm not making any promises."

Sandra's blood was boiling. Once again, this infuriating man was not actually *hearing* her. She had no intention of ever allowing Ryan to repeat the assignment. She needed for the school board president to understand. "Ewan, read my lips. I am not letting this go."

"Okay! Fine! Got it! I will talk to her!" Ewan hissed.

Maya and Sandra could almost feel his blood pressure rising.

"Thank you, Ewan. Now, if you don't mind, we have important cases to work on," Sandra snipped as she crossed to the door and opened it for him to leave.

"Right, right, sorry," Ewan sputtered, discombobulated. This was not how he had expected the meeting to go. He was used to always running roughshod and getting his own way.

With a perfunctory nod toward the two women, he hurried out as Sandra slammed the door behind him so hard the window nearly shattered.

Maya sensed Sandra was on the verge of exploding. "Hey, why don't you dump that coffee in the sink—I don't think you need any more caffeine at this point—and let's take a field trip to update our clients on our current case."

Sandra stared at her full cup of coffee, then marched over to the small kitchenette in the corner and emptied it into the sink. "Good idea. I could use some fresh air."

A trip across town sounded like a good way to calm her nerves. But unfortunately, they'd had very little progress to report to the Fanelli family. Even with Rocco advancing to the county competition, the mystery threat was still out there. They were no closer to identifying the perpetrator who wrote that note, which meant he or she could still strike again at any moment.

And that made Sandra exceedingly nervous.

# Chapter 9

When Maya pulled her Chevy Bolt, with Sandra in the passenger seat, over to the curb in front of the Fanellis' home, they immediately heard shouting in the otherwise quiet residential neighborhood as they got out.

Maya stopped to listen to the heated, raised voices. "Where's all that yelling coming from?"

Sandra pointed toward the back of the Fanellis' single-story, nondescript home. "Sounds like there's some kind of fight going on in the backyard."

Maya and Sandra hurried up the front lawn, circling around the side of the house to the backyard, where they spotted Eugenio Fanelli wagging a piece of paper in front of a man whose face he was blocking. There was a half-finished wooden fence between them with a small pile of lumber stacked up on the next property.

Eugenio shouted at the top of his lungs, "You

take this down right now or I'm going to call the police!"

"Go ahead! They can arrest you for harassment and disturbing the peace," the other man roared.

Maya and Sandra hurried up to the two feuding men, enough to finally get a glimpse of the neighbor, instantly recognizing him as Doug Chastain-Wheeler, one of Annabelle's fathers.

"Okay, let's calm down," Maya urged. "What seems to be the problem here?"

Eugenio swiveled around, surprised to see Maya and Sandra appearing suddenly in his backyard. He angrily waved the piece of paper he was clutching in his hand at them. "He's trespassing. He knows it and he doesn't care!"

Doug dropped his head, frustrated. "Look, Eugenio . . ."

"That's *Mister* Fanelli to you!" Eugenio barked.

"Mr. Fanelli," Doug seethed. "Please be reasonable. We're building this fence just as much for you as for us." He turned to Maya and Sandra, hoping to get them over onto his side. "We have two dogs we let out and we don't want them wandering over here and digging up their garden or leaving deposits for them to have to clean up."

"But their fence is on *my* property line," Eugenio cried. "They're inching their way, trying to take over the whole area."

"As I have explained to you about a dozen times now, that red maple tree is in the way, and we can't build the fence around it, so we had to move the fence forward, less than a foot," Doug said through gritted teeth.

"Onto my property," Eugenio snorted. "They didn't even ask me!"

"We thought you would like having the fence separating our properties, and we're willing to pay for the whole thing."

Eugenio shoved the piece of paper at Maya and Sandra. "Look, here is the deed. It clearly shows where the property line is and he's obviously crossed it!"

Sandra plucked the paper from Eugenio, glancing at it, unable to make heads or tails of it. "Maybe you should have a surveyor come out and do a proper inspection."

Doug threw up his arms. "Thank you! That's what I have been trying to tell him."

"I don't need a surveyor!" Eugenio bellowed in his thick Italian accent as he snatched the paper back from Sandra and waved it again in front of Doug's face, nearly nicking his nose with a paper cut. "I got this!"

Doug retracted his head, his face incandescent. "This is what I think of your stupid deed." He grabbed the piece of paper from Eugenio and tore it up into pieces, igniting Eugenio, who lunged at him, wrapping his hands around Doug's neck. As the two men grappled, stumbling to the ground and rolling around in the grass and dirt, Maya and Sandra sprang forward to try to pull them apart.

The spouses of both men, Lucia and Noah, apparently having been watching the ugly scene from their respective kitchen windows, came flying out their back doors, screaming for their husbands to stop fighting. As Sandra bent down to grab Eugenio by the shirt collar, he reared back to strike Noah, clocking Sandra in the eye with his elbow. She staggered back, throwing a hand over her face. Maya, enraged, moved in and wrapped an arm around Eugenio's neck, securing him in a headlock and allowing Doug to scramble out from underneath him and crawl to his feet, where Noah pulled him away from Eugenio, who by now was red-faced and embarrassed by being quickly subdued by a woman.

Maya loosened her grip slightly. "If I let you go, do you promise to calm down?"

Eugenio nodded and she released him. He sprang up, rubbing his neck and looking defeated.

Lucia shook her head in disgust. "Look at what you've done, Eugenio! You let your emotions get the best of you and you hurt a woman."

Eugenio glanced at Sandra, who was still covering her eye with her hand. Mortified, he rushed over to her. "Mrs. Wallage, I'm so sorry, are you all right?"

"You just assaulted the wife of a US senator, Fanelli. I hope you go to prison!" Doug screamed.

Maya stepped between them to stop any further fighting. "Mr. Wheeler, I think it would be best—"

"It's Chastain-Wheeler! Doug Chastain-Wheeler! I'm Chastain and Wheeler is my husband! We hyphenated when we got married!"

"Right, my apologies, Mr. Chastain-Wheeler. But don't you think it might be for the best if you and your husband just go back inside your house now and allow things to cool down?"

Doug hesitated until Noah tugged on his shirt-sleeve, signaling to him that he agreed with Maya. They needed to retreat from the battlefield and live to fight another day.

"Mark my words, Fanelli, you will be hearing from my lawyer," Doug warned before turning on his heel and storming off back to his house, Noah scampering after him.

These wealthy, helicopter parents sure did love their lawyers.

Lucia angrily shoved her husband. "Eugenio, what in the world were you thinking? Now they're going to sue us!"

Eugenio took his wife's face in his hands. "Lucia, I'm so sorry. I just lost my temper, I couldn't help it."

"Yes, you could! I have told you since the day we met that your hot head would one day get us into trouble. If you are so convinced that fence is on our property, let them hire a surveyor to prove it. Don't ever resort to violence."

Eugenio's shoulders sank and he respectfully nodded at his wife. "Yes, dear, you're right. What can I say, I'm Sicilian."

"You're not Michael Corleone and this isn't *The Godfather*! You work in a bakery, for heaven's sake," Lucia snapped. "Enough of this tough-guy act." She turned to Maya. "I've never seen him like this. He's usually so docile. He cries at Hallmark Movies."

"It's because of those two," Eugenio sneered,

pointing over the half-finished fence into the Chastain-Wheelers' backyard. "I know it's them. I know in my heart they're somehow behind that note in Rocco's locker. They would do anything, no matter how underhanded, to make sure their precious daughter Annabelle wins the county spelling bee."

"We don't know that for certain," Maya warned.

"Well, we hired you to find out for certain, so why haven't you?" Eugenio sniffed.

Lucia's eyes widened, dismayed. "He didn't mean that! We know you're working hard to find the culprit, and we know we're not paying you your usual rate. We're very grateful for everything you're doing." She slapped Eugenio on the arm so hard it left a welt. "Aren't we, Eugenio? Tell them!"

"Yes, thank you," Eugenio murmured, eyes downcast.

"I know the county competition is tomorrow, but please, just give us a little more time. We *will* find the person responsible, I promise," Maya assured them.

She glanced back at the house to see Rocco watching everything from his second-floor bedroom window on the far end of the house. When he spotted Maya looking his way, he quickly retreated, closing the curtain.

Lucia grabbed her husband by the back of the neck and shoved him forward. "Now say you're sorry to poor Mrs. Wallage."

"Please forgive me. I didn't mean to strike you, it was an accident," Eugenio said quietly.

"It's okay, Eugenio," Sandra said, removing her hand. "I'm fine."

Except her left eye was bruised, swelling and bloodshot.

"Wait. Don't go. I may have a steak in the freezer," Lucia declared, hustling back toward the house.

"We can't stay," Sandra called out to her.

"They're not inviting us to lunch." Maya chuckled. "It's for your eye."

# Chapter 10

Principal Birdie Munn was ecstatic to learn that her middle school had been selected to host the Cumberland County Spelling Bee Competition in their newly renovated auditorium, which was large enough to host all the contestants, their families, and their respective cheering sections. The top two spellers from this event would go on to compete in the state competition, to be held at Hannaford Hall at the University of Southern Maine campus. The winner of that event would represent the state of Maine at the televised Scripps National Spelling Bee in early June at the Gaylord National Resort & Convention Center in National Harbor, Maryland, just outside Washington, DC.

The big win for her school just put added pressure on Principal Munn to ensure everything went smoothly on that day. She had paid overtime to the janitorial staff to work through the night before the event to sweep, mop, and clean the auditorium, hallways, and classrooms throughout the school until everything was spotless. She doted on the judges, making sure they had everything they needed to avoid any temper tantrums or needless drama. But most of all, she just had to cross her fingers and hope there was no further fallout from the threatening note left inside Rocco Fanelli's locker.

Maya and Sandra also knew from a conversation with her that Birdie Munn was very concerned with the erratic behavior of her spelling bee coordinator and host of the event, Ellie Duncan. She had seriously considered replacing her with a teacher less controversial but feared that if she did, Ellie would explode with more fiery rage than the supervillain Thanos in all those *Avengers* movies. Stopping short of acknowledging Ellie's precarious mental state, Munn had concluded the risk was far greater removing her at the last minute than allowing her to take the stage and simply hope for the best.

Ellie, for her part, took Munn's paralyzed inaction as a sign that she was free to do and act as she pleased. She flitted out on stage, relishing her role as the queen bee at the county competition.

Maya and Sandra, who were signed in as guests of the Fanelli family, managed to hang around backstage and keep a watchful eye on the proceedings as they tried melting into the background, not wanting to draw attention to themselves.

Maya studied Sandra's black eye. "Wow, it looks a hell of a lot worse now than it did yesterday."

"Thank you, Maya, for that truly helpful, encouraging observation."

"Hey, I never claimed to be a coddler." Maya laughed.

"Well, at least it doesn't hurt. The only thing seriously damaged yesterday was my pride. I broke up literally dozens of fights between Jack and Ryan when they were growing up without once getting poked in the eye. I must be getting soft."

"I haven't seen the Fanellis. Are they even here yet?" Maya inquired, checking the time on her phone. "The competition is supposed to start in a few minutes."

"They went outside for a last-minute practice session with flash cards. They were here a little while ago, but Ellie Duncan kept staring at them, trying to psych them out, so I suggested they go someplace else, out of her sight."

"Smart move," Maya said. "She clearly has her favorites. Annabelle and Hunter can do no wrong, while Rocco and Phoebe are basically pariahs."

"It's so unfair, they're just kids," Sandra groused. "Why does she have to be so mean?"

Ellie suddenly stalked past them, eyeing them distrustfully before bowing her head to study the note cards in her hand on which she had probably scribbled her opening remarks.

"Listen, why don't you go out and check on the Fanellis and I will hang around here and keep an eye on things?" Maya suggested.

"No, you go. I want to stay put," Sandra said firmly.

Maya raised an eyebrow. "Sandra . . ."

"What? I'm an adult. I'm not going to confront Ellie again and cause a scene. I'm perfectly capable of staying in the background observing, like any good private detective."

"Okay," Maya said warily. "See you in a few."

She paused, trying to read Sandra's stony face, then smirked and walked through the wings of the auditorium and out into the hall.

Sandra carefully scanned the backstage area where the children from the surrounding county schools, including Falmouth, Scarborough, and Freeport, huddled with their parents and siblings, reviewing possible difficult words and quietly trying to spell them correctly in anticipation of what might come up during the competition. Sandra spied Phoebe sitting by herself in a corner, arms clasping her knees, her face full of apprehension and worry.

Sandra wandered over to her and knelt down beside her. "Why are you sitting all alone, Phoebe? Where's your dad?"

She shrugged, distraught. "I don't know. He said he would be here, but I haven't seen him. It's okay. I know he's superbusy."

Sandra knew that was a lie.

The poor girl was devastated.

She gently touched Phoebe's shoulder. "Don't worry. He'll make it in time."

Sandra was not sure why she had said that.

She had no way of knowing if Don Talbot would show up or not. He was hardly known as an attentive father you could always count on; accruing massive amounts of wealth seemed to be his top priority in life, a notch above raising his two motherless kids.

Just then, Ellie glided past, muttering under her breath but loud enough for Sandra to hear, "New tutor, Phoebe? Good luck with that."

Sandra felt her cheeks burning.

*No,* she told herself. *Hold your tongue. Do not get involved.*

But then, unable to let the cutting remark go, she shot to her feet and chased after Ellie, a voice inside her head screaming at her to adhere to Ewan Murphy's warning and just back off.

But that proved impossible.

She was appalled at how this revolting, puffed-up woman was trying to rattle an innocent sixth grader who was about to step on stage and try to win an intense competition that was going to require her complete focus and concentration.

It was inexcusable.

Ellie stopped suddenly, shuffling her note cards, and Sandra nearly rammed right into the back of her. Sensing her presence, Ellie slowly pivoted to face her.

"May I help you?" Ellie said with a sickeningly insincere smile.

"Just who do you think you are? Do you honestly believe that we both didn't hear what you said back there?"

"I was just wishing Phoebe luck. Is that a crime?"

"We both know that's not true. You were intentionally trying to throw that poor girl off her game. What's the matter with you? Why do you have to be so heartless?"

Ellie recoiled, stunned. "Heartless? You think I'm the heartless one because I don't indulge and curry favor with the kids who have an unfair advantage because of their ridiculously rich parents?"

"That's not what this is about and you know it!" Sandra lashed out.

"Oh, it's not? Why do you keep chasing after me, constantly attacking and harassing me? Is it because I gave your son a big fat *F*? One he wholeheartedly deserved? Is that why you've got a bee in your bonnet, no pun intended?" Ellie gave her a smug, self-satisfied look.

Taken aback, Sandra stood motionless.

"Oh dear, have I spoken out of turn? I can only guess from the astonished look on your face that Ryan hasn't yet shared the news that he *will* be flunking geography this semester?"

"I-I thought it was just one report," Sandra stammered.

"He cheated on the assignment. I would hate to give other students the impression that you can plagiarize a paper and just skate by unpunished. No, they need to learn there is a high price to pay. I think it only fair that he repeat the course this summer," Ellie said in a singsong voice, her eyes twinkling with glee.

This had gone far enough.

Sandra was about to move forward and get right up into Ellie's face to give her a piece of her mind when Dory Baumgarten, the math teacher at the high school and one of the judges of the county competition, hastened toward her, noticing Sandra shaking with fury.

"My goodness, Sandra, what's wrong?" Dory asked, full of concern.

Sandra brushed her off. "Nothing, Dory."

"But you look so distressed. Something is obviously troubling you."

Sandra faced her with a look of irritation. "I'm fine. Really! I just can't talk right now."

Stunned, Dory immediately backed away.

When Sandra whipped her head back around toward Ellie, she was already bouncing away, secure and content in the knowledge that she had thrown Sandra for a major loop.

Sandra began running after her.

As far as she was concerned, they were not yet finished with this conversation. She had to defend her son, who she knew was innocent of cheating. But then, Ewan Murphy suddenly strolled backstage, inserting himself in between Sandra and Ellie, who was now in the midst of an argument with someone else Sandra could not identify because of Ewan in her face, blocking her view of them.

"Anything I can help you with, Sandra?" Ewan asked with a snakish smile.

She knew she had to keep her mouth shut and just walk away in order to avoid further trouble from the school board.

"Everything's hunky-dory, Ewan," Sandra assured him, forcing a bright smile. "Just here to cheer the kids on."

"Happy to have you," Ewan said, although she hardly believed him. "I'm sure all our spellers appreciate your unbridled enthusiasm." He casually glanced over at Ellie, who was angrily gesticulating in front of someone none of them could see, and then walked away to greet some other parents.

Maya had been right.

She was coming in too hot.

She had to calm down or risk getting kicked out of the auditorium. Whether she liked it or not, this was Ellie Duncan's turf today, and it would not be wise to engage her any further.

She sensed someone fumbling next to her.

It was Dory Baumgarten, whose face looked stricken.

Sandra's heart dropped. "Dory, please forgive me. I'm just having a really bad day and I took it out on you, and that was inexcusable."

"Of course, Sandra, I was just worried seeing you so upset and out of sorts; it's just so out of character."

*Not so much lately*, Sandra thought to herself.

She was really letting Ellie Duncan get to her.

Mostly out of her mama bear's instinct to protect one of her cubs, who had fallen prey to this predatory wolf on the hunt and looking to attack.

Sandra hugged Dory. "I owe you a long, wine-soaked lunch. Let's catch up soon. I'll email you some dates."

"I would love that," Dory gushed.

Dory hustled off to take her place at the judges' table, which had been set up in front of the first row before the stage. Sandra spotted Maya returning from the hallway, passing Ellie, who was still berating someone who had now taken a step to the right and was fully visible. It was a beefy, barrel-chested man with tattoo sleeves on both arms, gripping a paint can in one hand and a wooden brush with the other. Although they had never

met, Sandra had heard about this man named
Rudy Holmes. He was an ex-convict who had served
his time for a botched burglary attempt in the early
aughts, during some especially hard times, and
was now trying to turn his life around. Although
rumors swirled around the community about
Rudy's violent past, Sandra had observed just from
seeing him around that he was, on the surface at
least, a docile man who was unfailingly polite to
everyone. Which begged the question, what had
he done to ignite the short-fused temper of Ellie
Duncan?

Sandra moved forward quickly, intercepting
Maya so they were both close enough to eavesdrop
on the argument.

"Look at my blouse! You splashed paint on it!"
Ellie roared.

"I'm sorry, Ms. Duncan, but you just came up
behind me so fast you startled me and I jumped. I
didn't mean to get paint on you."

"You should have finished this job yesterday!"

"We ran out of paint. I had to get approval to
buy more at Home Depot so I could get rid of all
the scuff marks on the walls before the spelling
bee," Rudy calmly explained.

"Look around you, Rudy; see all these people?
They're here for the spelling bee. It's too late!
Now gather your things and get out of here. I
don't want you hanging around making the parents uncomfortable."

She glared at the tattoo sleeves on his arms.

Rudy grimaced.

He knew what she was implying.

Everyone was aware of his criminal past and they certainly did not want him anywhere near their kids.

Which was a lie.

Most parents Sandra knew firmly believed in second chances and had no concerns about Rudy working at the middle school.

The hurt in Rudy's eyes gave way to defiance. "You want me to stop, you're going to have to talk to my supervisor, Burt Denning. He's the one who sent me here."

"Okay, where is he?" Ellie demanded to know.

"He's around somewhere." Rudy sighed.

Ellie stared fiercely at Rudy, full of hostility, then marched away in search of Burt, who was the head custodian at the middle school.

Sandra fought every urge to chase after Ellie Duncan again. How dare she treat Rudy Holmes, who was just doing his job, so discourteously, with so little respect! She then realized Maya was physically holding her back by the arm like she had with Don Talbot.

She blinked at Maya. "What?"

"I've known you long enough now. I can tell what you're thinking. As they used to say at the police academy, you need to stand down."

Maya was right.

She was in enough trouble already.

# Chapter 11

With a five-minute warning until the start of the annual Cumberland County Spelling Bee, Sandra hurried down the hall for a quick bathroom break. She was washing her hands and checking her makeup in the mirror when she heard someone sniffling from inside a stall. A woman barreled out of another stall from the far end, whom Sandra recognized as Hunter Hamlin's mother, Keri, a dour, humorless woman with a sour face that looked as if she was constantly sucking on lemons.

Keri ignored Sandra at the washbasin until Sandra finally spoke up. "Good luck out there!"

Keri seemed to notice her for the first time and answered curtly, "Excuse me?"

"I was just wishing your son Hunter luck."

She reared back. "Oh, well, thank you." It seemed to pain her to have to engage in an actual conversation, so she awkwardly turned away and placed her hands underneath the air dryer for a few seconds before scurrying out of the restroom without saying another word.

The sniffling in the stall behind Sandra persisted.

After applying some lip gloss from her purse, Sandra pivoted and walked over to the closed stall, where she could hear the sounds coming from. She paused, turning an ear to listen. There was more sniffling and crying.

She gently knocked on the door. "Are you okay?"

The sniffling and crying suddenly stopped.

"Is there anything I can do to help?"

More silence.

The latch on the stall door slid open. Sandra took a step back as it swung open, revealing Phoebe Talbot wiping her runny nose with her forefinger, her eyes wet from sobbing.

Sandra bent down. "Phoebe, what's the matter? Why are you crying?"

Phoebe stared at the tiled floor and shrugged.

Sandra had a pretty good idea what had upset her.

"Are you sad because of what Ms. Duncan said to you earlier?"

Phoebe nodded slightly, sniffing and wiping away the tears from her face with the palm of her hand.

Sandra tenderly took her by the arms. "You shouldn't take her words to heart. Ms. Duncan was acting very unprofessional. She knows you didn't break any rules by working with a tutor. She had no right to make you feel bad about it."

Phoebe choked back more tears. "She thinks I'm a cheater."

Sandra grimaced. "Well, she's been making those accusations about a lot of people lately, which is unfair and inappropriate and hurtful. So I want you to forget all about Ms. Duncan and just do your thing. You're a world-class speller, with or without a tutor, so go out there and show everyone what you're made of. You got this!"

Sandra studied Phoebe's face, wondering if her pep talk had had any effect.

Phoebe kept her eyes glued to the floor.

Sandra tried another tactic. "Win or lose, I know your dad is very proud of you."

Finally, Phoebe raised her eyes to meet Sandra's. "He's not here."

"What? Where is he?"

"I don't know. He said he'd be here. But he's not."

Given what a scene Don Talbot had caused with Ellie over her efforts to disqualify Phoebe for using a tutor, Sandra was surprised he was now a no-show. Still, she got the sinking feeling that this most likely happened a lot.

"He's a very busy man, but I'm sure he'll make it. He's probably just running a little late."

It felt odd to be defending Don Talbot.

Sandra did not even know him that well.

But she just could not bear the disappointed look on Phoebe's face. It was unfathomable to think Don was going to blow off this incredibly important day for his daughter. He had to be on his way. Still, deep down. she suspected work always came first.

"He'd never miss one of Cooper's football games," Phoebe muttered with a hint of resentment.

Sandra straightened up, glimpsing the wall clock. "We better get you backstage. The spelling bee is about to start." She took Phoebe by the hand, guiding her out. "Don't worry, every time you spell a word correctly, I will be sitting in the front row, the loudest cheering section you've ever heard!"

Inside the auditorium, when Ellie Duncan took to the stage, introducing all the students followed by the esteemed judges, the competition swiftly got underway. Two kids, one from Scarborough and the other from Freeport, were knocked out in the first round, missing easy words like "rhythmic" and "exaggerate." The top four, Rocco, Phoebe, Annabelle, and, surprisingly, Hunter Hamlin, remained strong, each nailing every word one of the judges threw at them, effortlessly slaying the rest of the competition.

By the fifth round, Sandra held her breath when Dory Baumgarten gave Phoebe her next word.

"Paraphernalia."

Phoebe gulped.

This obviously was not a word she had practiced.

"May I hear it in a sentence, please?" Phoebe squeaked.

Dory Baumgarten answered, "The detective found various pieces of drug paraphernalia throughout the suspect's apartment."

Phoebe stood motionless, her eyes closed, as she tried spelling the word in her head.

The clock was ticking.

Sandra held her breath.

And then Phoebe's eyes popped open. "P-a-r-a . . ." She stopped, whispered some letters to herself before continuing. "p-h-e-r-n-a-l-i-a. Paraphernalia."

The wait for a response was interminable.

Sandra's stomach tightened from the suspense.

"Correct," Dory said to thunderous applause from the audience.

Sandra leapt to her feet, clapping so hard the palms of her hands turned red.

Beaming, Phoebe returned to her seat.

It was Rocco's turn. He apprehensively stepped over to the podium and leaned into the microphone. Both Hunter and Annabelle had spelled their last words correctly as well, so if he missed this one, he was out of the competition.

Another judge read from a card. "Acquiesce."

All eyes were upon him.

Sandra detected the corners of his mouth lifting up into a sly smile. He knew this word by heart. He had practiced it.

He then confidently rattled off, "Acquiesce. A-c-q-u-i-e-s-c-e. Acquiesce!"

"Correct."

Wild applause as Rocco waved at Eugenio and Lucia, who were jumping up and down cheering, before turning around and bounding back to his seat.

All four kids were still in the game.

But only two of them would advance to the state spelling bee. The competition at this point was fierce, and all their families, not to mention Sandra in the front row and Maya hovering backstage, were on edge to see who would be the last pair standing.

# Chapter 12

During a fifteen-minute break, Maya milled about backstage, watching Doug and Noah Chastain-Wheeler crouched down in front of Annabelle and quizzing her, hurling words at breakneck speed, which she dutifully spelled as fast as she could. They were intensely focused on preparing her for the next round. Other kids were making TikTok videos or Instagramming live. Sandra was sitting on a folding chair next to Phoebe, quietly giving her another pep talk because her father, Don Talbot, was still a no-show. Eugenio and Lucia Fanelli as well as Hal and Keri Hamlin were standing around, looking confused. Their sons, Rocco and Hunter, were nowhere to be seen.

Maya walked out into the hallway where the audience was taking advantage of a table set out with coffee and pastries. She looked around but saw no sign of the two boys. Then she walked down toward the gymnasium and poked her head in. The gym was empty, but she heard low voices. Creeping across the basketball court, she rounded the bleachers and stopped short at the sight of Hunter Hamlin standing menacingly over the much-smaller Rocco Fanelli, having pushed him up against the wall and with his hand wrapped around his throat.

Maya rushed forward. "What's going on here?"

Startled by her presence, Hunter immediately withdrew his hand and Rocco rubbed his neck.

"Nothing," Hunter spat out.

As a former police officer, Maya knew she could be intimidating, so she used that to her full advantage. She gripped Hunter by the arm and knelt down so she was right up in his face. "What I just witnessed here is assault. That's a crime. Do you know how long you can go to prison for that?"

"N-no," Hunter stammered, his cheeks reddening.

"A long time. So think hard before you decide to touch anyone like that ever again, do you hear me, Hunter?"

He nodded, petrified.

"Now get out of here. Your parents are looking for you."

He tried to make his escape, but she twisted him back to make eye contact. "Just remember, I'm always watching you."

He nodded slightly, his body shaking, and then he bolted out of the gym. Maya stood back up and rested a hand on Rocco's shoulder. "Want to tell me what just happened? I thought you two were starting to become friends."

Rocco did not want to discuss it, but he knew

Maya was not about to drop the subject. Resigned, he mumbled, "He was mad I got him into trouble."

"For getting caught leaving the note in your locker?"

Rocco nodded again.

"That's a mess of his own making. He's just trying to scare you, throw you off your game. Don't let him get to you."

But she could see the boy was rattled.

"Are you going to be okay?"

"Yes. I'd better go find my parents."

He scooted away, embarrassed.

Maya hoped Rocco would rally in the next round, prove to Hunter that he would not be bowed by any more of his bullying. But alas, whatever underhanded tactics Hunter had decided to employ to disrupt Rocco's concentration and performance appeared to be working. When Rocco stepped up to the podium ten minutes later and was given the word "vengeance," a relatively simple word to spell, especially for someone of Rocco's exceptional skill level, he forgot the second *e*.

"Vengeance. V-e-n-g-a-n-c-e. Vengeance."

Dory Baumgarten, the judge who had given him the word, deflated. "I am sorry, Rocco, that is incorrect."

Annabelle suppressed a smile.

Phoebe felt bad for him.

Hunter remained stone-faced, frozen like a statue, worried Maya might still be watching him.

Rocco fled the stage in tears, passing Maya, who was standing in the wings, and retreated to a corner. Eugenio and Lucia hurried backstage to con-

sole their son, with Sandra following closely behind them.

As Eugenio and Lucia enveloped Rocco in a
tight hug, whispering encouraging words and
telling him how proud they were of him, Sandra si-
dled up next to Maya, who turned to her, fuming.

"I happened upon that punk Hunter Hamlin
bullying him. It threw him and he got nervous;
that's the only reason he missed an easy word like
'vengeance.' We need to report this to the judges
and get that kid disqualified."

"No," a man's voice said.

It was Eugenio.

Maya gaped at him, surprised. "Why not?"

"Rocco's done. He just wants to go home," Eugenio said, defeated. "It's over."

Maya could not let it go just yet. "But if we explain what happened—"

Eugenio cut her off. "It probably won't make
any difference anyway. All these kids are under a
lot of pressure. In the end, he misspelled a word.
End of story. I appreciate all you two have done."

Maya felt horrible. They had actually done very
little. After nearly a week since the Fanellis first
came to their office to hire them, they were no
closer to identifying the person responsible for
writing the threatening note.

"Please, let us continue with the investigation a
little while longer," Maya begged.

"Rocco is out of the competition. What's the
point? We just want to move on. I will Venmo the
rest of your fee later today. Thank you."

Eugenio's tone was final.

He turned on his heel and rejoined his wife and

son. Hugging them with each arm, he escorted his family out.

Maya was not ready or willing to let it go. "I don't care what Eugenio wants, I need to find the cretin who threatened the life of an innocent twelve-year-old boy."

"Maya, I know you're passionate about this, but we just got fired," Sandra said calmly. "Our job is finished."

Maya stewed some more, but she knew Sandra was right.

If they continued investigating crimes with no client to pay them, they would soon go out of business.

Both women were curious to see how the rest of the competition shook out, so they hung around backstage, watching from the wings.

Annabelle was at the podium.

The third judge, a college professor from the University of Southern Maine, read from his card. "Pterodactyl."

Annabelle grinned from ear to ear.

She obviously was very familiar with this word.

The judge smiled. "Would you like to hear it in a sentence?"

"No need," Annabelle announced confidently.

Doug and Noah were on the edge of their seats, beaming expectantly.

"Pterodactyl," Annabelle proceeded. "P-t-e-r-o-d-a-c-t-e-l. Pterodactyl."

There was a long pause.

"I am afraid that's incorrect," the judge lamented.

Gasps came from the audience.

One of her dads, Doug, jumped to his feet, a

hand over his mouth, realizing she had misspelled the word.

Annabelle remained at the podium, shell-shocked.

The unthinkable had just happened. Her dream of going to the National Spelling Bee was now dashed.

Her eyes welled up with tears and she rushed off the stage, her doting fathers running out of the auditorium to meet her and comfort her.

There were now two left standing.

Phoebe and Hunter.

If both kids spelled their words correctly, they would advance to the state competition.

Phoebe spelled "descendant" with little effort.

Then it was Hunter's turn.

Dory Baumgarten picked up a card. "Pedestrian."

Hunter leaned forward at the podium. "Pedestrian. P-e-d-e-s . . ."

Suddenly, there was earsplitting feedback from the microphone as Hunter completed spelling the word. None of the judges or anyone in the audience were able to hear the rest.

"Hunter, you're too close to the microphone. Could you take a step back, please?"

He did as he was told.

"I'm going to have to ask you to repeat the spelling of the word so we can accurately record it," Dory instructed. "In the official record, so far we have p-e-d-e-s. You may resume where you left off or start again with the whole word."

"Okay, I'll start again." Hunter mumbled. "Pedestrian. P-e-d-a . . . Wait, no, I meant to say e. P-e-d-e-s-t-r-i-a-n. Pedestrian."

The audience applauded warmly, under the impression that the spelling bee was now over, but the clapping soon died down as the judges conferred among themselves for an extraordinarily long period of time. Soon there was silence as everyone waited with bated breath to find out what was happening.

Finally, Dory Baumgarten broke from her two fellow judges and stood up. "I'm sorry, Hunter, but there is a hard-and-fast rule that a contestant will be disqualified if, while spelling the entire word, they utter any letter different from what the Bee official recorded and read to the speller."

Hunter blinked at Dory, confused. "I-I don't understand."

"He got the word right!" Ellie Duncan blurted out, unable to contain herself.

"Again, I'm sorry, but we have to follow the rules," Dory said pointedly, irked by Ellie's sudden outburst. She was supposed to be hosting the spelling bee dispassionately, without favor, and clearly Hunter was one of her prized pets.

Annabelle came bounding back onstage, eager for a second chance. She practically shoved Hunter away from the podium to take his place. The college professor announced her word, which was apropos of her current situation. "Reprieve."

Annabelle turned to her two fathers, hovering in the wings, near Maya and Sandra.

"Reprieve. R-e-p-r-i-e-v-e. Reprieve!"

"That is correct. Congratulations, Annabelle. You and Phoebe will be advancing to the state competition."

The audience erupted.

Ellie stormed offstage, furious that only one of her picks was moving on, ticked off that Phoebe Talbot had somehow managed to squeak through. As she blew past Maya and Sandra, they heard her muttering to herself, "Descendant? A five-year-old could spell that. It was a gift from the judges!"

Descendant.

Phoebe's winning word.

She slammed out of the side door into the hallway, stopping to berate the head custodian, Burt Denning, who was cleaning up a coffee spill with a mop and pail of soapy water. "I told you I didn't want that dangerous ex-con you hired anywhere near the school during the spelling bee today. It's disconcerting for the parents, and it makes the entire school look bad."

"Rudy's paid his debt to society, Ellie, and he has a right to make a living—"

She was tired of listening to him. "Sure, whatever, just have him paint the walls at night when no one's around."

"That's cruel. He's a decent man . . ."

Maya noticed Annabelle and her two dads nearby, making a self-congratulatory video with Annabelle's phone for her social media accounts as their attention slowly drifted over to the altercation between Ellie and Burt.

Ellie's nostrils flared. "I noticed some trash that needs to be swept up near the teachers' lounge. Perhaps you should spend less time defending a known criminal and more time focusing on your job. Otherwise, Burt, we may have a problem that will have to be brought up at the next school board meeting."

She stomped off in a huff.

Burt Denning trembled with rage.

He grabbed ahold of his mop and began violently pushing it up and down the floor, cleaning up the spill.

Sandra shook her head. "That woman is a monster. She doesn't even work at this school."

Maya nodded in agreement.

They both were thinking the same thing.

Ellie Duncan was just unhinged enough that perhaps she had been the one who wrote the death threat and then paid her little henchman, Hunter Hamlin, to leave it in Rocco's locker.

Ellie as a possible suspect was not that far out of left field. And paid or not, Maya especially wanted to keep digging to finally learn the truth.

# Chapter 13

Phoebe Talbot and Annabelle Chastain-Wheeler both stood awkwardly on the stage, waiting to be awarded their first and second place trophies for the county competition, which were displayed on a card table stage left, opposite the two girls. The audience murmured restlessly. The judges were huddled together, chattering. Sandra and Maya were both backstage wondering what was causing the long delay. Finally, with a few parents shouting at the judges to wrap this thing up so everyone could finally go home, Dory Baumgarten ambled up on the stage, winking at the two winners before taking to the podium and speaking into the microphone.

"Hello, everybody. I want to thank you for your patience. Unfortunately, the host of today's event, Ellie Duncan, has done a disappearing act. We can't seem to locate her and she is not answering any of our texts, so if you'll just bear with me, I will be happy to present the trophies to our winning students." Dory marched over and lifted up the second place trophy, carrying it back to the podium. "I would like to present this second place trophy to Annabelle Chastain-Wheeler, who will represent our school and all of Cumberland County at the Maine State Spelling Bee Competition at the Merrill Auditorium right here in Portland next week. Congratulations, Annabelle!"

As Annabelle pranced over to collect her prize, grimacing slightly for not coming in first, Maya and Sandra slipped out the side door from the wings.

Maya looked around the empty hallway; everyone was presently inside the middle school auditorium for the awards presentation. "So where do you think Ellie snuck off to?"

"I haven't a clue. It's not like her to give up the spotlight to Dory Baumgarten. This was her big moment. I hate to say it, but I have a sickening feeling," Sandra said, worry lines forming on her forehead.

"I'll check outside. Why don't you look around the school? Text me if you find her," Maya suggested, spinning on her heel and heading toward the exit to the parking lot.

Sandra hastily made her way down the corridor toward the classrooms, rounding a corner and running smack into Rudy Holmes, who jumped back, surprised. He had on a dark coat, his hands thrust deep inside the front pockets, and a gray, flat cap on his head. By the worn-down, drawn look on his face, he had obviously endured a very long day.

"Rudy, I'm sorry, I didn't mean to startle you," Sandra said.

"No problem," he spat out, stepping around her, anxious to get out of there.

"Wait, before you go, have you seen Ellie Duncan?"

He stopped in his tracks.

He did not turn around.

"Yeah," he grumbled. "About ten minutes ago. She passed me on her way to the restroom, I think."

Sandra found it odd that he did not turn around when he spoke to her, as if he did not want to reveal the expression on his face to her. She guessed it was probably not one of genuine concern. It was no secret he abhorred Ellie.

"Did you talk to her?"

"Nope. She talked to me, though. She started yelling at me about something else she thought I did; I couldn't tell you what, though, because I've learned to just tune her out. Is that it? Do you want to know anything else? I'm late. I need to report to my parole officer."

"No, that's all. Thank you, Rudy."

He hurriedly hustled off.

Sandra watched him go, then continued on down the hall to the restroom, where she popped her head in through the door. "Ellie?"

No answer.

Sandra crouched down to look underneath the row of stalls and didn't see any pair of feet. The bathroom was empty. She let go of the knob, allowing the door to close and turned to see Lucas walking toward her with a broad, cheerful grin on his face.

"Damn. You're a sight for sore eyes," he said, wrapping his arms around her waist and brushing her lips with a kiss. He gazed into her eyes and went in for a second kiss, but she gently pushed him away.

"We shouldn't be doing this here!" Sandra cried.

"No one's around. They're all in the auditorium."

He pulled her in closer to him, his eyes dancing. "Man, you're beautiful."

Sandra extricated herself from his grasp. "Lucas, please. Not now. Later. What are you even doing here?"

"The school was short on equipment for the girls' softball team, so I brought over some mitts and balls and even an extra scoreboard from the high school for their home game next week. I was just dropping them off in the gym." He placed his hands on her hips. "Now, how much later are we talking about? Do I have a shot at taking you out for a romantic dinner tonight?"

She ignored his question. "I need to find Ellie Duncan."

"Why?" Lucas scoffed. "Most people I know want to lose her in a crowd, not find her."

"She's missing," Sandra said ominously.

Her phone buzzed.

It was a text from Maya.

**No sign of Ellie but her car is still in the parking lot. Either she left on foot or she is still somewhere in the building.**

Sandra took Lucas by the hand. "Come on, you can help me look for her."

They checked all the classrooms, the teachers' lounge, the remaining restrooms, even the administration offices to no avail. Finally, after a thorough search of the premises, Sandra was about to give up when she noticed a door slightly ajar at the far end of the hall.

"What's that?" Sandra asked.

"A supply closet. It's usually locked. Only the teachers and janitorial staff have keys."

Sandra's heart pounded as they slowly approached.

She gripped the door handle and swung it open.

"Whoa!" Lucas cried.

Sandra threw a hand to her mouth, suppressing a scream.

Lying on the floor in a heap was the crumpled-up body of Ellie Duncan. Her head was twisted around and she had a glassy-eyed, vacant look on her waxy face.

The despised spelling bee coordinator was most definitely dead.

Murdered.

Someone in the vicinity had just spelled "A-E-I-Kill-U!"

# Chapter 14

Detective Beth Hart, a true force of nature, ordered the phalanx of police officers to corral everyone into the gymnasium so they could all be formally questioned. Hart was a no-nonsense, keen-eyed, serious woman with whom Maya had served at the South Portland Police Department for almost five years before Maya resigned under a cloud of controversy.

Maya loved her time as a cop, but when her husband, Max, was arrested for corruption, her continuing on at the department proved untenable. She would forever be stained by her husband's mistakes and misdeeds, which led her to leave the force altogether and open her own business as a private investigator.

Beth had always been a reliable ally, and Maya felt comfortable contacting her for advice on a few cases from time to time. Beth had been promoted to homicide detective not too long ago, so Maya knew the pert, tiny, auburn-haired woman was out to prove herself by solving all her cases in short order and impressing the chief, as well as other South Portland community leaders.

Maya sensed, as the officers cleared the area near the crime scene, that she would not be allowed to loiter and observe, but she was hoping Beth might cut her a break and ignore her hanging around as the forensics team set about doing their work, combing the supply closet for clues and evidence.

Maya felt a firm hand on her arm. "Ma'am, I'm going to have to ask you to join the others in the gymnasium to wait for further instructions."

The officer who held her by the arm was barely old enough to shave.

"I'm a private investigator," Maya informed him, knowing full well it would make no difference.

"I understand, ma'am, but you can't be here."

Maya's eyes shot toward her friend Beth, who was crouched down, inspecting the body. "Beth?"

Beth just shook her head, not even looking in their direction. "It's all right, Kaplan. She can stay. She's a former colleague."

The young officer carefully studied her. "I recognize you. Didn't your husband . . . ?" His voice trailed off as the realization sunk in, and then he gave her a curt nod and hurriedly walked away.

Maya made her way over to Beth. "Thanks for letting me stay."

"Don't make me regret it, Maya," Beth said sharply.

Maya stared down at Ellie Duncan's still body.

The terrified look on the victim's face made

Maya's whole body shudder as she examined her disheveled appearance.

"The bruising on her neck suggests she was strangled," Maya said, although she assumed Beth had already reached the same conclusion. There were also office supplies strewn about, indicating some kind of a struggle.

"They also found skin fragments underneath her fingernails, so the killer may have left with some scratches," Beth said matter-of-factly.

A woman's shrill voice suddenly punctured the air. "Excuse me! Excuse me! Let me through, please!"

Maya spun around to see Dory Baumgarten, one of the spelling bee judges, trying to push her way past the young officer who was valiantly attempting to block her path.

"Ma'am, you can't be here. Please, go back to the gymnasium."

"I need to speak with the officer in charge," Dory persisted. "I have very important information."

Detective Hart sprang to her feet. "Let her through, Officer Kaplan."

The officer stepped aside, allowing Dory to bustle down the hall to Detective Hart and Maya. As she opened her mouth to speak, her eyes fell upon the dead body of Ellie Duncan, and she let out a short gasp. Detective Hart took a step to her left, blocking Dory's view of the corpse. "How can I help you?"

"Actually, I'm here to help you. I know who killed poor Ellie!" Dory exclaimed.

Maya and Beth exchanged curious glances.

Dory paused, drawing out the suspense for dramatic effect.

Beth eyed her impatiently. "Yes? If you have any pertinent information, I would appreciate—"

"It was Sandra Wallage," Dory blurted out.

Maya scoffed, "That's preposterous!"

Dory shrank back.

Beth shot Maya a look of warning. "Maya, calm down."

"Sandra is my partner; there's no way—"

Beth interrupted her. "You are here at my discretion. I can easily have you removed if you can't hold your tongue."

Maya threw up her hands in surrender and reluctantly took a small step back.

Beth spoke gently to Dory. "What is your name?"

"Dory Baumgarten. And I'm a witness. I saw her!"

Beth cocked an eyebrow. "You saw Mrs. Wallage attack Ellie Duncan?"

"No! I saw her threaten her. Just a little while before she turned up dead."

Beth took this information in, then signaled for the young officer who was hovering a few feet away to come forward. "Officer Kaplan, would you escort Ms. Baumgarten into that classroom?" She pointed to the science room across the hall, then she returned her attention to Dory. "I'll join you in a minute so we can discuss what you saw further, is that all right?"

"Yes, thank you." Dory gave Maya a cautious glance. "I'm only trying to help. I don't mean to cause anyone trouble. I just thought it was my duty to report to the police what I witnessed in order to assist with the investigation."

"And we certainly appreciate it," Detective Hart assured her as Officer Kaplan led her away.

Maya could not help but scoff again. "You honestly don't believe Sandra had anything to do with this, do you?"

"Honestly? No."

"It's ridiculous, Beth. Sandra couldn't possibly be the killer."

"You were a cop. How many times has someone said that and then turned out to be proven wrong?"

Maya's mouth dropped open in shock. "Beth, come on!"

"Look, Maya, I am obligated to follow up on every lead in a murder case, even if that includes your BFF, so you need to back off and let me do my job, okay?"

Maya knew she was flying off the handle and needed to keep a level head. "You're right, Beth. Sorry."

"It's okay." Beth lowered her gaze to Ellie's body on the floor, now covered with a white sheet by one of the forensics team. "I know this is a lot to deal with. I'm going to go talk to the witness."

As Beth strode away, Maya tried to compose herself. The thought of Sandra Wallage as the killer was an absolutely absurd notion. Still, she was going to have to break the news to her partner that she was, at present, the number one suspect.

# Chapter 15

As the police cleared the area near the supply closet where Ellie Duncan was found, Don Talbot muscled his way through the crowd of rubber-neckers in the hallway behind some yellow police tape, trying to get a glimpse of the body.

"Where's my daughter? Where's Phoebe?" Don bellowed.

Sandra rushed to intercept him. "Don, all the students have been escorted to the gymnasium. I'm sure you'll find her there."

"What the hell happened? What's going on?"

"There's been a murder," Sandra explained solemnly.

Don's eyes widened in shock. "What? Who?"

"Ellie Duncan."

"Oh my God," Don muttered. "How?"

"I don't know many details yet, but the police are combing the scene for clues as we speak."

"It could have been anyone," Don remarked,

shaking his head. "There wasn't a teacher or student in this school that didn't despise that woman."

"Yes, Don, we're all aware of that, but it's still an unspeakable tragedy."

Don glanced at Sandra with a knowing smirk, as if to say, *Is it, though?*

Sandra ignored him. "Come on, I'll take you to the gym and help you find Phoebe."

Don stopped her. "Wait. What about the spelling bee? Did they postpone it when the body was found?"

Sandra stared at him incredulously. "No, Don, it was already over."

"How did Phoebe do?"

"She aced every word and will be advancing to the state competition." Sandra sighed, astounded by his complete lack of sensitivity.

Don lit up, a wide smile stretching across his face. "That's my girl. I knew she'd kill it!" He caught himself. "Sorry, poor choice of words."

Don bounded off toward the gym with Sandra by his side. They found Phoebe standing by herself, watching Annabelle receive hugs and congratulations from her two adoring dads. Sandra felt sorry for her, but Don seemed oblivious that his daughter was all alone after her big win.

"Baby doll, you did it! I am so proud of you," Don shouted, running over and enveloping her in a warm hug. Phoebe stood stiffly as her father squeezed her, eyes downcast.

"Where were you?" Phoebe muttered. "I tried to find you in the audience, but I didn't see you."

Don let go and nodded, guilt-ridden. "I know, I know, I tried to get here on time, but I had a work thing and I just couldn't sneak out in time to make it."

By the exasperated look on Phoebe's face, Sandra knew the girl had probably heard this excuse many times before today.

"But I'm here now, and we need to celebrate. How about we corral a few of your friends and I will take everyone out for pizza? How does that sound?"

Phoebe shrugged. "No. I think I just want to get my trophy and go home."

Sandra suspected Phoebe did not have any friends to invite but was reticent about telling her father that sad fact, fearing his resounding disappointment in her lack of popularity.

Don checked his watch and turned to Sandra. "When do you think they'll get around to awarding the trophies?"

Sandra's mouth dropped open. "Um, I don't expect they'll be handing out any trophies today, Don, not with everything that's going on."

"That's too bad. Leave it to Ellie Duncan to spoil things for everyone."

"To be fair, it wasn't Ellie who messed things up, it was the person who killed her," Sandra reminded him.

Don was unmoved. He took Phoebe by the hand. "Come on, baby doll, let's get you out of here."

"Hang on, Don, I'm not sure we're allowed to leave just yet. The police want to question everyone."

"They certainly don't need to talk to Phoebe.

She was on stage in the auditorium the whole time, right?"

"I certainly don't think you have to worry about Phoebe being a suspect." Sandra paused. "But they may be interested in you, given your ill will toward the victim."

Don chortled. "*Me?*"

"You certainly took umbrage with her treatment of Cooper."

"Well, then, I guess it's lucky I have an alibi. I was in a meeting with my entire staff and a major client. I can't think of anything more airtight than that."

There was no arguing him on that point.

"And I'm not the only parent around here who had an issue with Ellie Duncan's teaching style, am I right, Sandra?"

"I admit I was not a part of Ellie's fan club, but I had no desire to see her dead."

Don leaned in with a conspiratorial smile and whispered in her ear, "Oh, come on, let's be real for a second. Neither of us is going to lose any sleep tonight over this."

Sandra recoiled. "Don't lump me in with you, Don. We are not the same. I am truly upset by this."

Don raised an eyebrow, skeptical.

"Don't look at me like that. I am not even remotely a suspect. I was the one who discovered the body," Sandra snapped.

"Can we talk?"

The voice came from someone standing directly behind her.

Sandra spun around.

It was Maya, looking slightly disturbed by something.

"Sure," Sandra said, curious. She turned back around, winking at Phoebe. "Congratulations, Phoebe. You were awesome today."

"Thank you," Phoebe muttered as her father put his arm around her, pulling her close to him.

Sandra followed Maya over to the bleachers, where they could talk in private. "What is it?"

"I just want to give you a heads-up. Detective Hart is considering you a suspect."

"What? That's crazy!" Sandra cried. "I was just telling Don that Lucas and I were the ones who discovered the body."

"Dory Baumgarten told the police that she witnessed you and Ellie having a heated fight shortly before she was killed."

"Yes, but I would hardly call that a fight. It was a disagreement. It's not like we exchanged blows. Come on!"

"I'm just the messenger here, Sandra," Maya said calmly. "I only want you to be aware."

"Beth Hart knows me. How could she even have me on her radar as a possible murderer?"

"I don't know, but she does. And it doesn't help that Ellie lodged a complaint against you with the school board, accusing you of harassment shortly before she turned up dead."

The blood suddenly drained from Sandra's face.

She had forgotten all about that.

It was circumstantial evidence but evidence nonetheless.

And unlike many of Ellie's other enemies, most notably Don Talbot, Sandra did not have an airtight alibi at the time of the murder. She was wandering around the school.

Sandra now had a sinking feeling that her life was about to take a very dark turn.

# Chapter 16

When Ryan sashayed down the stairs and into the living room of the Wallage home to model his garish black-and-gold-paisley tuxedo, spinning around to give Vanessa and his mother a 360-degree view of his prom outfit, Vanessa crinkled her nose, unimpressed.

Ryan immediately noticed her less-than-glowing reaction. "What, you don't think I look good in this?"

Vanessa shook her head. "Um, I thought we decided to go with a classic black tux."

"Yeah, I know, but then the guy at the rental shop showed me this, and I thought to myself, *I'm going to really stand out wearing this one.*"

"I won't argue with that." Sandra chuckled.

"It was between gold and purple, but I didn't want to wear purple paisley because then people would think I was trying too hard to channel Prince."

"Ryan, you look good wearing anything," Vanessa said in a measured tone. "But that jacket is going to clash with my dress. Gold and turquoise do not go well together."

"Well, you've been keeping your dress under wraps like some big state secret, so how would I know that?"

Vanessa sighed, frustrated. "Because it's bad luck to show your date the dress you're going to wear before the prom."

"I thought that only applied to weddings," Ryan argued. He struck a pose. "Mom, what do you think?"

"I think I should stay out of this discussion. This is between you two. I will support whatever you both decide to wear to the prom."

"Just like Dad, always the politician," Ryan cracked.

Sandra ignored that last remark. "Vanessa, are you planning to stay for dinner?"

"No, I have to get home and work on my valedictory speech. So far all I have is, 'My fellow students, parents, friends, family, and faculty, today marks a very important day.' That's it. That's all I've written. I have no idea what else to say."

"You'll come up with something great," Sandra assured her. "I have complete confidence in you."

The doorbell rang.

"I'll get it," Ryan said, bounding out of the living room.

"Number one in your class," Sandra marveled, smiling at Vanessa. "I know your mother is extremely proud."

"She's more nervous about my speech than I

am," Vanessa said. "But that's because she's terrified of public speaking."

Ryan came back into the living room. "Uh, Mom, there is a detective at the door who wants to talk to you. She says it's important."

Sandra's stomach tightened. "Oh?"

Not wanting to spook the kids, Sandra stood up from the couch and casually crossed out of the room. "Stay here. I will be right back." She caught Ryan and Vanessa exchanging concerned looks. Sandra circled into the foyer to see Lieutenant Beth Hart, flanked by two uniformed cops, standing in the doorway.

"Detective Hart," Sandra said, eyeing her warily. "How can I help you?"

"Sorry to bother you, Mrs. Wallage, but I was hoping you would accompany me down to the precinct so I can ask you a few questions."

"Why don't you come inside and I'll make some coffee and you can ask your questions here?" Sandra offered, glancing at the two cops staring at her with stone-cold expressions.

"I would prefer it if you came with us," Lieutenant Hart insisted.

Sandra knew what was going on.

Because she was the wife, or soon-to-be ex-wife, of a US senator, Hart did not want to allow any concessions that might be open to criticism. She wanted to avoid any favoritism or special treatment toward anyone perceived to be an elite member of the community. She was determined to treat Sandra just like any other suspect of a crime, and that meant grilling her in an interrogation room, Hart's home turf.

"I see," Sandra mumbled. She grabbed her coat from the rack next to the door and cranked her head around to see Ryan and Vanessa peering around the corner, watching the scene. "Ryan, there's a frozen pizza you can pop in the oven for dinner. I will come home just as soon as I can."

"Okay," Ryan said. "Should I call Dad?"

"No, that won't be necessary."

She saw Vanessa already on her phone, presumably texting Maya, which would be far more helpful given her personal history with Beth Hart at the department.

Sandra threw on her coat and followed Hart down the walkway to her car, which was parked in the driveway behind Sandra's Mercedes. One of the officers opened the door to the back seat and she slid inside. He slammed the door shut so hard she jumped. Detective Hart sat in the passenger's seat and the other officer got behind the wheel and backed out, driving toward the South Portland Police Station without another word. Sandra knew the silent treatment was designed to keep her on edge and off-balance with the hope, the expectation, that her nerves might cause her to say something incriminating. Even though Sandra had nothing to hide, the tactic seemed to be working. She was definitely on edge.

Within twenty minutes, Sandra found herself sitting on a rickety old metal chair, face-to-face with Detective Hart, blinded by harsh fluorescent overhead lighting. The officer who had driven the squad car stood by the door as if he was stationed there to prevent her from trying to escape.

Detective Hart slurped from a can of Diet Coke

and then set it down on the metal table separating them. "Sure I can't get you something to drink?"

"I'm fine, thank you," Sandra said in a clipped tone.

"Sorry to drag you all the way down here . . ."

Sandra squinted underneath the harsh lighting. "Are you?"

Hart smirked knowingly, then continued. "I just have a few questions, and then Officer Willey over there will be happy to drive you home." She gestured toward the cop by the door, who stared straight ahead, refusing to crack a smile. "So, according to your statement at the scene, when you discovered the body of Ellie Duncan, you were with . . ." She checked her notes. "Lucas Cavill?"

"Yes, that's right."

"And you were with him the whole time?"

"Yes." Sandra paused. "I mean, no. When everyone realized Ellie was missing, we fanned out to try to find her. That's when I ran into Lucas in the hallway. I asked him to help me find Ellie, and after that we came across the body."

Hart scribbled some notes. "Uh-huh. And what is your relationship with Mr. Cavill?"

This one caught Sandra by surprise. "What do you mean?"

"What's the nature of your relationship? Friend? Boyfriend? Partner?"

"I don't see the relevance here."

"It's just a question."

Sandra sighed. "Friend."

Hart cocked a doubting eyebrow.

"Maybe a little more than just a friend. We're still trying to figure all of that out," Sandra explained, humiliated. She loathed anyone knowing the details about her personal life, especially since her divorce with Stephen technically was not yet final.

She could tell Hart already knew she and Lucas were dating.

Which meant she had probably already interviewed Lucas and was trying to catch her in a lie, a contradiction from what Lucas had previously told her in his own statement.

"Did you know that Ellie Duncan had filed a complaint with the school board?" Hart asked, locking eyes with Sandra.

"Yes. Ewan Murphy came to my office to inform me. I told him it was a ridiculous claim. I was simply trying to reason with her. She gave my son Ryan an unfair grade in geography."

"Ellie told the school board that you were strong-arming her into giving your son a passing grade so he could graduate with his class, and that if she did not comply, it would be a bad look for the esteemed Wallage family."

"That's a gross mischaracterization. Ryan is a good student. If anything, she was punishing him *because* of his family name."

"Okay," Hart said quietly. She lowered the reading glasses she was wearing to the bridge of her nose as she conferred with her notes. "Just so I get the timeline right. After Ms. Duncan filed a complaint, that was when Dory Baumgarten witnessed you threatening her?"

"I did *not* threaten her. You're twisting everything around to make me look guilty!" Sandra exploded.

A knowing smile crept across Hart's face. "I'm just asking a few simple questions, Mrs. Wallage. No need to get emotional."

Sandra sat back, agitated. She was playing right into Hart's hands. This was the whole goal of the interrogation. To get her upset enough that she might confess. But to what? She definitely did not strangle Ellie Duncan.

Sandra leaned forward and asked tensely, "Do I need to call a lawyer?"

Hart put down her papers on the table and threw her hands in the air. "Why would you need to call a lawyer if you have nothing to hide?"

"If you plan on arresting me tonight, I want my lawyer here as soon as possible."

"No one's getting arrested tonight," Hart said, clasping her hands. "We're just trying to get to the bottom of what exactly happened to Ms. Duncan."

"I wish I knew, but I don't. I just discovered the body."

"With your friend, maybe a little more than a friend, Mr. Cavill," Hart could not help but remark.

Sandra seethed.

She was over the innuendo, the humiliation.

Luckily, at that moment there was a knock at the door. A disheveled man with rolled up sleeves and wrinkled pants entered and marched over to Hart. Maya assumed he was one of her plainclothes detectives. He bent down to whisper something in her ear.

Before she could respond, Maya appeared in the doorway to the interrogation room. "Come on, Beth, enough is enough. You don't have jack squat to book Sandra on a murder charge, so let's just end this worthless cross-examination and call it a night, okay?"

Sandra was surprised Hart did not push back. But she also knew Hart respected Maya despite the circumstances of her leaving the department under a cloud of suspicion when Max, the former chief, was arrested.

Hart knew she was not going to get anything more out of Sandra tonight, so she gave Maya a brief nod and then got up, barely glancing in Sandra's direction. "Don't leave town."

And then she blew past Maya and out the door, followed by the plainclothes detective and the uniformed officer.

Maya rushed to Sandra. "How are you holding up?"

"I have certainly had better days. I just want to go home now," Sandra moaned, climbing to her feet.

"We can't go out the front. There is a crush of reporters outside, waiting for you. Someone in the department tipped off the press that you were down here being interrogated for the Ellie Duncan murder. It's all over the news."

Sandra's heart sank. "*What?*"

"It happens. I'd like to think it wasn't Beth, but this could be her way of applying pressure. In any event, we should be able to avoid the circus out front. I got Oscar parked in the back alley in his Prius to drive you home safely."

Oscar Dunford was a fellow cop and IT guy at the police department with a huge crush on Maya.

Maya hustled Sandra out of the interrogation

room and down the hall, avoiding several officers who perked up at the sight of Maya, formerly one of their own.

Sandra kept her head down as Maya led her to a back door and out into the alley and bundled her into the back of Oscar's black Prius.

One lone reporter spotted them and bounded toward the car, shouting questions. "Sandra, did you murder Ellie Duncan? Does Senator Wallage know what's happening?"

Any angle that worked in her powerful husband was a boon to any news story, true or not.

"Evening, Mrs. Wallage," Oscar said, smiling through the rearview mirror. "Nice to see you again. I wish it was under more pleasant circumstances."

"Hi, Oscar," Sandra mumbled, ducking down in the back seat as Oscar slammed his foot down on the accelerator and sped out of the alley and away from the precinct.

On the fast, bumpy ride home, Sandra knew she had to come to terms with the fact that as of now, she was a suspect in a very high-profile murder investigation. And it wouldn't be long before the aforementioned Senator Wallage would find out, if he had not already been informed by a gleeful reporter.

# Chapter 17

It was an unusually frosty morning for the month of May in Maine and Sandra wriggled deeper under her bedcovers to stay warm, slowly drifting off to sleep again. She never had to set her alarm because she always naturally popped awake at the crack of dawn like clockwork every morning. But today, after an exhausting interrogation at the police station and a late night reviewing the facts surrounding the Ellie Duncan case with Maya over the phone before turning in, Sandra was in desperate need of sleep. When she finally stretched her body and tossed off the covers to grab her phone from the nightstand to check the time, she was shocked. It was already nine thirty. She had slept right through her typical morning routine, rousing Ryan out of bed, making him breakfast, and steering him out the front door with enough time to catch the school bus down the block. She could not bring herself to listen to the over ninety voicemail messages, most no doubt from nosy reporters eager for a statement.

After a quick, invigorating shower, Sandra slipped on a blouse and slacks and padded down the stairs, where the coffee maker heated what was left in the pot. Pouring herself a cup, Sandra plopped down at the kitchen table, downing the caffeine, hoping to revive herself. She texted Maya to let her know she would be late arriving at the office, which she assumed Maya knew because she would normally already be there with a bag of bagels from the bakery on the corner.

After finishing her coffee and rinsing the cup out in the sink, Sandra was about to find her purse and head out the door when she heard a rustling sound outside. She glanced out the window. The neighborhood appeared quiet. Not even Mr. Fraser from two doors down was out walking his beagle, Reckless. She was surprised there was not a scrum of reporters gathered on her property, ready to shout questions at her like there had been the previous evening at the police station, but she could only assume that, with the shift in news cycles, the press had found another shiny object on which to focus their attention, at least for the moment.

Sandra remembered it was garbage pickup day, and so as she rushed out the door to her Mercedes, which was parked in the driveway. She grabbed the brown bin from the side of the house and hauled it down to the curb. On her way back to retrieve the blue recycle bin with her empty bottles and cans, she stopped suddenly.

She felt a presence behind her.

Someone breathing heavily.

A chill shot up Sandra's spine.

Was it a reporter?

No, a reporter would not bother sneaking up on her. They would just swoop in and start pummeling her with rude questions.

Sandra slowly, methodically reached into her purse to extract some pepper spray, then whipped around, aiming her weapon, ready to nail whoever seemed poised to pounce.

Rudy Holmes, the ex-convict employed by the middle school to perform odd jobs as part of his community service and rehabilitation program, was hovering just a few feet away. He took a step back, raising his hands in surrender. "Mrs. Wallage, I'm sorry, I didn't mean to frighten you."

Relieved, Sandra lowered her pepper spray. "Rudy, you nearly gave me a heart attack. What are you doing here?"

"I called your office, but your partner said you weren't in yet, so I thought I would try to find you at home. I know I shouldn't just show up on your doorstep, but I had to speak to you. It's very important."

"What's wrong? What's happened?"

"You haven't been on social media this morning?"

"No," Sandra replied, not wanting to admit she had been asleep until about ten minutes before.

Rudy gravely handed her his phone.

She scrolled down the screen of a local chat app designed for parents and teachers and students to communicate about news and events at the middle school. All the comments were about Rudy Holmes.

> *How can Principal Munn in good conscience allow this convicted criminal to be roaming the halls of the school ready to do God knows what?*
> *I agree! The man is a danger to others! In what world is it appropriate to allow him to be around innocent children?*
> *Get this menace to society off the streets!*

Stunned, Sandra handed the phone back to Rudy. "I don't understand. You've been working at the school for months now with no problem. Where is this suddenly coming from?"

Rudy, eyes downcast, devastated, said in a defeated voice, "A parent posted on this site last night, claiming to have seen me with Ellie Duncan shortly before she was strangled. Once the other parents saw it, everyone started to panic because of my prison record and started fanning the flames, so now everybody thinks I did it!"

"Is there any truth to the rumor? Were you with Ellie at any point before she was murdered?"

He hesitated, but then nodded slightly. "Yes. She was upset that I hadn't finished my job painting the walls before the spelling bee. She came at me out of nowhere, yelling at the top of her lungs, and I was so startled, my hand shook and a few drops of paint flew off the brush and onto her blouse. That just made her even madder. But then she just kind of ran out of steam and stormed off."

"I was there. I saw the altercation. Was that it? Did you follow her after she left?"

"No, ma'am. I just kept my head down and went back to doing my work," Rudy promised, wiping his nose with his thick, tattooed forearm. "I never saw her again."

"So where is this coming from?"

"I got a rap sheet, Mrs. Wallage. Of course they're going to point fingers at me anytime something like this happens. People will always just assume I'm guilty," he said matter-of-factly, without a hint of self-pity. "No matter what the truth is."

Sandra knew Rudy was right. Given his past, many in the community were going to automatically jump to conclusions.

"I admit I was no fan of Ms. Duncan. She was suspicious of me and always looking at me like I was going to try to rob the school or something. But I know who I am now. I paid my debt to society, I'm on a new path, and I want to make a decent life for myself, maybe do some good. I would never risk that by causing harm to anyone. You *have* to believe me, Mrs. Wallage."

"I do, Rudy," Sandra assured him. "You need to keep your head down, avoid talking to reporters, just do your job and let the murder investigation play out."

Rudy bowed his head. "I'm afraid it's a little late for that."

Sandra's eyes narrowed. "Why do you say that?"

"I got a voicemail from Principal Munn earlier this morning. Once she was alerted to the outcry from the parents, she told me it would probably be best if I took an unpaid leave from the school until everything blows over and they find the real killer. But I could tell from her tone she was lying. She thinks I did it. She doesn't want me near the school ever again."

"I'm sorry, Rudy, that's not fair."

Rudy's eyes welled up with tears as he fought vigorously to hold them back. "I don't know what I'm gonna do. I counted on that paycheck. If I can't pay my rent, I'm gonna have a problem with my parole officer. I can't go back to prison, Mrs. Wallage, not after I've come this far."

She felt sorry for him.

It was hard enough for ex-convicts, facing discrimination and unjust treatment based on their past mistakes, despite their efforts to make a fresh start. She did not want Rudy Holmes falling through the cracks because of an unfounded rumor. "You know, maybe I can help you out."

Rudy frowned. "Mrs. Wallage, I'm not looking for a handout."

"Who said anything about a handout? I have some odd jobs that need to be done around here. A leaky faucet in my son's bathroom. A running toilet in the guest room. Some scuff marks on the walls in the den that need to be touched up. And I'm guessing you come cheaper than a plumber or my regular handyman."

Rudy nodded gratefully. "I appreciate the opportunity."

"Good. Come back tomorrow morning and I'll get you set up. How does twenty-five bucks an hour sound?"

"Sounds like a lifeline," Rudy answered, smiling.

"And don't worry. My partner Maya and I plan on running our own investigation into Ellie Duncan's murder to find out who the real guilty party is."

"You would do that for me?"

"Honestly, no. I'm doing it for myself. In case you haven't heard, Rudy, you and I have something in common."

Rudy pursed his lips, curious. "What's that?"

"We're *both* suspects in this murder case."

# Chapter 18

When Meredith McKinley swept into the tiny coffee house in the Old Port, Maya, who was sitting at a table in front of the window, marveled at just how much the young woman had changed. Maya had known Meredith when she was in her midtwenties, working as a weekend dispatcher at the South Portland Police Department while studying for her master's in business administration at the University of Southern Maine. They had worked together during Maya's tenure as a beat cop, long before she was forced to resign.

Meredith usually showed up for her shift in a sweatshirt and jeans and with no makeup. Her smoky, alluring voice became famous with hundreds of Maine residents who had a police scanner in their homes to keep up on all the calls the department received. But now, in her early thirties, Meredith had glammed herself up, with her shiny brown hair pulled back in a sleek bun, a smart, classic gray-heather business suit with lightweight shoulder pads and expensive-looking Christian Dior glasses, and just enough makeup to show that she cared to make an effort but not too much so as not to be taken seriously. Meredith McKinley had transformed into the perfect corporate executive. Maya had watched her pull into an empty parking space out front in a BMW, not the banged-up, used Ford Fusion that was always breaking down that her grandparents had gifted her with when she graduated from high school.

She had come a long way from her days as a scrappy, part-time police dispatcher who shared a one-bedroom apartment with two other room-mates, living paycheck to paycheck.

And Meredith had one person to thank for this monumental life change.

Don Talbot.

He had been the one to take a chance on her and hire her right out of grad school to work at his asset management company, first as an entry-level project coordinator, but then eventually working her way up to the coveted position of a private equity specialist dealing directly with the wealthiest clients. She still lived with one of those early room-mates, but now he was her husband and they had three kids, two dogs, and a gecko in a tony New England Colonial mansion not too far from the Wallage home.

Meredith lit up at the sight of Maya and rushed over to greet her. "Maya, I was so delighted to get your call."

The two women hugged and then Maya gestured for her to sit down and handed her a white paper coffee cup with a brown sleeve. "I took a chance and ordered you a sugar-free vanilla latte, your drink of choice back when we worked together."

"Good bet," Meredith said, accepting the latte and taking a sip before setting it down on the table. "How have you been?"

"Hanging in there," Maya said with a shrug. "Vanessa's graduating high school this year."

Meredith's eyes widened. "No! I can't believe it. It seems like yesterday she was running around the station stealing candy out of my desk drawer while I was busy on the radio. Is she still the same firecracker I remember?"

"And then some. She's also the valedictorian of her class," Maya boasted proudly.

"Wow," Meredith replied, impressed.

"I know, I can't even begin to guess where she got her smarts. Not from me and Max, that's for sure."

Meredith's smile tightened slightly. "I heard Max got out of prison. Do you see him often?"

Maya nodded, not sure she was comfortable with this line of questioning but not willing to avoid it either. "All the time. Max and I are back together. He's living with us."

"Oh," Meredith gasped, surprised, but then she quickly collected herself and covered with a big smile. "That's wonderful. And I hear you have your own business now."

"Yes." Maya nodded. "A private detective agency."

"How very *Charlie's Angels* of you!" Meredith quipped.

"Except there's no Charlie," Maya quickly added.

"Actually, that's one of the reasons I wanted to reach out to you."

"I figured you contacting me might be connected to one of your cases. We haven't exactly kept in touch these past ten years, and as far as I know, no one we have in common has died, so there were only so many reasons I could think of why you'd call me."

"I'm sorry. I am happy to know you're doing so well, and that you're married and have a beautiful family—"

Meredith cut her off. "But you want to talk about my boss, Don Talbot."

She was a smart cookie.

And there was no getting around it.

Maya had to be forthright.

"Yes. I'm sure you're aware of the murder that occurred at the middle school recently?"

"How could I not? It's all over the news."

"Did you know Don had an intense dislike of the victim, Ellie Duncan?"

"Of course. So did everybody else in the office. It was all he would talk about. How she was unfairly targeting his son, Cooper, and how he was going to find some way to bring her down if it was the last thing he did."

"So he was that open about it?"

"Oh, yes. He was not shy about discussing the bad blood between them. He'd spend hours musing on how he was going to make her life miserable by suing her and the entire school board for the mistreatment and abuse of a student. He never expected to win, not given the education laws, but he was ready to pour money into enough litigation hearings to bleed them all dry, and we both know he has plenty of money to do it."

"It sounds like he was obsessed with her."

"He was. But let's be clear: He did not kill that woman. Someone else did. The police already questioned him at the office and cleared him. He was presenting a pitch to a client on Zoom at the time of the murder. I was there, along with about a dozen other account executives and employees. There was no way he could be in two places at once."

"What time did the meeting wrap up?"

"Not until close to four. Then he had to dash out to the school to see Phoebe compete in the spelling bee, but unfortunately, I heard he ran into some traffic and didn't show up until after it was already over."

Maya nodded.

The timeline did add up.

Which meant Don Talbot could not have been the one who strangled Ellie Duncan.

"I feel bad for Phoebe," Meredith moaned, slowly shaking her head. "That poor girl always gets the short end of the stick, if you know what I mean. If it had been Cooper in that spelling bee, Don would have moved mountains to be there. It's a shame. She's such a nice, intelligent, thoughtful girl. Just like her mother, God rest her soul. And then there's Cooper . . ."

Maya perked up. "What about him?"

"He's the exact opposite. Spoiled, entitled. I remember him showing up at the office one day after school, stomping around and yelling at his dad, demanding he do something about that teacher.

Everyone was embarrassed for Don, but he still went on indulging Cooper, spoiling him with whatever he wanted, encouraging him to behave that way." Meredith leaned in closer to Maya. "If you ask me, the police should be questioning Cooper, not Don. Cooper was the one who really had it in for his teacher."

"Did Don ever mention where Cooper was the day Ellie Duncan was killed? Was he at the middle school to cheer his sister on?"

"Are you kidding?" Meredith scoffed. "It would never have even occurred to Cooper to show any support for his little sister. No, if it wasn't all about him, it didn't exist. I think Don mentioned at one point that Cooper was at baseball practice at the high school, two miles away from the crime scene. But I can't be one hundred percent sure." Meredith was anxious to change the subject. She obviously did not want to dwell too much on the personal life of the man who signed her paychecks or his family. "Hey, I heard a rumor that Senator Wallage's wife Sandra also had a beef with the murder victim and is being considered a suspect."

"It's not her," Maya assured her, unwilling to get into the details of Sandra's role as a partner in Maya's private investigation agency. It would take far too long to explain and she had more leads to follow up on.

She sat with Meredith twenty more minutes, making small talk, and then finally extricated herself and headed to her car. She had a gnawing feeling in the pit of her stomach about Cooper Talbot, and she was now determined to give his alibi a test run to see if there were any potential problems.

Instead of returning to the office, Maya swerved left at the first traffic light and headed to Sandra's home, where she knew she would be. Maya hopped out of her car and strolled up the walkway to the front door and rang the bell.

When Sandra opened the door, dressed in a bathrobe and slippers even though it was not even six o'clock in the evening, Maya did not waste any time commenting but got right to the point. "We need to look into Don Talbot's son Cooper and where he was—"

Sandra shot a hand up to silence her, nervously glancing back inside the house, before whipping her head back around and saying to Maya in an urgent whisper, "Cooper Talbot is in my living room at this very moment."

Maya stumbled back, surprised.

She could hear Cooper's voice bellowing from the living room. "We cannot let your mother drive us to the prom in her Mercedes. This is *our* special night. We need a stretch limo and a driver to take us to all the after-parties. Don't worry, I'll get my dad to pay for it."

Sandra stepped outside and quietly shut the door behind her. "He and Ryan are friends. They're here with Vanessa and Cooper's girlfriend, Chloe, planning prom night."

A Jetta pulled into the driveway and Coach Lucas Cavill, looking casually dashing in khakis, a light purple dress shirt, and a dark navy cashmere sweater, slid out. His face fell at the sight of Sandra in her robe and slippers. "What's happening? Why aren't you dressed yet?"

"Sorry, I'm running a bit late. What time's the reservation?"

"Seven, but I thought we'd grab a cocktail first at Blyth and Burrows beforehand," Lucas said, disappointed.

"It's my fault," Maya apologized. "I stopped by without calling. We're working on a case and I'm just trying to follow up on a few alibis."

"The Ellie Duncan murder?" Lucas guessed.

"Yes," Sandra jumped in. "Maya, why don't you come to dinner with us and we can go over everything? Would that be okay with you, Lucas?"

"Um, sure," he lied. "I could call the restaurant and see if they can add a person on the reservation."

"No, I am certainly not crashing your date," Maya insisted, then lowered her voice. "We can talk about Cooper's whereabouts at the office first thing in the morning."

"I know where he was. Ryan said that Cooper told him he was at baseball practice."

"That's what his father said as well," Maya confirmed.

"He wasn't."

Sandra and Maya turned to Lucas.

"How do you know?" Sandra asked, curious. "You were with me at the middle school the whole time. We discovered the body together."

"Yeah, it's kind of hard to forget that. But I left my assistant coach, Eddie, in charge of practice, and Eddie is a stickler about his attendance sheet. I distinctly remember that Cooper Talbot skipped practice that particular day. I was planning to punish him with a set of two hundred push-ups before Saturday's batting practice, but with all the drama that went down after Ellie's murder, I forgot all about it."

"Then Cooper is lying," Maya said, more to herself than to either Sandra or Lucas.

Now she needed to know why.

# Chapter 19

Lucas merrily bounded into the living room, interrupting the prom night strategy session. "Cooper, glad I caught you here. I want to show you some video of last week's game against Sanford, when you scored the winning home run. I also have a few new plays I want to go over with you, if you have the time."

Maya slid into the room, hovering off to the side.

Cooper shot up in his seat, setting down his phone on the arm of the couch. "Uh, sure, Coach. That would be great."

"I sent you the video just now."

Cooper picked up his phone again and typed his passcode to check.

Maya surreptitiously memorized the six-digit number.

"Yeah, I just got it."

Lucas sensed the consternation from Vanessa and Chloe, who obviously did not appreciate the intrusion. Ryan just sat back, arms folded, amused. He liked having Lucas around.

"Awesome, but while you're here, there are a few things I'd like to show you," Lucas crowed, scooping up the TV remote and turning it on before tapping his phone with his index finger to bring up the video and screen mirror it to the fifty-six-inch television monitor mounted on the wall.

"Cool," Cooper replied, setting his phone back down on the armrest.

With all eyes glued on Cooper stepping up to the plate on the TV and thwacking the first pitch with his bat, sending the ball soaring into the air and over the head of a Sanford right fielder who couldn't stretch his mitt up high enough to catch it to the roar of the home team crowd of spectators, Sandra arrived with a steaming plate of nachos and drinks for the four teens.

Ryan eyed his mother suspiciously, not quite sure what her game plan was. She never served snacks this close to dinner, but he was not about to make an issue of it, especially because her nachos tasted so good.

Lucas prattled on about how amazing Cooper played that day, drawing him in, stroking his ego to keep him content and distracted; then he rewound the video to study a few plays from the opposing team he wanted Cooper to memorize for the next game.

Maya quietly hovered off to the side as Lucas played the role of overenthusiastic coach before quickly reaching down and pocketing Cooper's phone off the armrest of the couch. She made a beeline for the downstairs office that Stephen once used to run his local political campaigns. Closing the door, she typed in Cooper's passcode on his phone and then inserted a USB drive adapter to download the information directly from the phone. She could hear everyone cheering Cooper on in the living room. She was particularly interested in location services to find out where Cooper had gone the day he skipped baseball practice. When she had downloaded 76 percent of the phone data, the living room quieted down as the video of the game ended. Lucas was still talking a mile a minute, trying to keep all of them engaged, when suddenly she heard Cooper say, "Hey, what happened to my phone?"

Eighty-two percent.

"I set it down right here on the armrest," Maya heard Cooper declare.

"It's got to be around here somewhere," she heard Sandra assure him as they all began moving around to look for it.

Ninety-eight percent.

Maya was out of time.

She had to get the phone back.

One hundred percent.

Maya yanked out the USB drive and stuffed it in her jeans pocket and then hurried out of the office and back to the living room. "Did you leave any nachos for me?"

They were all on their feet, circling the living room in search of Cooper's phone.

"I lost my phone!" Cooper wailed.

Maya stood on the exact spot next to the couch where she had been before, bent down, and with the phone already pressed into the palm of her right hand, pretended to find it lying on the floor. "It's right here. You must have knocked it off the armrest when you were watching yourself score a home run."

Cooper was so grateful to have his phone back in his possession he did not bother to question how it went missing.

"Can we get back to discussing the prom now?" Chloe sighed.

"Yes, we all know Cooper is a superstar hot jock, but the prom is this weekend and we need to nail down our final plans!" Vanessa insisted.

"Right, sorry. Cooper, just keep those plays in mind before practice tomorrow and we can bring the rest of the team up to speed, okay?"

"Got it, Coach," Cooper beamed, proud to have been brought into Coach Cavill's inner circle and trusted enough to be consulted outside of a typical practice.

"Vanessa, I have to run an errand. Do you want me to swing back here and pick you up on my way home?" Maya asked.

"Uh, no, that's okay, Ryan can give me a ride."

Maya then turned to Sandra. "I will call you later."

Sandra smiled and nodded. She knew exactly where Maya was going. She was off to pay a visit to Oscar Dunford, IT extraordinaire and the one person they knew would have no trouble analyzing the contents from Cooper's phone.

Maya dashed from the Wallage house, jumped into her car, and sped across town to the Forest Glen apartments, where Oscar resided in a small one-bedroom.

Maya rapped a few times on the door to the first-floor apartment before Oscar opened it to greet her. He was a geeky, short man, around five foot four with a slight build, around one hundred and thirty-five pounds. The sight of Maya on his doorstep made him smile so big, it looked as if his face might split in two.

"Dreams really do come true!"

"This isn't a social call, Oscar, but I know you're off this week and this can't wait," Maya said sharply.

"Please, come into my humble abode," Oscar said, opening the door wider.

Maya got a whiff of his smelly apartment, a disconcerting mix of dirty socks and sticky beer, but she bravely entered to a sight of empty Budweiser cans, discarded pizza boxes, and dishes piled high in the sink. Maya threw Oscar a look. "You get paid a decent wage. Why not invest in a cleaning lady once a week?"

"If I knew you were going to drop by, I would've scrubbed the place spotless myself. Can I offer you a drink, maybe something to eat? I was going to DoorDash some curry noodles from that new place downtown."

"I can't stay, Oscar, I just need a favor," she said, handing him the USB drive. "I need you to go over the data and tell me where this phone has been. Specifically, last Thursday afternoon."

"And what do I get out of it?" Oscar pouted.

"Will you settle for my sincere gratitude?"

"No! Not this time. You only come to me when you want something, and it's very demoralizing. I need more out of this relationship."

"What? I have taken you to dinner to show my appreciation multiple times. That's all you're going to get. There is no romance on the horizon for us. Seriously, dude, I'm married, and this fawning admirer act of yours is getting old."

"This is your way of charming me into helping you?" Oscar huffed. "You might want to rethink your strategy."

Maya softened a bit and took his hand. "You're a sweet guy, and I know I count on you a lot for favors, and I really am grateful for all you do for me, so how about I show you how much I care by . . ."

Oscar leaned in closer, intrigued, squeezing her hand. "Yes?"

"Hiring a maid service to get this dump back into tip-top shape. Really, Oscar, if you want to find a real girlfriend, you need to at least make an effort."

Oscar threw his hands up in the air. "Fine. Whatever. One day when I'm, like, Elon Musk, rich and famous with tens of millions of X followers, you're going to regret not taking a chance on me."

"It's a risk I'm willing to take," Maya joked.

Grimacing, but then unable to stop himself from giving Maya an adoring wink, Oscar ambled over and plopped down in front of his computer and inserted the USB drive. After a few clicks, he glanced back at Maya. "What time are you interested in from last Thursday?"

"Late afternoon. Between three and four."

He tapped some more keys and then swiveled around in his chair and said, "Easy-peasy. Pine Street."

Maya gasped. "Pine Street? Ellie Duncan lives on Pine Street. But she wasn't home at the time. She was at the middle school."

"Yeah, I know. Getting strangled," Oscar said, eyes fixed on his computer screen. "According to Google Maps, there is a house with a security camera directly across the street from Forty-Six Pine Street, where I pinpointed the phone's location."

"Thanks, Oscar. I will call the maid service to make an appointment tomorrow," Maya said as she dashed out the door.

"Make sure she's single!" Oscar called after her.

Maya jumped back in her car and drove immediately to Pine Street, a residential section of Downtown Portland. She parked in front of 46 Pine Street, which turned out to be a petite pied-à-terre studio situated on the first floor of the brick row-end condo where Ellie had lived, which now had a FOR RENT sign in the window. Across the street, Maya spied the security camera hanging above a garage door attached to a single-family brick home. It was aimed toward the street and would have recorded any comings and goings on the day in question. Maya hustled over to the front door and rang the bell.

A hunched-over, elderly woman, wearing a heavy

gray wool sweater to keep herself warm, opened the door and offered Maya an expectant smile. "Yes, how may I help you?"

"Hi, my name is Maya Kendrick and I am a private investigator."

Her smile slowly faded. "If this is about Grady, you're barking up the wrong tree. I won't fink on my own nephew! I don't know anything about what groups he might belong to. He's never said one word about overthrowing the government!"

Maya reared back, stunned. "No, I'm not here about Grady. I just noticed you had a security camera."

"Grady installed it. He said we needed to have surveillance in case the Black Ops showed up to try to take away all our weapons."

"I see; well, I am certainly not here to do that," Maya promised. "I was hoping you might allow me to take a quick peek at your footage, specifically from last Thursday. I'm working on a case and it would be very helpful."

The woman eyed Maya warily. "So you're not FBI? Or CIA?"

Maya vigorously shook her head. "Most certainly not."

The woman appeared to relax a little, then looked both ways up and down the street to make sure Maya was alone. "All right, come in then; don't be loitering out here where the deep state spy satellites can see you!"

Maya noted Grady's influence on his doddering, sweet old aunt and how paranoid his delusions had made her. But if she had expected this woman, who introduced herself as Gladys, to just allow Maya to view her footage for free, she was dead wrong. Gladys charged Maya a hundred bucks. Cash. Luckily, Maya had just enough in her wallet to cover the expense.

Gladys made a pot of coffee and set up Maya in front of Grady's computer in the tiny guest room. Maya quickly scanned through the footage before Grady returned home from his meeting of the brotherhood of whatever the conspiracy theory of the moment was. Gladys also offered her a plate of her sugar cookies, which Maya gratefully accepted, fearing the consequences if she refused. She slowed down the footage to see Cooper walking down the street, looking over his shoulder to make sure he was not seen by anyone. Then he pulled a can of spray paint out of his coat pocket and began to write the word "bitch" on the front door of Ellie Duncan's condo. He nervously glanced around for any witnesses and, seeing none, dashed off.

Maya sat back, chewing her sugar cookie. Cooper was a vandal but not the killer. She rewound the footage, spotting a mailman dropping off a stack of mail through the slot around ten in the morning, continuing backward until she was at 7:35 a.m., when Ellie's front door opened and a man stepped out, his back to the camera. Ellie was in a baby-blue, thigh-length negligee, barefoot, with a mug of coffee in her hand. The man was dressed in a wrinkled white shirt and khaki pants. He threw on a windbreaker and leaned down to plant his lips on Ellie's face. It was a long, languorous kiss. Then he drew her in for a tight hug. She placed her hand on his left butt cheek and squeezed. They shared a laugh, and then the man turned around and headed across the street to his car, which was parked directly in front of Gladys's house.

Maya finally had a clear view of the man's face.

It was Ewan Murphy.

President of the school board.

And, apparently, Ellie Duncan's lover.

# Chapter 20

Maya and Sandra spotted Ewan Murphy far down to the right in the crowd that had filled the dock just off Commercial Street in the Old Port to listen to local fishermen and politicians speaking at a rally to protest a federal judge's ruling to allow the National Marine Fisheries Service, a part of the National Oceanic and Atmospheric Association, to impose new restrictions on how the local lobster industry could fish to protect an endangered whale species.

With Maine's lobster industry the lifeblood of many residents of the state, the reaction to the new regulations was swift and furious, sparking an angry outcry from the community on both sides of the political spectrum.

When Sandra had called his wife, Beverly, she had told her that Ewan, whose brother was a lobsterman, had gone to the rally to show his support. So Maya and Sandra had hopped in Sandra's

Mercedes and driven straight to the Old Port to track him down.

When they weaved their way through the riled-up crowd, a lobsterman stood at the podium, his fishing boat anchored at the dock behind him, waving his fist in the air, and yelling into the microphone, "I'm fed up! We're all fed up! None of these new regulations are based on sound science! The people who are making up these rules have never been to Maine, have never talked to any fishermen! These idiots aren't saving whales; they're telling the whole world not to buy Maine lobsters. They're putting us all out of business and we just won't stand for it!"

There were raucous cheers and applause from the defiant crowd, including Ewan Murphy, who cupped his hands around his mouth and shouted back to the fisherman, "Give 'em hell, Harry!" He was pumped up and excited, caught up in the fervor of the protest, but his mood quickly darkened at the sight of Maya and Sandra sidling up next to him.

"What do you want?" he spat out.

"We need to talk," Sandra told him solemnly.

"Can't you see I'm busy? That's my brother up there speaking right now! This is a real crisis in our state."

Maya crossed her arms. "We'll wait."

Ewan tried to return his attention back to the rally, sneering in Sandra's direction, "Your husband is responsible for this whole mess."

"How do you figure that?"

"His kind have never met a rule or regulation they didn't love. There have been zero documented whale entanglements in Maine lobster gear since 2004. Zero! These guys aren't killing off whales! But it's politicians like your husband who fall under the spell of overreaching, uninformed environmental groups!"

"My husband is a conservationist and an environmentalist, but in this case, because you're throwing around wild accusations, I suggest you consult his X feed. He came out on the side of Maine's lobster industry this morning. He supports this rally one hundred percent," Sandra explained evenly.

"Then why isn't he here with us?" Ewan snarled.

"Maybe because he needs to fight this battle from Washington where it originated; did you ever think about that?" Maya snapped, quickly losing patience.

Sandra noted Maya's growing annoyance. "Ewan, is that how you and Ellie initially bonded, over your mutual hatred of my ex-husband, Stephen?"

He turned toward her, eyeing her warily. "What are you talking about?"

"We've recently become aware of the nature of your relationship with Ellie Duncan," Sandra said.

Ewan scoffed, "You don't know anything. Ellie and I were friends. Yes, we shared a love of certain political issues. I know if she was still alive, she'd be down here today. We were friends, nothing more than that, and if you try to suggest otherwise to take the heat off you as a suspect, Sandra, you're sadly barking up the wrong tree."

Maya could not suppress a knowing smile.

He had just given them a full-throated denial.

Checkmate.

She gleefully pulled out her phone and brought up the security cam video she had just obtained from Ellie Duncan's neighbor from across the street. She hit Play and held the screen up in front of Ewan.

He swatted it away. "Get your phone out of my face. I'm trying to listen to my brother's speech."

"This is a show worth binging, believe me," Maya said, again shoving it in front of him and forcing him to watch.

Before he could avert his eyes, he caught the exact moment he had left Ellie's house, the long, romantic kiss, the sweet goodbye, her hand on his left butt cheek.

The cheeks on his face suddenly drained of color.

"How did you—?"

"It looks like we may be barking up the right tree, don't you think so, Ewan?"

Ewan attempted to snatch the phone out of Maya's hand but, anticipating the move, Maya quickly yanked it out of his desperate reach.

"You can't show that to anyone!" Ewan cried.

Maya glanced down at the video still playing on the phone. "That's a very sexy negligee Ellie is wearing. Was that a gift from you, Ewan?"

"I'm serious! I don't know how you got ahold of that video, but Beverly can *never* see it. *Please!* I'm begging you."

"So you admit to having an affair with Ellie?"

Ewan looked around feverishly, fearful someone might be listening in on their conversation. Then he stepped away from the crowd, toward the far end of the dock, with Maya and Sandra trailing him. Once he was secure enough that no one could hear them talking, he hissed, "Yes! Yes! We were seeing each other for a few months before she was killed. Are you happy now? But I am a married man! No one, especially Beverly, can ever know about the affair. Ever! Look, Beverly and I have been deeply unhappy for nearly a decade now and we've had discussions about an official separation."

"Then why are you so worried about the affair becoming public if the marriage was already practically over?" Maya asked.

"Because Beverly can be very vindictive. It's one thing for us to separate; it's quite another to discover I was cheating on her. She will take me to the cleaners in any kind of divorce proceeding."

"Not to mention you were cheating with a teacher who answered to you as president of the school board. That brings up a whole host of power dynamic problems for you," Sandra reminded him. "Especially in this day and age."

"I *never* coerced Ellie! She was the one who pursued *me.*"

"I'm not sure the Maine State Board of Education will see it the same way," Sandra said.

"What do you want from me?" Ewan wailed.

"We want to know if you told the police about your affair with Ellie," Maya pressed.

Ewan reared back, still wildly surveying the area for potential eavesdroppers. "What? No! They never asked me, so I did not feel I had an obligation to tell them."

"They might ask once they see this," Maya said, holding up her phone.

"I was protecting my reputation. If word of my infidelity ever got out, not only would Beverly suck me dry financially, I would probably get fired to boot."

"And shoot straight to the top of the list of suspects in her murder," Maya added.

He nodded, ashen-faced. "I-I was praying that our secret would stay one after Ellie died."

Maya tapped her phone to stop the video and stuffed it in the back pocket of her jeans. "Guess you didn't pray hard enough."

Ewan's shoulders sank. His defeated gaze drifted over to the podium, where his brother had just finished his rallying cry to thunderous applause. But he could not join in cheering his brother because he was suddenly hit with the realization that his life was about to dramatically change from this moment forward.

# Chapter 21

After leaving the rally, Maya and Sandra swept through the front door of the Wallage home only to be immediately overtaken by the wafting aroma of Indian spices.

"Something smells delicious!" Sandra said, shedding her coat and hanging it on the rack in the foyer.

"Chicken coconut curry," Maya replied. "I'd recognize Vanessa's specialty anywhere. She must be cooking dinner."

The women wandered into the kitchen to find Vanessa boiling some rice and stirring a large pot of curry with a wooden spoon as Ryan hovered around her holding a smaller spoon, trying to scoop some out to try, but she kept pushing him away with her left hip.

"Stop! It's not done yet," Vanessa scolded.

"It smells so good. I can't keep my hands off it. Or you," he said with a flirtatious wink, then nuzzled the back of her neck with his face, causing her to giggle.

Sandra loudly cleared her throat, startling both of them. Ryan instinctively jumped back from Vanessa, bumping her arm. She dropped the wooden spoon on the floor, splattering some curry on the oven door. She quickly grabbed a rag off the counter to wipe it clean.

"Were you two just going to stand there spying on us all night?" Ryan huffed.

"Who's spying? I live here. We just came home from work," Sandra countered. "If you're feeling guilty about something, that's on you."

Sandra glanced into the adjacent dining room to see five place settings on the table. Before she could ask, Ryan explained, "Cooper and Chloe are staying for dinner, if that's okay. They're in the living room."

"Of course," Sandra said, turning to Maya. "Why don't you stay too? Looks like there's plenty to go around."

Maya shrugged. "Why not? Max is working late at the garage and I have no other plans, so long as the chef has no problem serving her mother. . . ."

"Of course not, Mom." Vanessa sighed. "But you can't complain about my curry being too spicy." She turned to Sandra. "She's always telling me I make it too hot and it burns her mouth, but you would think given her Latin heritage, she'd be used to spicy food."

"Please, it has nothing to do with race. Your father is as Anglo-Saxon as they come and he eats ghost peppers like they're Lay's Potato Chips," Maya said.

"I'm going to go say hello to your friends," Sandra said, leaving the kitchen and going down the hall, turning the corner in time to see Cooper and Chloe quickly moving away from each other on the couch, settling a few feet apart, both with flushed cheeks and guilty looks. It did not take Sandra's investigative skills to conclude what they were doing before she walked into the room, especially with two pillows on the floor, no doubt knocked off when the teenagers were writhing and grinding and kissing on her couch. Fully clothed, thank God. She'd just had the upholstery cleaned.

"Hi, Mrs. Wallage," Chloe muttered.

At the sight of Sandra, Cooper's expression went dark, and he angrily stared straight ahead.

Chloe picked up on the sudden mood change and touched his knee with her hand. "Everything okay, Coop?"

"Yeah, everything's fine," he spat out.

Clearly to those watching him in the room, everything was definitely not fine.

"Chloe, would you do me a favor and go set another place at the table for Maya? She's going to join us for dinner."

"Uh, sure," she said tentatively, standing up and eyeing her rattled boyfriend worriedly before heading out to the kitchen to scrounge up an extra plate and set of silverware.

Sandra waited until she was gone and then turned to Cooper. "Something's obviously bugging you, Cooper. Does it have to do with the security cam footage we found?"

That was the trigger he needed.

Cooper jumped to his feet, eyes blazing. "Why

did you have to send that tape to my dad? You ratted me out!"

"I had no choice, Cooper. And you're lucky you just have to answer to your dad. A bonehead move like vandalizing a teacher's home could have gotten you expelled."

"I'd rather be expelled from school than make my dad mad. I thought he was going to kick me out of the house. He called me a brainless idiot for getting caught doing something so stupid."

Sandra was taken aback by the focus of Don's anger. He should have been more upset about the actual act of vandalism than the fact that his son did not get away with it.

Not exactly a teachable moment.

But Sandra was hardly surprised by Don's twisted priorities when it came to his parenting skills.

She wanted to explain that he should be more ashamed of his behavior than getting caught, but she feared her words would, unfortunately, fall on deaf ears. Cooper's whole focus in life was not disappointing his father. Nothing she could say now would ever shake that resolve. She just had to accept that she had a whole different parenting style than Don Talbot.

"How did your father punish you?" Sandra asked curiously.

Cooper gave her a blank look. "What do you mean?"

"Did he ground you? Take your car away?"

"No, he just told me to be more careful next time and not embarrass him ever again." Cooper shrugged.

Okay, another completely lost teachable moment.

"Well, I hope your anger toward me snitching on you doesn't keep you from sitting down to dinner with us in a few minutes. You're always welcome in our home."

Cooper exerted himself to keep a frown on his face, but she could hear his stomach grumbling and knew he would throw whatever grievances he had with her out the window when the dinner bell rang.

Sandra walked back to the kitchen, where she found Ryan at the island tossing a salad and Maya pouring herself a glass of Cabernet. Vanessa was still at the stove, stirring and tasting the curry.

Maya grabbed another wineglass and poured one for Sandra, handing it to her. The two moms clinked glasses and took a sip before Maya lowered her voice as she spoke. "I had a little chat with Chloe when she came in to get another place setting. She's on cloud nine about going to the prom with Cooper."

"You do not want to know what I almost caught them doing when I came into the living room just now." Sandra sighed, shaking her head.

"Mom, Vanessa and I are standing right here. We can totally hear what you're talking about," Ryan cried.

"I'm not trying to keep it a secret," Sandra said before glancing in the dining room to make sure Chloe was out of earshot and then whispering, "I just think she deserves better."

"Come on, Cooper's not that bad," Ryan said in a hushed tone. "He just had a momentary lapse in judgment. I mean, you can hardly blame him. We were also dealing with the wrath of Ellie Duncan, remember? I'm not saying she deserved what happened to her, but she certainly took a perverse pleasure in making people's lives miserable when she was still alive."

Ryan was not wrong.

Vanessa put down her wooden spoon and darted her eyes in the direction of the dining room. Chloe was no longer there. She must have circled back into the living room to rejoin Cooper. Vanessa turned to Maya and Sandra and spoke in a barely audible voice. "Look, we know Cooper can be a jerk, but for whatever reason, Chloe adores him, so Ryan and I have decided to support the relationship. Believe me, I've said about a dozen times Chloe deserves better, but she's been going through a lot lately with her dad, and Cooper is the one bright spot in her life."

The news struck Sandra like a thunderbolt. "Her dad? What's going on with her dad?"

Chloe's father was Burt Denning, the middle school custodian, who had also been near the scene on the day of Ellie's murder.

"They've been pretty much keeping it under wraps. Her dad doesn't want anyone to know because he's afraid he might get fired. But he's sick," Vanessa said solemnly.

A sense of dread was building inside Sandra. "Sick? Sick from what?"

"She doesn't really like to talk about it," Vanessa whispered under her breath. "But we think it's cancer."

Maya gasped. "Oh no."

"From what we've been able to get out of her, the outlook is pretty grim. Chloe is just hoping he lives long enough to see her graduate."

Sandra and Maya were both stunned into an unsettling silence.

# Chapter 22

Ewan Murphy sat behind the long conference table that had been set up in the middle school auditorium, flanked by his fellow school board members. He had just been drowned out by loud jeering from the parents in attendance after remarking that the results of the recent spelling bee competition would not be changing under any circumstances. This did not sit well with a few irate parents, especially Hal and Keri Hamlin, who staunchly believed that Ellie Duncan and the judges had unfairly disqualified their son, Hunter, and that the only course of action would be a redo of the whole regional competition.

Ewan, his lips pursed, with a hangdog expression on his face, waited for the shouting and jeers to die down a bit, but his steady silence and obvious inaction only seemed to agitate the parents more.

"The whole thing was rigged!" Hal Hamlin cried

out to a smattering of applause from a few of the parents in his corner. "Ellie Duncan was always playing favorites. She knew in advance who she wanted to win."

A parent called out from the back, "Yeah, and everybody here knows your son was one of them! He blew his chance all by himself. Don't blame her or the judges!"

Hal Hamlin whipped around, furious. "Who said that?"

Don Talbot jumped to his feet. "Look, we all had our issues with Ellie Duncan, but my daughter Phoebe won, fair and square, and I don't appreciate you trying to take that away from her, so sit down and shut up, Hal!"

Hal's nostrils flared. "You think just because you're an arrogant, highfalutin one-percenter you can talk to me like that, Don?"

"Hal, I don't think I'm better than you. I just think my daughter is a better speller than your son," Don remarked with a patronizing grin.

Hal clenched his fist and his wife, Keri, grabbed him by the arm to stop him from lunging at Don.

More parents stood up yelling their general displeasure with the school board.

Ewan grabbed a wooden gavel he'd probably purchased on Amazon and started banging it on the table for order. "Please! Please! One at a time! We'll never get anywhere if you all continue to talk over one another."

"I have the floor!" Hal roared, stomping his foot.

"You've had it long enough!" Don hollered. "I'm sick of hearing your voice."

Keri's hand tightened on her husband's arm as he tried diving again at Don, who seemed to almost enjoy the testy back-and-forth exchange.

"I'm warning you, Hal," Ewan cried, banging the gavel again. "If you continue to get out of hand, we have security standing by to escort you off the premises."

A pleading look from Keri finally managed to calm Hal down, although he kept staring daggers in Don's direction.

"It's not right. Hunter was robbed. He a lot better at spelling than Don's kid! He should be the one going to the state competition."

"I swear to God, Hal, if you don't stop trashing my daughter, I will sue you for defamation, and believe me, with the crack team of lawyers I have on retainer, I *will* win!" Don warned before casually sitting back down.

Now it was Doug and Noah Chastain-Wheeler who stood up to be heard. Seated directly behind them were Maya and Sandra. Although neither of them had children in the middle school, they knew attending the school board meeting was an effective way of sizing up everyone who was at the spelling bee and near the crime scene when Ellie Duncan was strangled.

"I would just like to say . . ." Doug muttered.

"Louder!" Hal Hamlin bellowed.

Doug cleared his throat and raised his voice. "I would just like to say, I think we're avoiding the elephant in the room. The results of the spelling bee should not be the priority topic at this meeting."

"That's only because your kid is already going to the state competition," Hal howled. "You just don't want to rock the boat. You're afraid she might lose her spot if there's a redo!"

"No! Come on, Hal, a teacher at this school was murdered! The safety of our children is at stake here," Doug wailed. "I, for one, am very concerned that there is a dangerous killer on the loose."

*Finally,* Sandra thought, *a voice of reason.*

"The police are investigating, let them handle it." Don shrugged.

Noah stepped forward, concurring with his husband. "And yet so far there have been no arrests. That's unacceptable. Doug and I are very concerned that the police are not working fast enough. Why haven't they arrested Rudy Holmes yet?"

Sandra, much to Maya's surprise, popped to her feet. "What does any of this have to do with Rudy Holmes, Noah?"

Noah spun around to face Sandra. "He's an ex-convict. Apparently dangerous enough to be locked up for years. And in its infinite wisdom, the school hired him to do odd jobs around our kids. Our Annabelle! What on earth were they thinking?"

Rousing applause came from most of the parents.

Ewan banged his gavel some more, "This has all been taken care of, Mr. Chastain."

"Wheeler-Chastain," Noah sniffed.

"Mr. Wheeler," Ewan huffed. "I mean, Wheeler-Chastain. It's a whole new world. Give me time to adapt. Look, everyone, there is no need for hysteria. Principal Munn dismissed Rudy after the murder. He's no longer allowed on school grounds."

"He never should've been allowed in the first place!" Keri Hamlin shrieked.

"And he's still out on the streets, free to do whatever he pleases. What's stopping him from coming back here with some kind of weapon to get revenge on Principal Munn for firing him? Our precious kids could be caught in the crossfire," Don lamented.

Sandra circled around front to address the unruly crowd, leaving Maya to watch with rapt attention. "Now, hold on! Rudy is a decent man who has paid his debt to society. He should not be punished for the mistakes of his past."

"Easy for you to say. You don't have a kid enrolled at this school," Noah snapped.

"No, I don't, but if I did, I would have no problem with him being around Rudy. Full disclosure, I recently hired Rudy to do some work around my house because no one should be penalized based simply on rumor. Whatever happened to innocent until proven guilty?"

"He's already guilty. That's why he spent the last decade in prison," another parent in the back shouted, followed by more mounting outcry from the spectators.

Ewan was banging his gavel again in an almost Pavlov's doglike response.

Hal yelled over the din of the audience, "She's right. Give poor Rudy a break. I've talked to the guy; he's just trying to piece his life back together."

Don turned with a smirk. "And if he was the one to wring Ellie's neck, I say he did the world a favor."

Gasps from the crowd.

Followed by more jeers and booing.

Complete pandemonium.

And Ewan banging his gavel until the handle snapped in two.

Giving up, Sandra returned to her seat and plopped down next to Maya. "I suspect this is what the Salem witch trials looked like."

"We came here to see if anyone acted suspicious or out of the ordinary to narrow down our list of suspects," Maya noted. "But if you ask me, anyone of them could have done it."

Sandra nodded in agreement.

Everyone in the auditorium with a grudge against the murder victim was playing the blame game, pointing the finger in every direction except back at themselves. Which, in Sandra's mind, meant that Hal and Keri Hamlin, Don Talbot, Doug and Noah Chastain-Wheeler—half the parents in the room, for that matter—they all could have something to hide.

# Chapter 23

"What's the verdict, Rudy?" Sandra asked in the doorway of her bathroom, just off the main suite.

Rudy Holmes had unscrewed the handles, taken off the stem nuts, and was inspecting the O-rings of the pair of his-and-her faucets, which both had slow drips that were driving Sandra mad the last couple of months. She'd just been way too busy to get them fixed. "No corrosion, gaskets look good, very little mineral deposits; I'd say the washers just need to be replaced. I can swing by Home Depot right now and pick up a couple."

"You're a lifesaver, Rudy," Sandra gushed.

Rudy smiled as he wiped his hands on a rag. "I sure do appreciate you taking a chance on me, Mrs. Wallage. I need to pick up as many part-time gigs as I can manage to pay my rent and meet my parole requirements."

"You're the one doing me a favor, Rudy. Neither my ex-husband nor I have ever been handy around the house, and we just let the minor repairs pile up over time, hoping they might fix themselves. Stephen always said you could drop him in the middle of Afghanistan and he would find his way to the Kabul Airport, but faced with a leaky pipe underneath the sink, he's balled up in a corner, frozen in fear."

Rudy chuckled.

"And I can't say I'm any better, so I'm very thankful you're here to help me out."

Rudy's phone rang.

He stared at the screen, surprised. "It's my neighbor. Hold on, I should take this." He pressed the Answer button. "Yeah, this is Rudy." He listened. His face suddenly darkened. "What do they want?" His face scrunched up. "Are you serious? No, don't call the police. They're probably parked across the street watching the whole scene right now. Just ignore them. They'll go away eventually. Okay, thanks, Evie." Rudy sighed and pocketed his phone. "I'm going to head to Home Depot. Be back in a bit."

He started to head out of the bathroom, but Sandra stopped him. "Rudy, wait. What was that phone call about?"

He grimaced, not anxious to discuss it. "It was nothing, really. A couple of parents from the school showed up at my place and started banging on my door, demanding I turn myself in to the police for Ellie Duncan's murder."

"*What?*" Sandra gasped.

"It's happened a few times when I haven't been home. My poor neighbor, Evie, in the apartment next door usually calls me in a panic. I'm worried the landlord is going to evict me if this keeps going on."

"That's harassment, Rudy," Sandra said, furious.

Rudy shrugged. "Not much I can do about it. Can't call the cops. I've noticed a squad car parked across the street this past week keeping my place under surveillance, like they're waiting for me to trip up, make some mistake, hand deliver them some kind of evidence so they can arrest me for the murder."

"That's so unfair. How can they target you like that? You had no real personal relationship with Ellie. What would your motive be to want to kill her?"

Rudy immediately averted his eyes away from Sandra's, as if he did not want to admit something. It was subtle, but Sandra caught it.

"Rudy, is there something you're not telling me?"

Rudy vigorously shook his head and blurted out defensively, "No!" Then he regained his composure and offered her a weak smile. "I better get over to the Home Depot. Parking there is a bitch on Saturdays." And then he flew out of the bathroom.

Sandra knew there was more to the story.

But Rudy was not about to share any details with her.

Sandra hurried over to the nightstand next to her California King bed, scooped up her phone, and called Maya, who picked up on the first ring.

"Hey," Maya answered.

"Hi. Is Max working at the garage today?"

Max's new career after his own prison sentence was as a mechanic in an auto body shop owned by an old colleague from his time in law enforcement.

"No, he's home today. We were just about to head out to the Old Port to grab some lunch," Maya said.

"Why don't you come here? I'll make us a spring salad and some sandwiches."

"That's very nice of you, but my investigative prowess tells me that there must be an ulterior motive for this very sweet last-minute invitation," Maya pressed.

"Rudy Holmes is here working at the house. Didn't Max serve his time in the same prison where Rudy was incarcerated?"

"Yes, Max told me they knew each other; not well, but very casually from rec hours in the yard. Why? What's up?"

"Rudy had a very strange reaction when I mentioned his relationship with Ellie Duncan, and he clammed up when I pressed him to elaborate on the details. I was hoping Max might be able to get him to open up because they have a longer history together."

"It's worth a shot. Max likes egg salad."

"I'm on it!" Sandra chirped.

She raced down to the kitchen to prepare a fresh spring salad and an assortment of sandwiches. Maya and Max arrived before Rudy returned from the Home Depot and were sitting in the kitchen enjoying lunch by the time Rudy's truck pulled up in the driveway. They heard him enter through the front door and start to trudge up the stairs.

"Rudy!" Sandra called to him.

"Yes?"

"Could you come in here for a sec?"

They heard him pound back down the stairs and tramp into the kitchen, stopping short at the sight of Maya and Max seated at the kitchen table.

"Max," Rudy said with a startled look.

Max stood up and shook Rudy's hand. "Good to see you again, buddy. It's been a while."

"You look good, Max," Rudy remarked uneasily. He did not run into fellow cons from his time in prison all that often.

"We were just sitting down to lunch. Would you care to join us?" Sandra offered.

He eyed the sandwiches hungrily but thought better of it. "No, thank you. I'd better get to work on those faucets."

"Please, there's plenty. We have ham and cheese, egg salad, roast beef and provolone, and I have some tuna in the fridge."

They could tell his resolve was starting to melt.

"Max lives in a houseful of women," Maya said. "He's dying to talk to someone with a little testosterone."

That was all it took.

"Okay." Rudy sat down at the table and grabbed a roast beef sandwich as Sandra served him salad with some tongs. Maya and Sandra were careful to keep the conversation on mundane topics, carefully avoiding the subject of Ellie Duncan's murder. Max's initial questions had more to do with how Rudy was adjusting to life on the outside, and they shared stories on the challenges of parole and how in many ways it still felt as if they were serving time, having to answer to other people.

Once lunch was finished and Sandra set down a plate of cookies and poured some coffee, she and Maya retreated, excusing themselves under the guise of having to discuss a case they were working on and leaving the two men alone.

They stayed within earshot of the two men in the kitchen, and it did not take Max long to steer the topic of conversation to recent events at the middle school. Rudy almost seemed relieved to be able to talk to someone who might understand what he was going through.

"I feel like I'm the only person the cops are looking at. They're so convinced in their minds that I did it. Is it ever going to get any easier?"

"You're asking the wrong dude," Max said, shaking his head. "I'm a dirty cop *and* an ex-con. It's like a double whammy. Nobody is ever going to trust me again."

"It's tough, man. I'm just trying to keep my head down and stay out of trouble, but the world keeps conspiring against me. I loved working at that school. It felt good getting up every morning and doing my job there. The kids liked me. Principal Munn seemed happy. But then it all went to hell."

"When Ellie Duncan got murdered?"

"No, before that."

Maya and Sandra exchanged expectant looks.

There was a long pause.

Max took his sweet time, allowing a casual lull in the conversation, not wanting to press him too hard.

Maya and Sandra could hear Rudy chewing a cookie and then swallow.

Max finally spoke up. "What happened, if you don't mind me asking?"

Rudy took a beat before responding. He was probably making sure Maya and Sandra were not hovering around nearby, eavesdropping, which they most certainly were.

"She wouldn't leave me alone," Rudy explained.

"Who?" Max asked.

"Ellie."

"She didn't want you working at the school?"

"No, nothing like that. She wanted to date me."

Sandra had to cover her mouth with her hand to stop herself from gasping out loud.

"Seriously?" Max asked.

"Yeah, but I had no interest in getting involved with her. Hell, I had no interest getting involved with *anyone*. That job was too important to me. I didn't want to make any waves. So I told her I was flattered, but it was a violation of my parole and I could be sent back to prison."

"Which isn't true," Max said.

"No, it's not. I just wanted her to stop and go away. But she didn't. She kept bugging me. She wouldn't let it go. So I finally told her I just wasn't interested in her that way."

"Which didn't sit well with her, I suppose?"

Rudy scoffed. "I'll say. It set off an explosion.

She started tormenting and bullying me, making unwanted contact, lodging complaints about me. I tried to explain what was happening to Principal Munn, but it was my word against Ellie's. Who do you think she was going to believe?"

"I'm so sorry, buddy," Max whispered.

"After that, I just kept my mouth shut and prayed she'd find someone else to focus on and finally just leave me alone. But then she was murdered. I was terrified people were going to think I did it, given all the complaints. I tried to keep a very low profile, but that didn't do any good. Of course, within days the cops were showing up at my door, the parents were in an uproar, and I lost my job. I thought that was the worst that could happen to me. But now I'm afraid that was just the beginning. I hear the DA is building a case against me. He's bound and determined to file murder charges and ship me straight back to prison."

"That's not going to happen, Rudy," Max assured him.

"How do you know that?"

"Because my wife and her pal Sandra are two of the sharpest detectives I have ever run across, and they will get to the bottom of who actually did kill Ellie. I promise you, you're not going to have to go back to prison."

Max's tone was confident and comforting.

He had absolute faith in Maya and Sandra.

But Sandra worried he was being too generous in his assessment of their investigative skill set.

So far, she and Maya had not even discovered the identity of the person who had left the threatening note in Rocco Fanelli's locker, let alone the one who strangled Ellie Duncan and left her body in the school supply closet.

They were still a very long way from saving poor Rudy Holmes from another stint in prison, this time no doubt with a life sentence.

# Chapter 24

Carl Duncan sat at the picnic table in Ellie Duncan's tiny backyard and stared at Maya and Sandra with a puzzled expression. "Excuse me?"

"Isn't that why you called our office and asked us to come by for a sit-down? Don't you want to hire us to find out who killed your sister?" Maya asked.

"Uh, no, that's not why I contacted you," Carl mumbled.

Sandra looked at him, confused. "So you don't want to hire us?"

"No, I definitely want to hire you, but it has nothing to do with my sister."

When Maya and Sandra had received a voice-mail from a man claiming to be Ellie Duncan's younger brother, requesting a meeting at their earliest convenience, they had just assumed he wanted to employ their services to find out who strangled his older sister. According to a quick Google search,

Carl Duncan had left Maine the day he graduated from SoPo High and moved to Boston to attend bartending school. He had a number of accounts on Instagram, X, and TikTok and, according to his most recent posts, Carl was quite the party animal. He was young and devilishly handsome, always with a twinkle in his eye in his photos, surrounded by an army of gorgeous young women and a few muscular bros at the college bar where he worked in Cambridge, or on a boat sailing off Cape Cod, or playing the drums with his band at Wally's Cafe Jazz Club. Based on his social media footprint, he came off as roguishly charming and loved by all who knew him.

Nothing like his sister Ellie.

When Maya and Sandra had arrived at Ellie's house, where Carl was staying, they found him sifting through all of his sister's paperwork as executor of her will. He was her only living family member, he explained, and that both their parents had died five years ago, his father of a heart attack, his mother following him six months later from a broken heart.

It was a beautiful spring day, so Carl had led them out to the backyard to talk. There were birds chirping and flowers blooming in Ellie's small garden. He had offered to serve them some of the pink lemonade he found in the fridge, but both Maya and Sandra had politely declined.

When Sandra had offered her condolences, Carl dismissed the gesture out of hand with a curt, "Thanks."

The cold-blooded murder of his older sister seemed to be the furthest thing from his mind.

"If we're not here to discuss Ellie, why are we here?" Maya asked Carl pointedly.

"Kathy McFarland," he replied matter-of-factly.

"Who's Kathy McFarland?"

"The one who got away," Carl said wistfully.

Carl picked up a high school yearbook he had next to him on the picnic bench and slapped it down on the table. He opened it and began thumbing through the pages, stopping and pointing to a senior photo of an attractive, bubbly girl with cascading strawberry-blond hair. "There she is. Isn't she beautiful?"

Sandra's face twisted in bewilderment as she glanced over at Maya, who appeared just as baffled. Then she redirected her attention back to Carl. "She's lovely. Is she missing? Do you want us to find her?"

Carl nodded. "In a manner of speaking. Don't get me wrong, I don't think anything sinister has happened to her. But she's not on social media, and when I Google her name, nothing much comes up. She could be anywhere."

"Why do you want to find her?" Maya asked.

"We dated in high school, our senior year, and it was starting to get serious, but Ellie didn't approve. She didn't like her for some reason, so she poisoned Kathy against me, told her I was into drugs and seeing other girls on the side, and Kathy believed her and dumped me. I didn't know why until much later, but by then I was living in Boston and had another girlfriend. We recently broke up, and I started thinking about Kathy again and tried to track her down, but so far I've had zero luck."

"To be honest with you, Carl, we thought you wanted to hire us to find your sister's killer," Sandra said.

Carl sneered, "Um, no. That's not really a priority for me right now. The killer could be just about anyone who ever met Ellie. She was an awful person. I mean, I'm sorry she's dead and all, but we haven't spoken in years. I'm surprised she named me as executor of her will. Of all people. We never got along."

"Actually, I don't think there was anyone else in her life willing to do it," Sandra said, feeling a little sorry for her.

"Well, once I get her cremated and settle the estate, I'm driving straight back to Boston," Carl announced. "Not that there is much of an estate. Once I pay off her two mortgages and sell her junk heap of car, I'll be lucky to pocket some loose change."

"She didn't have much in her savings?" Maya asked.

"Savings? Hell, no!" Carl scoffed. "Her bank account was overdrawn. My sister was a compulsive shopper. When I showed up here yesterday, there were about a dozen boxes from Amazon piled up on the front porch. She couldn't help herself."

"What about some kind of a memorial?" Sandra asked.

"There's no point. Who would come? She had no friends, no boyfriend. Most people couldn't stand being around her." Carl shrugged. "I'm not even sure what I'm supposed to do with her ashes. She never left any instructions. And quite frankly, I never paid her much mind when we were kids, let

alone when we were adults. And I will never forgive her for coming between me and Kathy."

"Why do you think she sabotaged your relationship?" Maya asked.

"Beats me. She was always jealous when she saw
other people happy. Not to speak ill of the dead,
but she was a vindictive, spiteful, nightmare of a
woman. But it's not like I'm telling tales out of
school. Everybody knew how terrible she was."

Sandra was not about to debate that point.

"I mean, I've been going through her stuff, and
the only person in her life she seemed to even care
about was some guy named Ewan."

Maya and Sandra's ears perked up. "Ewan? How
did you come across that name?"

"Her diary."

Maya leaned forward, suddenly animated. "She
kept a diary?"

Carl nodded. "Yeah, I found it in a dresser drawer
next to her bed. I didn't want to read it at first because I thought it would be an invasion of privacy,
but then I figured, what the hell? She's not going
to care anymore. She's dead. Most of it was just doodling and scribbling complaints about the people
she worked with at the high school, or students
she hated. . . ."

Sandra felt reasonably certain her entire family
was probably name-checked in Ellie Duncan's secret diary.

"But toward the end, all she could write about
was some dude named Ewan and how much she
loved him."

"Carl, can we take a peek at the diary?" Sandra
asked.

"Depends. You gonna take my case and try to find Kathy?"

"Once we solve Ellie's murder, we'll look into finding your ex-girlfriend," Maya promised.

"Why do you want to find Ellie's killer if no one's paying you?" Carl wanted to know.

"Because I happen to be a suspect," Sandra said flatly.

Carl's face lit up. "Cool!"

He stood up and led them inside the house. "Are you sure you don't want some lemonade? It's probably been in there for a while, but I had some earlier and it still tastes pretty good."

"No, thanks," Maya and Sandra said in unison.

He escorted them to Ellie's immaculate bedroom, sparsely decorated, the shades drawn, blocking out the sun. On top of the dresser was a stack of folders, presumably Ellie's bank accounts, mortgage documents, and health insurance information. A small pink diary with the lock broken sat on top of the pile of paperwork. Carl scooped it up and handed it to Sandra, who eagerly began leafing through it, Maya hovering over her shoulder, staring down at the flying pages.

Carl was right. There was a lot of mindless doodling. Not much in the way of entries. But a few pages were filled up with manifestos of why she despised a fellow teacher, followed by pages of rage-filled rants against misbehaving students in her geography classes. To Sandra'ssurprise, there was no mention of Ryan or Cooper Talbot. Finally, around mid-April, Ewan Murphy made his first appearance in Ellie's diary.

*April 18th. Attended school board meeting to discuss upcoming spelling bee. After the meeting was adjourned, Ewan Murphy gave me a hug and whispered in my ear that he liked my dress. He said the color brought out my beautiful blue eyes. What a shameless flirt. He's totally married. How inappropriate. Men are so transparent.*

*April 25th. Ran into Ewan again. The way he looked at me made me very uncomfortable. He wants to meet for coffee outside of school. I know what he wants and I will not bow to his charms.*

*April 28th. Met Ewan for coffee. He was very sweet. Very unhappy in his marriage. But I have no intention of engaging in any immoral behavior. He is a married man. I need to stay away.*

*May 1st. Ewan came over tonight. I made dinner. Veal parmesan, which he loved. Said it was the best he ever tasted. We split two bottles of wine. One thing led to another . . .*

*May 2nd. Ewan left early this morning. Told his wife he was on an overnight fishing trip. Called me an hour later to tell me how much he missed me already.*

*May 5th. Ewan and I spent three hours talking on the phone tonight. I think I may be in love.*

*May 7th. I wish Ewan would just divorce Beverly already. What an odious human being. The stuff he tells me she does, the way she treats him, it's all I can do not to write her a nasty letter and totally give her a piece of my mind. But I know Ewan would freak out.*

*May 10th. Ewan has stopped returning my calls. I don't understand why. We love each other.*

*Why won't he just file for divorce from Beverly so we
can finally be together? It's not fair to me! He must
understand that.*

*May 12th. Sent four texts to Ewan. All unan-
swered. I tried to start something with Rudy Holmes
to make Ewan jealous, but he's not being coopera-
tive. Stupid, useless ex-con. Why won't Ewan talk
to me? What's changed?*

Finally, the last diary entry.
The day before the regional spelling bee.
The day before someone strangled her to death.

*May 14th. I'm desperate. I told Ewan if he didn't
call me back I would go over to his house and tell
Beverly everything. Well, that did the trick. He called
me back in two minutes and told me to calm down,
not do anything rash. He said he still loves me, he
just needs a little more time to figure things out,
how to leave Beverly so we can be together. I told
him in no uncertain terms that he better think fast
because I'm losing patience. When is he going to re-
alize I'm the best thing that's ever happened to him?
He promised to come over tonight right after his
school board meeting. Luckily, that new negligee
and perfume I ordered from Amazon were delivered
today.*

After that, nothing but blank pages.
Maya and Sandra could confirm that Ewan Murphy did come to her house that night because he
was clearly seen on the camera across the street,
leaving the next morning.
Ellie was threatening Ewan.

She was going to upend his life.

Destroy his marriage.

A rocky marriage to be sure, but one he did not seem all that anxious to give up.

No, Ewan Murphy was panicked over what kind of trouble Ellie was going to stir up, which gave him a very strong motive to want to silence her permanently.

# Chapter 25

"I'm married," Meredith McKinley said sharply to Oscar Dunford after he attempted to flirt with her in Maya and Sandra's office.

"Happily?" Oscar asked, still holding out a bit of hope.

Meredith turned to Maya, who sat behind her desk, feet up on the desk. "Who is this guy?"

"A pain in my butt most of the time, but one of the best computer analysts I have ever known. I asked him to come over here and take a look at the recording you brought us."

Oscar, totally smitten, surveyed his ratty jeans and wrinkled T-shirt that said *Computer Whisperer*, commenting, "I usually like to present myself better, but it's my day off." Then he tried again. "You are one of the most beautiful—"

Meredith cut him off. "Married! Happily! With kids! And what part of the Me Too movement completely passed you by?"

Oscar finally backed off, chastened. "Sorry, I don't know what came over me. It's just that your eyes are like—"

Meredith sighed. "Is this guy for real?"

"You keep this up, Oscar, you're gonna make me jealous," Maya cracked.

Oscar's eyes widened. "Really?"

"No," Maya replied, deflating him. "Now that we've dispensed with the pleasantries, can we please get to the matter at hand? Meredith was kind enough to bring a recording of the client meeting Don Talbot presided over on the day of the Ellie Duncan murder."

Meredith extracted her laptop from a book bag and set it down on the desk in front of Maya. Sandra handed Oscar a cup of black coffee from the pot brewed in the kitchenette and then circled the desk behind Maya. Meredith tapped a few keys and brought up the recorded Zoom meeting with Don Talbot on the top row of participants, totaling nine people in all, calling in from their various homes and offices. The screen looked like the opening credits from *The Brady Bunch.*

"It's standard practice to record all our client meetings. It saves everybody the trouble of having to take notes, like in the good old days," Meredith explained. "I was at home watching the video last night because there were a few financial figures from the meeting that didn't add up to my own, so I wanted to make sure I had heard them correctly, and that's when I noticed the glitch."

She pressed down on a key and fast-forwarded through the meeting toward the end. She stopped as Don got up out of his chair and disappeared from the frame. They could still hear him talking off-screen. After about a minute and a half he returned with a bottle of water. As he sat down, the frame appeared to skip, freezing for a second, and then continued normally. Meredith paused the video. "See that? It stood out to me when I was watching. It might signify nothing, but I don't know, I just had a feeling in my gut that something was off."

"I'm glad you called," Maya said before turning to Oscar. "What does it look like to you?"

Oscar gestured for Maya to get up from behind her desk so he could take her place and carefully analyze the video himself. He rewound it, played it again, studying the image of Don leaving the frame and returning. He turned to Meredith. "Is this the only time he left the frame?"

Meredith shook her head. "No, he leaves two or three times, which is not unusual. Don can never sit still for very long."

Oscar played the video again to the part where it skipped.

"Maybe it was just a problem with the internet," Sandra suggested.

Oscar leaned in closer to hear Don talking while he was out of the frame. "Nope. It's definitely a prerecording," Oscar concluded.

"*What?*" Meredith gasped. "But that's impossible. It can't be. Don was actively participating in the discussion in real time."

"Yes, but if you watch closely, he only engages when he's off-screen. Look, most of the time he's just listening to the client when he's on-screen, but then he leaves the frame, presumably to get something to drink or stretch his legs. The glitch is him switching from the prerecording of him sitting at his desk listening to everybody else to the live feed of an empty chair with him talking off-screen. The audio level is too high. If he was getting a water from the fridge or looking for something across the room while he was talking, his voice would sound distant, away from the computer mic. But it sounds like he is right next to it. Which means he could be providing audio from just about anywhere in the world while everyone assumes he just stepped out of the frame for a few seconds. When he's done speaking he switches back to a prerecorded video of him returning with a water or a file or just sitting down after a brief break."

"Everyone in that Zoom meeting assumed he was there the whole time, providing him with the perfect alibi," Sandra marveled.

"Not so perfect. He didn't count on the mighty genius of Oscar Dunford to smack him down!" Oscar looked up at Meredith expectantly. "Did I impress you?"

"A little," Meredith had to admit.

Oscar beamed, proud of himself. "Has it in any way changed your first impression of me?"

"Not particularly." Meredith sighed. Her mind was now racing. "Now that I'm thinking about it, there was a strange moment when the client asked Don a question and he just sat there not saying anything. We all assumed his audio went out or something. But then he left the frame for a few seconds and we could all hear him give an answer."

"He could have been providing live audio commentary during the meeting while he was actually sitting in his car outside the middle school moments before sneaking inside and strangling Ellie Duncan!" Maya exclaimed.

"You're right. Why would Don go to such great lengths to cover up his whereabouts if he wasn't planning on doing something nefarious, like murder Ellie? We have him red-handed!" Sandra cried.

Maya folded her arms, not entirely convinced. "The evidence is damning but still circumstantial. A good defense lawyer will come up with some kind of plausible explanation as to why Don tried to pull a fast one on his team and the client. Plus, we still can't tie him directly to the crime scene. And what about Ewan Murphy? I think he also could have done it."

"And then there are all the parents who had it out for her. We certainly have no shortage of suspects," Sandra said. "It could be like that classic Agatha Christie novel, *Murder on the Orient Express.* Maybe they *all* did it!"

Maya grimaced.

Sandra had a point.

The classic Christie plot was fiction, but not all that far-fetched.

They kept stumbling across more and more people who would have been happy to see Ellie Duncan dead.

# Chapter 26

Sandra hated running late. She had always prided herself on her promptness, a skill she had honed as a politician's wife, where her responsibilities included keeping her chronically tardy senator husband on a tight schedule so he would not fall behind timewise on his various campaign stops and groundbreaking ceremonies with his constituents. She knew if Stephen alienated voters by making them wait too long, they might think twice about casting their ballot for him on Election Day. She was his secret weapon, and during the many years they were married, she had routinely polled at least ten points higher than him in popularity. She did not miss those days—not by a long shot— but she had retained the valuable lessons she had learned, which she applied to her new career as a private investigator.

Maya was far less draconian when it came to her

attitude on punctuality, explaining that puttering around in the morning allowed her precious time over coffee to muse on cases, maybe come up with a whole new angle in a current investigation. But Sandra knew better. It was just an excuse to relax until the caffeine finally started to kick in.

But today it was Sandra who was dawdling. She had been up half the night mulling over the Ellie Duncan case and wondering which of the top-two prime suspects, Don Talbot or Ewan Murphy, might be the guilty party. Both had strong motives, although at this point, given what they had discovered, Don had opportunity now that his alibi had blown up.

Sandra jumped out of the shower, toweled off, and slipped on some jeans and a casual, sea-green, mixed cable sweater. She decided to forgo makeup and pulled her hair back in a ponytail, then grabbed a pair of wedge mules and padded down the hall to Ryan's room to rouse him out of bed. When she poked her head in, she saw the bed already made—well, the covers were pulled up over his wadded-up sheets, which was Ryan's modus operandi. A half-hearted attempt to please his mother by completing the morning ritual, unlike his older brother, who was like a military recruit, his bed so flat and tucked in, Sandra could bounce a quarter off it like a trampoline. The door to the bathroom was ajar and it was empty, so Sandra could only assume Ryan was downstairs or had already left for school.

Descending the stairs, she could hear him talking in the kitchen. "No, he's really cool, I like him."

Sandra stopped short of entering, pausing to listen to the one-sided conversation.

"I don't know how serious they are. You're gonna have to ask Mom that question."

Sandra suddenly knew who Ryan was talking to.

His father, Stephen, who was pumping his son for information about Sandra's new boyfriend, Lucas.

When Sandra continued into the kitchen, where she found Ryan sitting at the kitchen table, on his phone, downing an English muffin slathered in butter and a glass of orange juice, he suddenly sat upright, as if he had been caught doing something he shouldn't.

"I'd better go, Dad. I'm going to be late for school. See you soon," Ryan said, eyeing his mother warily. "Love you too." He ended the call and set down the phone. "How much did you hear?"

"Enough," Sandra said, crossing to the coffeepot on the counter and pouring herself a cup.

"Did you hear the part about how much I like Lucas?"

"Yes," Sandra said evenly, sipping her coffee.

"I know I shouldn't be talking to Dad about your relationship with Lucas, but he keeps asking me about it. I had to tell him something."

The word "relationship" stuck with her.

She still did not know how to define whatever was going on with Lucas. She certainly liked him and enjoyed their company together, but the age difference still gnawed at her no matter how hard she tried to put it out of her mind.

"What you and your father discuss is none of my business," Sandra said, although deep down she was uncomfortable with Stephen pressing Ryan for details and wished her private life was not a hot topic of discussion between father and son. She decided to change the subject. "He's still planning on coming to your graduation, isn't he?"

"Yup. He promised."

Stephen had also promised to be there for Jack's graduation, but a Senate filibuster had kept him in Washington and he missed his train, arriving ten minutes after Jack had received his diploma. She had forgiven him at the time—a US senator's job can be unpredictable—but she also knew Jack had been sorely disappointed that his dad was a no-show.

"I know what you're thinking, but I trust him. He felt so bad about Jack's graduation. He'll move heaven and earth to be here for mine," Ryan said, feeling the need to defend him.

"I'm sure you're right," Sandra said. "I'm way behind this morning. I have to get to the office. Do you need a ride to school?"

Ryan shook his head. "Nope. Cooper's picking me up in his new Jag. When can I get a car?"

"When you can afford to buy one," Sandra answered crisply.

Sandra had made a pact with herself not to spoil her sons like Don Talbot, who showered his boy with expensive toys and privileges, most of which the kid did not even seem to appreciate. She wanted both Ryan and Jack to be responsible young men who earned whatever they wanted in the world with hard work. She was not happy about Ryan's friendship with Cooper, but she was not about to dictate who he could or could not hang out with; that was Ryan's choice. And she had enough faith in him to be his own man and not start emulating Cooper's troubling and entitled behavior.

The doorbell rang.

"That's probably Cooper. Bye, Mom." Ryan stuffed the rest of the muffin in his mouth, gulped down his orange juice, and bolted out of the kitchen.

Sandra finished the rest of her coffee and dumped the crumbs from Ryan's plate into the garbage as Maya walked into the kitchen, surprising her. "Oh, Maya, I wasn't expecting you. Did we decide to meet here instead of the office this morning?"

"No," Maya answered, her face clouded with concern. "Ryan let me in and then went upstairs to brush his teeth."

Sandra instantly sensed something was wrong. "What is it?"

"I just got a call from Oscar. He showed up for work at the precinct this morning and found out there has been an arrest in the Ellie Duncan case."

"An arrest? Who? Don Talbot?"

Maya shook her head.

"Ewan Murphy?"

"No. Burt Denning, the school custodian," she said gravely.

"*What?*" Sandra cried, letting out an unexpected gasp of disbelief. "Chloe's dad?"

"I drove straight over here to get you," Maya said. "We need to head down there right now and talk to Beth."

Sandra deposited the breakfast plate in the sink and raced after Maya. They hurried outside and hopped into Maya's Chevy Bolt, peeled out of the

Wallage driveway in reverse, and zoomed down the street.

By the time they arrived at the South Portland Police Department ten minutes later, there was a swarm of news trucks jamming the whole area. A large pool of reporters from the local news affiliates were gathered around the entrance where a podium had been set up for a press conference. Detective Beth Hart stood behind the podium, addressing the crowd.

"The community can be assured that there is no longer an ongoing threat now that we have arrested the man responsible for Ellie Duncan's murder," Hart announced.

"This is nuts," Maya whispered to Sandra before shouting above the din of the reporters asking questions. "What evidence do you have that Burt Denning did it?"

Hart zeroed in on Maya. She could plainly see the skepticism on Maya's face. "Mr. Denning has provided us with a full-throated confession."

Both Maya and Sandra were knocked back on their heels, flabbergasted.

# Chapter 27

Judge Constance Abernathy, a tiny but formidable woman in her late sixties with a stern face and a no-nonsense demeanor, lowered her wire-rimmed glasses to the bridge of her nose, her lips moving slightly as she read the indictment. There was complete silence in the courtroom. When she finished, she raised her head, eyes fixing on the defendant. "Mr. Denning, you have been charged with murder in the first degree. How do you plead?"

Burt Denning, in a rumpled suit, his wide-striped, blue tie slightly askew, was urged by his young, wet-behind-the-ears public defender to stand up from the table and face the judge. He mumbled something unintelligible to everyone in the courtroom.

"You're going to have to speak up, Mr. Denning," Judge Abernathy said.

Burt glanced at his lawyer, who gave him an encouraging nod. Then he looked back at the judge. "Guilty, Your Honor."

There were some scattered gasps.

Sandra, who was sitting in the front row with Ryan and Chloe, swiftly threw a protective arm around Burt's daughter as she sank down in her seat and began quietly crying.

When Ryan had returned home from school the previous day after Burt Denning's arrest, she had asked him about Chloe and how she was handling such devastating news. Ryan had told her that Chloe had been absent from school that day, so the two of them headed straight over to the Denning house, where they had found a shell-shocked Chloe slumped down on the couch, glued to the television as she watched the excruciatingly painful details of her father's sudden arrest and shocking confession. The local press was going hog wild with outlandish theories as to why the mild-mannered middle school head custodian had snapped and violently strangled Ellie Duncan, which ranged from Burt being a lovestruck stalker who could not handle Ellie's heartbreaking rejection to Ellie stumbling across Burt's botched attempt to steal some valuables from the school, although all of these breathless speculations were completely devoid of any hint of actual evidence.

Chloe was adamant that something was seriously wrong here. Her father was a gentle, kind, caring man. In her mind, he did not possess a single violent bone in his body. His confession was especially confusing. Why would he admit to a crime he did not commit? Ryan wholeheartedly agreed. He had spent enough time at the Denning house with Chloe, Vanessa, and Cooper to know the real Burt Denning, and he was not the man they were portraying on TV as some kind of unstable, rage-filled predator.

Sandra had done her best to be supportive, but she was used to dealing with the facts that were in front of her, and there was no getting around Burt Denning admitting to the murder. There was no suggestion he was being coerced. He had confessed of his own free will. And based on what Maya had been able to suss out from some of her former colleagues at the station, he had done so emphatically and without reservation.

So maybe he *had* done it.

Her more immediate concern was making sure Chloe was taken care of, so when Chloe had insisted on attending her father's arraignment, Sandra offered to accompany her to the courthouse, along with Ryan, for moral support.

As they walked into the courtroom, Sandra could see Chloe's whole body shaking with nerves. And at the moment her father pleaded guilty, it was clear from her gutted reaction that Chloe's entire life had just completely fallen apart. With her mother gone, and now knowing that she would soon be losing her father either to a prison cell or from a wretched disease, she was now facing the reality of finding herself completely alone in the world.

Judge Abernathy folded her hands and addressed the defendant. "Mr. Denning, do you understand that by pleading guilty you waive the right to a trial and you will have few options to appeal?"

Burt nervously cleared his throat and nodded. "Yes, Your Honor."

"All right, then, you will be remanded into custody and returned to jail until a sentencing hearing," Judge Abernathy said. "See you back here on . . ." She consulted a calendar in front of her. "July eleventh."

The towering, flabby bailiff hustled forward and snapped a pair of handcuffs on Burt's wrists behind his back and started to lead him out of the courtroom as his lawyer promised to do his best to advocate for a reduced sentence, given his acceptance of responsibility.

Before Sandra could stop her, Chloe vaulted up and made a mad dash toward her father, tears streaming down her cheeks. "Dad! Dad, why did you plead guilty?"

Burt jerked back when he caught sight of her. He had not expected her to be there.

The bailiff inserted his large frame between father and daughter, refusing to allow them any physical contact.

"Please, can I just give my dad a hug?"

The bailiff was sympathetic, but he had his orders. "No, I'm sorry."

Burt gazed at his daughter with sorrowful eyes, knowing what all of this was doing to her. Chloe tried to push past the mountainous bailiff to get to

Burt, but it proved to be impossible. The bailiff was not going to budge. Frustrated and angry, Chloe began screaming. "He didn't do it! Let him go! I'm telling you, he's innocent!"

The judge banged her gavel as a warning. "There will be no outbursts in this courtroom."

Sandra rose quickly and took Chloe firmly by the arm, pulling her back as the bailiff led Burt, who was unnerved by her presence, out of the courtroom to a holding cell until he could be transported back to jail. Before he disappeared out a side door, Burt turned back and mouthed the words, *I love you, Chloe.*

Chloe nearly melted on the spot, and Sandra quickly enveloped the despondent girl in a motherly hug, gently patting her back as Ryan looked on, feeling helpless. When the door shut and Burt was finally gone, Sandra led Chloe out into the hallway, Ryan following on their heels. The hall was bustling with jurors and lawyers and families of both plaintiffs and defendants. Sandra's immediate concern was getting Chloe out of there. "Come on, we're going to take you home with us. I will not have you staying alone at that house with your dad in jail."

Chloe did not put up a fight.

In fact, she seemed to take comfort in the fact that Sandra and Ryan were going to look after her.

"Mrs. Wallage, you have to help him. I don't know why he's saying he did it, but I know him. I can always tell when he's not being truthful. He must be covering for someone else," Chloe pleaded desperately.

"One thing at a time, Chloe," Sandra said as they headed down the hall to the door that led out to the parking lot. Chloe's phone buzzed and she glanced at the screen. "It's Cooper. He keeps texting. He's worried about me and wants to know if I'm okay."

Sandra could see that there was a crush of reporters outside, waiting to shout questions at them. She squeezed Chloe's arm. "You can return his text on the way. Right now I just need you to keep your head down and not say a word and follow me to the car."

Sandra steeled herself, breathing deeply, and then grabbed Chloe by the hand and burst out of the door right into the middle of the throng of press that eagerly swarmed around them.

"Chloe, is your dad a cold-blooded killer?" one insensitive reporter shouted.

"Did you know? Were you protecting your father?" another yelled.

"Chloe, over here! Look over here!" a photographer cried, aiming his camera, hoping for a good shot of her.

Sandra spotted Ryan elbowing the photographer as he passed by him. "Leave her alone!"

"Ryan, do not engage!" Sandra scolded. "Eyes straight ahead."

It was complete pandemonium.

Sandra thought they would remain trapped in the eye of the storm, but then, after battling their way through the mob of journalists, they finally made it to Sandra's Mercedes. They quickly piled in and sped away.

Behind the wheel, Sandra drove as fast as she could to the safety and security of their home, fearing Chloe's nightmare was just beginning.

# Chapter 28

"**B**urt Denning is a client, Beth, and we have a right to see him," Maya pressed as she and Sandra stood in front of Detective Hart in her office at the South Portland Police Station.

Hart sat behind her desk, arms folded in front of her, and gave them a withering look. "I am only obligated to allow his lawyer to meet with him, and I'm guessing if I checked with the Maine Board of Bar Examiners, your applications would not show up anywhere in their database, am I right?"

Maya threw up her hands in surrender. "Yes, we're not his attorneys. He's got an inexperienced public defender who has got about sixty other criminal cases he's working on handling his, and not enough time in the day to adequately serve his clients, so we're here to help pick up the slack."

"Does the public defender . . ." Hart glanced down at a file on her desk. "Kenny Madison . . .

You're right, he looks like he's twelve years old. . . ."
She pushed the file away. "Does Mr. Madison know
you're now working for him as his assistants?"

"Not yet. But even Perry Mason had an investigator on his legal team. And lucky for Kenny, he's
got two and we're very good at what we do," Maya
said.

"What about Mr. Denning? Is he aware of any of
this?" Hart asked skeptically.

"Of course," Maya fibbed.

Hart studied her face.

She had known Maya for years.

And it appeared as if she could tell when Maya
was not telling the truth.

Still, she decided not to make an issue of it.

"Everyone deserves an advocate fighting for
him," Sandra added. "We just need twenty minutes
to go over the facts of the case with him. You can
set a timer."

Hart sighed. "I'd love to help you out, but he's
not here."

Maya stiffened. "Where is he?"

"He was transferred to the Maine Correctional
Center in Windham to wait out his time before
sentencing, and they're much stricter than I am
when it comes to a sit-down with an inmate. There
is a whole process you have to go through."

Maya planted her hands on Hart's desk and
leaned in close to her. "Come on, Beth, it'll take
days for us to arrange a meeting. You must have
some pull over there. Help us cut through some of
the red tape. Make a call."

Hart hesitated.

"You owe me," Maya tossed out.

Hart did owe her.

Years earlier, when they were both rookies, Hart had frozen in fear when confronting a dangerous suspect twice her size, her hand clutching the gun in her holster, but she was too scared to draw. The suspect was wielding an axe and was about to take a swing at her head when Maya, thinking fast, took him down with a swift whack to the knee using her police baton, just months before the department issued an order to stop using them. When she filed her report about the incident, Maya purposefully left out the details involving Hart's botched role in the arrest. If those details had come to light, Hart could have been bounced off the force or shipped back to the academy for more training. Hart had thanked Maya and promised to do better. Maya instinctively knew Hart had a lot of potential and deserved a second chance, which was why she did not report her. And she was proved right. With time, Hart found her footing and eventually became a damn good cop and worked her way up the ladder with her sights on captain someday.

Maya and Hart engaged in a staring contest for a few seconds as they silently relived the past, and then Hart blinked, picking up the phone receiver as she began punching in a number.

"Consider us even," she barked.

Within two hours, Maya and Sandra had driven to Windham, about thirty-five minutes from South Portland, and were being escorted by a female corrections officer down a row of eight vacant, scuffed plastic chairs that were set up for each visitation booth. At the far end, the officer pulled a chair from another booth and dragged it over to the one in front of the last glass partition so both Maya and Sandra could sit down.

"Thank you," Sandra said to the officer, who gave her a curt nod and took a few steps back, close to an exit, where she would be presiding over the visit.

After about five minutes, on the opposite side of the booth, a door opened and a male officer escorted Burt Denning in. He wore a set of orange scrubs with a white T-shirt underneath. He appeared haggard and tired, his sad eyes watery and bloodshot, as if he had not gotten much sleep since his arrest. His head was shaved. His face registered surprise at the sight of Maya and Sandra behind the glass as he was told to sit down in a plastic chair opposite them. When the male officer retreated to stand guard at the other exit door in the visitation room, Maya picked up the phone on the wall next to her, waiting for Denning to do the same. But he just sat there for a moment, confused. Then, finally, after some prodding by Maya, he grabbed the phone and held it to his ear, but he did not speak.

"How are you doing, Burt?" Maya asked with concern.

He shrugged. "All right, I guess."

"We're here because we want to help you," Maya said gently.

"I didn't ask you to come here and I don't need your help," he growled.

"Okay, fine, Burt, but we're not just trying to

help you. We're also here for Chloe," Sandra added.

The mere mention of his daughter's name struck him hard. His hardened exterior seemed to melt away, replaced by anguish and concern. "How is she?"

"She's going to stay with me for a while until we can figure out next steps. She doesn't turn eighteen until August, so she's going to need a guardian. She says you have a brother in Arizona?"

"Yeah, Tucson, but he's not the parenting type. He's a mean, old, crotchety drunk. I don't want her going out there. She won't be happy."

Sandra sighed. "No other family?"

Burt shook his head with a sorrowful expression.

"Well, I'm happy to look after her until she heads off to college in the fall," Sandra assured him.

"You're going to miss out on a lot of your daughter's life, you know that, don't you, Burt?" Maya said gravely.

Burt's bottom lip began to quiver. "I know."

"She wants to come see you," Sandra said.

Burt's shoulders sank. "No! I can't face her right now. It's too much. Maybe in time, once she's settled in at college, making friends, starting a new life."

"She's convinced you're innocent. She wants to be by your side during the sentencing to show her support," Maya said.

"The sooner she accepts what happened, the better off she'll be, trust me. If you really want to help, try to make her understand that."

"What did happen, Burt?" Maya asked.

There was a long pause.

"I already told the police. I killed Ellie."

He averted eye contact and there was a catch in his throat.

Maya did not buy it for a second. "Why?"

"She was trying to get me fired."

"On what grounds?" Maya asked.

Burt shrugged. "She said I was lazy. She claimed I was ordering Rudy Holmes to do all the custodial work around the school while I goofed off. Sure, Rudy helped me out with some of the odd jobs, but I worked just as hard as he did, and he was only part-time. She was making it all up out of spite because for some unknown reason she had a big problem with me."

"And we'll never know why because she's dead now," Maya observed.

"Seems so," Burt mumbled.

Maya studied the worry lines on his forehead as if he was afraid they might not believe him. "You were in a panic that she was going to go to Principal Munn to try to get you terminated, so you decided to kill her?"

"No, I didn't come up with a whole plan, it just happened. She was railing on me the day of the spelling bee. She made it clear she was going to take the issue to Munn that day. I couldn't let her do that. I just snapped. If I lost my job, how would I be able to send Chloe to college? How would I pay for my meds . . . ?" He stopped, kicking himself for revealing too much.

Sandra wished she could reach through the glass window to touch him. "We already know you're ill, Burt. Do you want to talk about it?"

"No. It is what it is. I can't do much about it now. I may not even make it to the sentencing. That's why I want Chloe to move on, forget about me, and just get on with her life without me dragging her down."

Sandra exhaled heavily in frustration. "She won't do that, Burt. She loves you too much. Don't shut her out."

"Burt, I was a cop for a long time," Maya said evenly. "And I've gotten pretty good at knowing when someone's lying."

"So what do you want me to do, take a lie detector test so I can prove I'm guilty? I'm sure the judge will have a good laugh over that one. I confessed. It's over. Case closed." Burt hung up the phone and turned to the guard at the exit. "I'd like to go back to my cell now."

Sandra tapped on the window, pleading, "Burt, please, don't leave yet. . . ."

Ignoring them, he stood up as the guard approached to escort him out. They took a few steps before Burt turned back and reached over to snatch up the phone one last time. "You can do one thing for me."

Sandra grabbed the phone. "What's that?"

His eyes pooled with tears. "Give Chloe my love."

Then, overcome with emotion, he threw down the phone and marched away with the guard. The female guard on the other side of the visitation booth opened the door, signaling to Maya and Sandra that it was time to go.

The pair of women looked at each other as they rose to their feet, both thinking the same thing.

Burt Denning had not committed this crime.

But how were they ever going to prove it?

# Chapter 29

Boot Hill was a dingy biker bar located near an industrial park about a five-minute drive from Downtown Portland. Although it was only four in the afternoon, there were more than a dozen Harley-Davidson, Kawasaki, and Yamaha motorcycles lined up out front for the early happy hour, two-for-one whiskey shot special, according to the sign out front.

Maya rolled her car to a stop in the gravel parking lot and shifted gears into the Park position before turning to Sandra, sitting in the passenger seat. "You ready?"

"Are you sure she's still in there?"

Maya nodded. "I followed her here before swinging by your place to pick you up. That's her bike right over there." She pointed to a Harley-Davidson Iron 883 SuperLow, small enough for a woman to easily straddle, with a vanity Maine license plate that said 2FAST4U.

Sandra surveyed the half-sleeve, V-neck, floral

print blouse and capri pants she was wearing. "I wish you had given me more of a heads-up so I could do a costume change. I'm not exactly going to blend in at a biker bar."

"There was no time. We have a limited window to talk to her and I wanted to get her outside of the school, where she doesn't have to act so professional and on guard with what she says."

Sandra eyed the crumbling exterior of the dive bar. "It's hard for me to get my mind around her hanging out here to relax."

"According to my sources, she comes here after work at least three or four times a week," Maya explained. "I know, I was as surprised as you."

Maya opened the car door and got out.

Sandra followed.

As they crossed the gravel lot toward the bar entrance, Sandra sized up Maya, who was in distressed denim jeans, a black tank top, and leather boots. "At least you look the part. I'm not wearing *any* leather."

"Your belt's made of leather. That's good enough," Maya said, bursting through the door to the bar as Sandra tentatively tried to keep pace with her. This was definitely not the usual haunt for a US senator's wife.

Inside was dark and dank. The floor was sticky. A classic Allman Brothers song played on the jukebox. A few of the bikers turned in their direction as Maya and Sandra walked in. One raised an eyebrow in mild surprise at the sight of the more proper-looking Sandra. Most just leered ravenously. As they approached the bar, the shaggy-haired bartender, with sleepy eyes and a potbelly underneath his camouflage tank top, ambled over from the other side of the bar where he had been chatting with a couple of long-bearded customers who were dead ringers for ZZ Top. "Help you, ladies?"

"I'll have a Manhattan," Sandra said with a smile.

The bartender gave her a withering look.

Maya quickly jumped in, "We'll both try the whiskey shot special."

The bartender grunted and grabbed a couple of shot glasses, filling them both from a bottle of Jack Daniel's.

"That'll be seven bucks," he said, stone-faced.

Maya pushed a ten-dollar bill in his direction. "Keep the change."

He finally managed a slight smile. "Thanks."

Sandra was scanning the bar. Except for a buxom fake blonde in a black bustier making out with a 300-pound, leather-clad bald guy in a corner, there did not appear to be any other women in the bar. Sandra turned and whispered to Maya, "Where is she?"

"Over there, playing pool," Maya said, gesturing to the back of the room.

Sandra had to suppress a gasp at the sight of her. Sure enough, there she was, almost unrecognizable. Her hair was slicked back, she was in jeans and a white tank top, and she sported a tattoo of a skeleton wearing a motorcycle helmet and the words *Live to Ride* on her right arm. Sandra could not believe it. Never in a million years would she have ever expected to find middle school principal Birdie Munn playing pool in a rough and shabby biker hangout.

Maya, on the other hand, was hardly taken aback. She had seen it all and people rarely were capable of surprising her.

Birdie was chalking her cue, about to take on a scrawny, beak-nosed kid with an obvious crush on her, which she quickly used to her advantage, distracting him, making him miss his shots, until she easily put him down with one last masterful shot to the corner pocket. The kid ambled to the bar, the wager made that the loser buy the next round.

Maya and Sandra crossed over to the pool table where Birdie's back was to them as she placed the balls back inside the triangle rack.

"Cool tattoo," Sandra noted.

Birdie turned around, her face registering shock. "What the hell are you two doing here?"

"I love this joint. I come here all the time," Sandra cracked.

Birdie smiled. "Yeah right. And I'm Queen Camilla. Did you follow me here or what?"

"We just wanted to have a little chat outside your place of work, where there can be too many prying eyes and ears," Maya said.

"I hear that. I appreciate your discretion," Birdie said, noticing Sandra was still staring at the tattoo on her arm. "I got it when I was sixteen. I was a real rebel back then. Saved up all my money from waitressing that summer to buy my first bike. Granted, it was a Honda moped, but it got me on the road. By eighteen I graduated to my first real Harley. Called her Billie Jean. Man, what a great bike. Had her six years until I crashed her during a wild night of drag racing. Man, I was dumb back then. Took me years to get my act together."

"And now you're a middle school principal," Sandra marveled.

"Girl's gotta make a living. Turns out I'm pretty good at it. Nobody's more surprised than my mother. I put that poor woman through the ringer."

Maya cast a quick glance around the room. "Old habits die hard, I guess."

"And what I do on my own time is nobody's business but mine," Birdie said as she downed a whiskey shot special, handed to her by her scrawny pool opponent.

Maya followed suit and slammed her empty shot glass down on the edge of the pool table. "Birdie, we came here—"

"To talk to me about Burt Denning."

Before they could respond, the wiry pool player saddled up next to Sandra. "Hey, sweet thing, I'd love to take you for a spin on my bike and show you what freedom really feels like."

Sandra stared at him. "Really? That's the pickup line you decided to go with? Right now I just want to be free from you."

He chuckled, undeterred. "You're a feisty one. I like that. What's your sign?"

"Do not enter."

Maya burst out laughing.

"Beat it, Travis!" Birdie barked. "It's never going to happen. Not in this lifetime. Now go lick your wounds and leave us the hell alone."

The kid finally got the message and sulked off, tail between his legs. When he was finally gone, Birdie returned her attention to Maya and Sandra. "I gotta say, I was as surprised as anyone when Burt got arrested. I did not see that one coming at all."

"Do you think he did it?" Maya asked.

Birdie shrugged. "I mean, the guy confessed. That's pretty much that. But I never thought it would turn out to be Burt who killed Ellie. He just doesn't seem the type. Everybody at the school loved him."

"Except Ellie. From what we've learned, there was a lot of animosity between the two of them. Ellie was out to get Burt fired. She was threatening to lodge a complaint," Maya said.

"She never came to me about it. And I would not have just taken her word for it if she had. Ellie was a known troublemaker. I heard Principal Williams at the high school wanted to fire her, but she had the teacher's union behind her and they were not going to allow that to happen, so the school was pretty much stuck with her. As for Burt . . . well, he was doing such a bang-up job, I was actually in the process of trying to get him a raise. There was very little left in the budget, but I went to bat for him. I was keenly aware of his financial difficulties due to his medical condition."

"So he told you about his diagnosis?" Sandra asked.

Birdie shook her head. "I heard it through the grapevine. Burt pretty much keeps things like that to himself. He never wants to burden anyone with his problems, or make them feel uncomfortable. He's a good man. It boggles my mind that he confessed, especially because I initially thought it could not possibly have been him."

Maya perked up. "Why do you say that?"

"The timeline doesn't make sense."

"What timeline are you talking about?" Maya pressed.

"On the day of the spelling bee, right before Ellie did her disappearing act, one of the kids participating in the competition was overcome with nerves and threw up in the boys' bathroom. I found Burt, who was talking to Ellie, and told him to go clean up the mess. He must have been in there for at least twenty minutes between the point when Ellie disappeared and the body was discovered," Birdie explained.

"Do you think he could have slipped out of the bathroom when no one was looking and come back later?" Maya suggested.

"Yeah, maybe." Birdie hitched her shoulders, uncertain, before considering it some more. "But there were people everywhere. *Someone* would have seen him." She gestured toward Sandra. "After you found Ellie in the supply closet, I distinctly remember seeing Burt coming out of the boys' room with his mop and pail and cleaning fluid. He was looking around, confused, wondering what all the commotion was about."

A spark of excitement passed between Maya and Sandra as they made eye contact.

If Biker Birdie was recalling correctly, Burt Denning was nowhere near the scene of the crime.

Which meant he could not have committed the murder.

Burt Denning was an innocent man.

So why had he confessed?

# Chapter 30

"I'm not sure what it is you want me to say," Burt Denning said, shrugging his shoulders from behind the glass partition at the Maine Correctional Center.

Maya groaned in frustration, throwing up her hands.

Sandra, squeezed in next to her, leaned forward. "We have an eyewitness who saw you come out of the restroom where you had been cleaning up a mess *after* Ellie Duncan's body was discovered."

Burt grimaced, annoyed. "So?"

Sandra exhaled in exasperation. "So, Burt, you went into the bathroom with your cleaning supplies *before* Ellie disappeared and you didn't come out until *after* she was found dead, which means you clearly did *not* kill her."

Burt folded his arms, defiant. "Who is this supposed eyewitness?"

"Principal Munn," Sandra answered quickly.

This caught Burt by surprise.

He sat in his seat glumly, still holding the phone to his ear, his hand shaking slightly.

"That's right," Sandra continued. "The woman runs the entire middle school. She's your superior. I would say she's a pretty reliable witness. Now why would she make up something like that? What reason could she possibly have?"

"I don't know," Burt huffed. "Maybe she's confused about the timeline. All I know is, she's got it wrong. When I finished cleaning the bathroom I had plenty of time to . . ." He paused and swallowed hard before continuing, ". . . to commit the crime."

"You can't even *say* it!" Sandra snapped. "You can't even say you had time to *kill Ellie*! I don't understand why you won't be honest with us, Burt; we're just trying to help you."

"And I've told you, I don't need or want your help. I did it. End of story. I'm ready to accept my punishment," Burt insisted, his cheeks reddening.

Maya snatched the phone from Sandra. "Why are you lying? Who are you covering for?"

"I'm done talking!" Burt shouted, about to hang up the phone.

Sandra snatched back the phone from Maya. "Burt, wait!"

He hesitated, on edge but still listening.

"Chloe wants to see you."

He began to shake his head vigorously. "No."

"Come on, Burt, she's your daughter and she loves you, and she so desperately wants to support you."

"Like I said before, tell her she should forget about me and get on with her life. That would be best for both of us."

"She's never going to do that," Sandra said quietly. "You at least owe her the opportunity to say goodbye. Can you do that, Burt? Can you find it within in yourself to see your only child one last time?"

His bottom lip quivered slightly.

Sandra was finally getting to him.

As tears began pooling in his eyes, he hastily wiped them away, sniffed back his emotions, and then barked into the phone, "I'll think about it." Then he slammed down the receiver, hauled himself to his feet, and marched out of the room, followed by the guard at the door. When the door shut behind them, Maya checked her phone and climbed to her feet. "I told Oscar to text me when Beth is back at the station. She's there now. We need to get over there right away."

Maya dashed out past the female guard with Sandra on her heels. They drove from Windham back to Downtown Portland in less than twenty minutes on US Route 301 East. Parking out front and scurrying up the steps into the South Portland Police Station, Maya and Sandra literally ran into Detective Hart as she came barreling out into the reception area to leave, followed by a few officers in plainclothes.

"Beth, I'm so glad we caught you," Maya said.

"I can't talk right now. I have a meeting with the police commissioner in Augusta and we're already running late."

"Please, this will only take a minute," Maya insisted.

Hart checked her watch. "You got thirty seconds."

Maya launched into their theory on why Burt Denning could not have killed Ellie Duncan, including the problematic timeline and Principal Munn's eyewitness testimony as to Denning's whereabouts at the time of the murder. Hart listened impatiently, her jaw clenching slightly as Maya pressed on, insistent on making her point heard.

When Maya finished, Hart's gaze darted from Maya to Sandra and then back again. "What exactly is it you want me to do?"

"Release him," Maya said.

Hart howled.

Startled by the boss's sudden outburst, the officers flanking Hart chuckled alongside her, as if they were in on the joke.

Maya and Sandra remained stone-faced.

Hart's laugh slowly subsided and her smile faded. "And why would I do that?"

"Because he didn't do it," Maya stated emphatically.

"Ladies, I appreciate your enthusiasm for this case. But I have a signed confession and Ellie Duncan would not get the justice she deserves if I simply ignored that fact and just let the man go."

Sandra could not stay silent anymore. "What about the evidence?"

"I don't need evidence. He confessed. He wants to accept responsibility and pay for his crime. I heard Birdie Munn hangs out at biker bars guzzling beer and getting drunk every day after work. Who's to say she didn't down a few at the time she claims to have seen Denning, supposedly putting him in the clear? A good prosecutor would no doubt tear her testimony apart. I understand you have a soft spot for Denning and his daughter, but read my lips, ladies: This case is closed. It's time for you to move on."

One of the officers hovering behind Hart poked his head over her shoulder and held up his phone. "I just checked Waze and there is construction on the I-95, so we should probably get going."

Hart nodded and then redirected her attention to Maya. "Look, we've been friends a long time, and I know how passionate you can get about your causes, but I'm warning you, don't bring this up with me again. I can be very helpful to you when it comes to future cases, so you may not want to risk burning that bridge. Have a nice day."

She blew past them out the door, followed by her phalanx of officers in lockstep. The sergeant at the reception desk who had been listening the whole time quickly dropped his head, pretending to review paperwork.

Sandra turned to Maya. "Was that a threat?"

Maya stamped her foot in annoyance. "Yes. Classic Beth Hart. But she's right. If we alienate her too much, she'll freeze us out, and we are definitely going to need her at some point down the road on some other case."

"So what do we do now?"

Maya wearily rubbed her temples with her thumb and forefinger. "Maybe we let it go. Burt's got his reasons for confessing. He's obviously not going to budge. It's starting to sound like we're done."

"But what about Chloe?"

"If Burt's going to stick to his guns and go to prison for murder, there's nothing much we can do. She's just going to have to accept the situation."

As cold as it sounded, Sandra knew Maya was right.

They could not save a man who did not want to be saved even if his daughter would wind up as collateral damage.

Maybe it was time they just walked away.

# Chapter 31

When Sandra dragged herself through the front door, drained, she heard excited voices coming from the kitchen. Dropping her bag and shedding her coat, she plodded in to find Ryan, Vanessa, and Chloe sitting around the kitchen table, wolfing down a large pepperoni pizza.

"I was going to make dinner," Sandra said.

"Sorry, Mom," Ryan said with his mouth full. "I thought you'd be working late tonight and we got hungry."

"Help yourself," Vanessa offered.

Sandra scooted over and scooped up a slice. "Thank you. I'm ravenous."

Sandra's eyes drifted over to a store-bought cake on the counter with a package of candles next to it. "Is it somebody's birthday today?"

"No, we're just celebrating," Chloe piped in with a sunny smile.

It was nice to see her smiling.

Sandra chewed some pizza and swallowed before asking, "Celebrating what?"

The three teens exchanged happy, knowing looks.

Chloe leaned in, bumping arms with Vanessa. "Do you want to tell her?"

Vanessa shook her head. "It's your news. Go ahead."

Chloe tried drawing out the suspense for a few moments, tongue in cheek, her eyes dancing, but then she could no longer contain herself and blurted out, "I got a full scholarship to Bates!"

Sandra threw up her arms and exclaimed, "That's wonderful, Chloe! Congratulations."

"I honestly didn't think I had a chance. I mean, I was supposed to hear back a week ago, but then today, out of the blue, I got an email from the dean herself, informing me that I had been given a full four-year scholarship including tuition, room and board, even a budget for living expenses. It's so crazy! Just when I was about to give up hope of even going to college."

"I'm so happy for you," Sandra cooed. "This does call for a celebration. I think we have some ice cream in the freezer to go with the cake. I'll serve." Sandra went to the cupboard for some plates and a knife from the butcher block. Setting them down on the counter, she retrieved a carton of vanilla ice cream from the subzero freezer and a scooper from the utensil drawer.

"I swear, I tried applying for a bunch of student loans to at least get me through the first year, which would give me enough time to try again for some kind of academic scholarship, but I got turned down flat. I wasn't surprised. My family's financial history would scare any lender off, believe me."

Ryan grabbed the last slice of pizza from the box. "I knew something would happen. If anyone deserves to go to college, it's you. You're always studying so hard."

"If I didn't believe in miracles before, I sure do now!" Chloe shouted with a broad grin.

Sandra cut slices of the chocolate cake, placing the pieces on the plates. "Where's Cooper?"

"I texted him like six times today, but he's not answering. He's been in such a foul mood lately. He's still pissed about getting suspended for vandalizing Ms. Duncan's . . ."

Chloe's voice trailed off.

No one wanted to discuss who it was who technically turned him in. In Cooper's mind, Sandra was a rat.

"I don't know why he won't text me back," Chloe pouted. "I know once he hears my news, he'll be so happy for me."

Sandra finished scooping ice cream onto the pieces of cake and served them to the kids before clearing the table of the empty pizza box. "I know someone else who is going to be very happy for you."

Chloe gave her a knowing nod. "I tried calling Dad today to tell him, but he wasn't available. They said I should try to schedule a visit, but I'm not sure he even wants to see me. It's like he's so ashamed he can't even look at me. But I know he didn't do it. I just know it!"

Sandra carried her own plate of cake and ice

cream over to the table and sat down with them. "Your father's going through a very rough time, but we're working on him. I can't guarantee anything, but hopefully you'll be seeing him real soon."

"It was Dad's dream for me to be the first one in the family to go to college. At least now, when he . . . when he . . ." Chloe began to choke back tears. "When he, you know, goes, he'll know that at least one of his dreams came true."

Sandra reached over and put an arm around her to comfort her, but Chloe refused to break down sobbing. She quickly got control of herself by pushing those emotions back inside of her and defiantly standing up from the table. "Enough with the touchy-feely crap. This is a day to dance. I wanna play that new Harry Styles video." She grabbed what was left of her cake and dashed off to the living room. They heard the giant flat-screen TV on the wall above the fireplace turn on and, seconds later, the thumping upbeat intro to Styles's latest hit.

They heard Chloe calling from the living room. "Come on, you two! You know I hate dancing alone."

"Harry Styles?" Ryan moaned.

Resigned, Ryan pushed back his chair from the table and hauled himself to his feet. He had scraped his plate clean and was now eyeing Vanessa, who had only eaten a few small bites of her own cake.

An unspoken exchange passed between them before Vanessa slid her plate over to Ryan. "Yes, you can have the rest of mine."

"Thanks, boo." Ryan winked at her and grabbed

her plate and then danced out of the kitchen to the muffled, pounding beat coming from the living room.

Sandra turned to Vanessa, who appeared to be hanging back. "Hey, I've seen your moves at home with Maya; are you afraid of showing them up out there?"

"No, I wanted to talk to you," Vanessa answered ominously.

"Vanessa, come on! We're making a video for TikTok!" Chloe yelled from the living room.

"Be right there!" Vanesa redirected her gaze to Sandra. "Something's not adding up."

Sandra gave her a puzzled look.

Vanessa leaned in closer to her. "The scholarship. There's something not right."

"How do you mean?"

"Chloe is like one of my best friends. We talk about everything all the time. That girl has applied for over a dozen scholarships and she has gotten turned down by all of them because her grades just weren't good enough. I mean, it's not like she was flunking out, but she was getting average scores. Not nearly good enough to warrant a full four-year ride. It doesn't make any sense. A girl in my class got a full scholarship to Bowdoin, but she still has to get a part-time job at Starbucks to pay for her living expenses and she has a four point zero average."

"What kind of scholarship is it? Who's sponsoring it?"

"That's another strange thing. Ryan asked her and she was very vague. She referenced some super-wealthy Bates alumnus, but she didn't give us a name. I don't know why she's acting so cagey about the whole thing. I'm telling you, Mrs. Wallage, something weird is going on."

Sandra had no doubt Vanessa was right.

But what was it?

Who was this mysterious benefactor willing to foot the bill that at minimum would total over $240,000? Bates ranked in the top one hundred most expensive colleges in the nation.

And was all of this in any way related to the pig-headed, irrational behavior of her father, who seemed hell-bent on going down for first degree murder?

# Chapter 32

O vercome with emotion, Burt Denning planted
the palm of his hand against the glass partition separating him from his beloved daughter,
Chloe, at the Maine Correctional Center. Tears
streamed down his cheeks as Chloe raised her own
hand, pressing it against the glass, his larger hand
outlining her own. Sandra and Ryan crowded in
on either side of Chloe for the heavily anticipated
reunion. Chloe had asked them to accompany her
for moral support because this was going to be,
without a doubt, an intensely emotional day for all
concerned.

Despite Burt's bark and bluster and vociferous
demands that Chloe be kept far away from him, he
had finally relented when Chloe wrote him a long
letter telling him how much she loved him and
wanted to be there for him, which Sandra was more
than happy to deliver to him. But it was her threat
of not accepting the scholarship if he refused to see

her that finally convinced him to allow Sandra to set up a meeting. There was no way Burt was going to risk his daughter purposely throwing away her future because of him. He had managed to get word to Sandra that she should go ahead and put in a visitation request, which she promptly filed with the lobby officer two days prior. Chloe had gone through a wide range of emotions waiting for this day, from elation to apprehension to confusion as to why they were in this terrible situation in the first place.

At the moment, neither was able to speak.

They just sat across from each other, staring at each other through the glass, both crying.

Sandra and Ryan remained silent out of respect for their private time together.

Chloe noticed some deep scratches on her father's right arm that were just beginning to heal. She sniffed, wiping her nose with the back of her hand. "How did you get those serious cuts on your arm, Dad?"

Burt glanced down at them, covering them with his left hand. "Oh, those? They're nothing. Don't worry about them."

Chloe was unconvinced. "They look pretty serious to me. Did someone assault you?"

Burt hesitated long enough for Sandra to know Chloe had just nailed it on the head, but he was not about to cause her any more worry and pain.

"No, honey, no, it was just an accident. I tripped and fell against a concrete wall, scratched the hell out of my arm on the way down. I'm fine. Totally fine."

Sandra, Ryan, and Chloe all strongly suspected

that his story was made up because the wounds were too deep to be caused simply by scraping skin against a rough concrete surface. No, they appeared more like wounds from an altercation, perhaps someone wielding a sharp-edged object. But none of them questioned it out of fear that Burt might cut the reunion short and bolt for the exit so as not to further upset his daughter by admitting he was in constant danger behind bars.

Chloe decided to change the subject. "Mrs. Wallage tells me Principal Munn came forward with exculpatory evidence that could clear you."

Burt threw Sandra an irritated look. "Mrs. Wallage is wrong, although I appreciate her enthusiastic efforts to prove my innocence. I hate to break it to you, sweetheart, but Principal Munn is confused about when she saw me. I wish it was true, that I was nowhere near the crime scene, but I was. I did it, honey. And I'm so, so sorry. I just lost control. She was making all kinds of threats about getting me fired. I couldn't risk losing my job."

"Dad, I don't understand. How could you do something like that? You haven't got a violent bone in your body!"

Burt averted his gaze, ridden with shame. "I don't know. I guess I just snapped." He then sat up with renewed purpose. "But at least when this failing body of mine finally gives in to the godforsaken cancer, I'll go knowing my girl is going to get a degree from Bates College. Imagine that. Pretty damn impressive, baby girl. I couldn't be prouder."

Burt spent the rest of the visit steering the conversation toward much safer topics, like Chloe's prom dress, the upcoming graduation ceremony, her summer plans before Bates, any subject that did not have anything to do with his incarceration. When the guard signaled that their time was up after forty-five minutes, Burt suddenly filled with emotion again as Chloe stood up to leave. They pressed their hands together against the glass one more time, Burt telling her how much he loved her, and Chloe promising to come visit him again, although Sandra was not sure if Burt would allow that. He was so determined that she move on and pretend he had already died behind bars.

Ryan and Chloe began to shuffle out, but Burt asked Sandra to stay behind for a second.

When she turned to face him, he conjured up the most menacing look he could muster. It did not work. He was not the least bit imposing or fearsome. In fact, his face was almost comical. "Sandra, I'm only going to say this one more time. Stop meddling in my personal business. Just leave it alone or else."

Sandra suppressed a smirk. "Or else what, Burt?"

He had not thought that far. It took him a minute to respond. "You don't want to know!"

Sandra nodded, showing no signs of being intimidated by him. His threat sounded hollow. "Honestly, Burt, you're never going to win any acting awards for this whole hardened-criminal performance. I'm just not buying it. But don't worry. If you really want to live out the rest of your days in an eight-by-six cell with a metal bed tray, a sink, and a toilet, that's your decision and I will abide by it. But I don't think Chloe is ready to give up on you just yet, so you'd better be prepared for that."

Before he could open his mouth to respond,

Sandra turned her back on him and marched out of the visitation room, then joined Ryan and Chloe in the hallway. Ryan had his arm around her as she collected herself.

Chloe raised her gaze to Sandra. "Did he look pale to you? I'm worried he's not getting his meds."

"I will find out. Ryan's father and I may be divorced, but I still have a little pull left as the ex-wife of a US senator."

"Thank you, Sandra."

As they headed down the hall toward the building exit, Chloe asked, "Do you and Mrs. Kendrick have any leads yet that might help prove my dad didn't do it?"

"We have one suspect whose alibi blew up, but it's been tough getting the police to take it seriously. Your father is making the situation extremely difficult. As long as he firmly sticks to his confession, the cops have no reason to follow up on any other leads."

Chloe quavered, confused. Sandra could tell her heart was saying one thing while her head was telling her another. She was at odds with herself. She could not believe her father was capable of murdering another human being in cold blood. That was not the dad she knew. And yet she could not completely discount the unsettling thought that they were all wrong, that he was actually telling the truth, and that maybe she did not really know her father after all.

# Chapter 33

"Good morning," Noah Chastain-Wheeler said warily as he opened his front door to greet Maya and Sandra. "How can I help you?"

"We would like to speak to Annabelle," Maya said.

Noah reared back with suspicion. "Oh? Regarding what? As her father, I think I have the right to know."

Sandra raised her hand. "Of course. That goes without saying. We're not here to cause any trouble. We think Annabelle could help us in our investigation of Ellie Duncan's murder."

Noah, still blocking the doorway to prevent them from entering his house, suddenly grew curious. "How so?"

"I noticed on that day, after Annabelle won, you were all backstage recording a video," Maya explained.

Noah nodded. "That's right. Annabelle has a lot

of fans who follow her on Instagram. We're talking tens of thousands. She's well on her way to becoming a highly paid social media influencer."

"Good for her," Sandra cheered, trying to suppress any hint of sarcasm. "We watched the video she posted online but were wondering if you recorded a longer version that she might have edited from."

Noah opened the door a little wider, ushering them inside. "Come in."

Maya and Sandra entered the house and he shut the door behind them.

"Doug is running a 5K today and won't be home until this afternoon." He wandered over to the foot of the stairs. "Annabelle, could you come down here, please? And bring your phone."

They heard feet stomping on the floor above and then a door slam open. "What is it? I'm watching cartoons."

"Just come down, please. It will only take a minute," Doug called out through gritted teeth.

There was some very loud, dramatic sighing and then Annabelle appeared at the top of the stairs in gray leggings and a pink rainbow T-shirt, her lips pouting, her phone firmly clenched in her right hand. As she stared down at Maya and Sandra, her body seemed to suddenly tense up. "Am I in trouble?"

"No, of course not, dumpling. Mrs. Wallage and Mrs. Kendrick are here because they need your help."

Annabelle's eyes flicked suspiciously back and forth between the two women. Then she boldly trudged down the steps, joining them in the living room, where Noah gestured for them all to sit down.

"Can I offer you some coffee?" Noah asked.

"No, thank you, this won't take long," Sandra replied.

Annabelle hugged the side of the couch, trying her best to stay as far away from Maya as possible. Maya turned to her and tried to muster the friendliest, most nonthreatening smile she could. "Annabelle, your dad tells us you recorded a longer video at school on the day of the spelling bee than the one you posted on Instagram, is that right?"

She jerked her head toward her father, not sure if she should answer. He gave her a slight nod. She turned her body toward Maya, rocking back and forth nervously, and then muttered as she stared at the floor, "Yeah."

"Would it be possible for us to take a look at it?" Sandra quietly asked.

Annabelle shrugged, then lifted her gaze to her father, who gave her another encouraging nod. She unlocked her phone and tapped the screen a few times before tossing it in Maya's direction. When Maya picked it up, the video was already playing. Sandra jumped up from her chair and raced over to watch the recording with her.

The phone appeared to capture everything that was going on backstage. Parents consoling their kids who had been eliminated. Phoebe being congratulated by her fellow students and a few teachers. Ellie Duncan lambasting Burt Denning before storming off. Even Maya and Sandra watching Ellie's despicable behavior toward Burt. Moments later, they could see Birdie Munn approaching

Burt about the mess he needed to clean up in the bathroom. Burt moved his supply cart in front of the bathroom, barring anyone from entering, and then he grabbed his mop and pail and disappeared inside.

"Wait, pause it right there!" Sandra exclaimed.

Maya tapped the red button on the video, freezing the image of Ellie Duncan walking into the frame.

"There she is," Sandra said, pointing with her finger. "At this point, after Burt has gone into the bathroom, Ellie is seen here, still very much alive. And he doesn't come out until after Lucas and I found her body."

Maya pressed the button again, and it resumed playing for a few more seconds, with Annabelle thanking her devoted fans for all their support, before she waved goodbye and the screen went to black.

"Is this the end? Did you record any more video that day?"

"No, once I posted the shorter version, we left school and my dads took me to dinner," Annabelle answered.

Sandra sighed, frustrated. "So there is no video that would prove Burt Denning did not leave the bathroom at any time before Ellie was discovered."

Annabelle sat forward, not so shy anymore. "Sure there is. There were tons of kids making videos that day. I can post something on Instagram, asking everybody to send me what they have."

"And we can put together a complete timeline! Annabelle, you're a genius!" Maya declared.

"We know," Noah interjected, beaming proudly.

It took Annabelle less than thirty seconds to post her request, and within two minutes TikTok and Instagram videos were pouring in. Annabelle was able to download them on her father's computer in his office and line them up on the home screen according to exactly when they were recorded. When she was finished, Maya, Sandra, Noah, and Annabelle crowded around the desk and watched them in order. Although taken from a variety of different angles, each one had the door to the boys' bathroom seen clearly in the background. Two other videos recorded at the same time Annabelle was making her own showed Burt pulling his cart in front of the door and grabbing his mop and pail before going into the bathroom. For the next twenty minutes, according to the time codes from the videos, no one was seen coming out of the bathroom.

Then, suddenly, there was pandemonium and confusion. People running around, checking their phones, huddling together gossiping, all occurring just moments from the exact time Sandra and Lucas stumbled across Ellie Duncan in the supply closet. Principal Munn was seen scurrying into view and calling 911. Seconds later, Burt Denning came out of the bathroom with a confused expression on his face, wondering what was going on. Munn yelled something to him and he reacted with shock. Like he had just found out someone murdered Ellie Duncan.

"There it is! He never left the bathroom. That's exactly the proof we needed," Sandra cried.

"Now hold on," Maya cautioned. "Is there a window in the bathroom? He blocked the entrance to the bathroom, so no one could come in. What if he crawled out a window, strangled Ellie, stuffed her in the supply closet, and then snuck back before she was found?"

Sandra deflated. "You're right. He would have had time."

"That's impossible," Annabelle insisted. "The window in the boys' bathroom is way too small for a grown man to squeeze through. Billy Tannenbaum tried skipping school by climbing out that window and got stuck. It took hours to free him, and he's only in the fifth grade."

Maya snapped her fingers. "And, if I recall correctly, there is a security camera set up outside the school building covering all entrances and exits, including that bathroom window. If Burt had come out through there, the cops, who I'm sure have already reviewed the footage, would have seen him. So unless he's Ant-Man and left through a tiny hole in the wall, there is no way he could have killed Ellie."

Sandra looked around the room, taking in all their expectant faces. "Did we just clear Burt Denning of murder?"

# Chapter 34

Burt Denning, now a free man, stood at the foot of the staircase in the Wallage home as his daughter, Chloe, descended in a gorgeous, glittering, off-the-shoulder tulle gown trimmed with a dramatic ruffled top. Her glamorous, tousled half-updo-with-curls hairstyle looked red carpet ready. Burt, overcome with emotion, raised his phone and began snapping a series of photos to capture this indelible moment. Just behind Chloe, Vanessa followed, her own glistening brown hair designed in a chic updo with a modern boho twist, looking smashing in an aqua, feather-trimmed sequin gown.

Maya, who was hovering behind Burt, put a hand to her mouth, stunned by her daughter's radiant smile, her poise and beauty. Sandra was preoccupied snapping photos with her own phone as Ryan and Cooper, in matching black tuxedos and each holding a plastic box with a wrist corsage inside, stood awestruck at how lucky they were to be escorting two such dazzling, knockout dates to their senior prom.

Burt, choking back tears, rushed to embrace his daughter as she reached the bottom of the stairs. "Chloe, you . . ." He sniffed back tears. "You remind me so much of your mother."

She embraced him and they hugged for a long time. No one spoke, allowing them to have this moment out of respect. The passing of Burt's wife several years before had left a heartbreaking void in the family that still hurt. Finally, Burt pulled away and placed his hands on Chloe's shoulders. "She would be so proud. She never stopped talking about how much she wanted you to go to college. And now, it's actually happening."

Cooper stepped forward with his corsage, plucking it out of the box and gently sliding it onto Chloe's wrist. As Ryan did the same with Vanessa, Sandra positioned herself with her phone camera to capture it all for posterity.

Maya watched Burt, who appeared unfazed by the fact that just eight hours earlier he was languishing in a jail cell. But presented with irrefutable proof of his innocence, Detective Hart had been left with no choice but to release Burt. Shortly thereafter, the prosecutor dropped all charges. Burt was no longer a suspect. However, Hart was infuriated over Denning's false confession, which she explained away in a press conference as the rantings of an emotionally disturbed man eager to worm his way into the public eye, a theory Maya found utterly ridiculous. Burt Denning had never shown any signs of somehow being a fame-starved, publicity whore. In fact, from what

Maya knew about the man, he appeared to be the exact opposite: an intensely private man who was painfully uncomfortable talking about himself, which was why his sudden murder confession seemed so out of left field. Maya was determined to find out why he had blatantly lied to the police and put himself into such a precarious legal position.

Cooper opened the front door and peeked outside before turning back to the group. "The limo's here!"

All four teens rushed outside to take some selfies in front of the fancy, silver stretch limousine. Sandra skittered out behind them, now recording a video on her phone. Burt was about to follow when Maya intercepted him, lightly gripping his arm. "Burt, wait. We really need to talk."

Burt grimaced. He knew what was coming and he clearly had a desire to cut the anticipated conversation off at the pass. "Listen, Maya, I appreciate all you and Sandra have done, but I just want to put this whole sordid mess behind me."

"I'm afraid that's not going to be possible, Burt," Maya warned him. "Detective Hart is not just going to forget all about your false confession. You wasted valuable police resources. She's threatening to arrest you again, this time for obstruction of justice."

Burt shrugged, unmoved. "If that's what she wants to do, I can't stop her."

Maya shook her head, incredulous. "How can you be so cavalier about this, Burt? Hart is dead serious. Do you want to wind up behind bars again, this time for a crime you actually *did* commit? Think of Chloe."

"I am thinking of Chloe," Burt spat out.

"Why would you take a risk like that? Chloe has already lost her mother. How is she going to cope if she loses her father too? It's not fair to her."

"Life isn't always fair, Maya. Take it from me."

Maya's face fell.

She suddenly felt sorry for Burt.

He was right.

The man had mere months to live.

If anyone knew just how unfair life could be, he did.

"The only thing I care about these days is Chloe's future. I've lived my life. She's just beginning hers."

"But don't you want to be a part of her life for as long as you possibly can?"

He did not have an answer. His mind was preoccupied as Maya waited for him to say something.

Anything.

Then he reared back, wiping away whatever unpleasant thoughts had been consuming him, and with a stiff upper lip, declared, "Yes. I'm here right now, aren't I? And I'm going to savor every minute of it. Chloe is happy, she looks beautiful, she's going to the prom with one of the most popular boys in school, and she has a full college scholarship. Tonight is a cause for celebration and I'm not going to worry about what happens tomorrow."

He marched out the front door to join Sandra and the kids and the limo driver, who was now posing with the two teen couples in the shot as Sandra recorded her video. Maya watched Burt excitedly hustle down the driveway, clutching his own phone to take more pictures. Sandra continued recording as Ryan and Vanessa and Cooper and Chloe all piled into the back of the limo and the driver jumped in front to spirit them away to their senior prom.

Burt waved goodbye to them from the sidewalk as if he didn't have a care in the world. But he was a smart man. So either he was deluding himself into thinking he had an easy road ahead or he was hiding something.

Maya firmly believed the latter.

Burt Denning was carrying around a deep, dark secret.

And she needed to find out what it was.

# Chapter 35

"Why are you calling me on a Saturday? The weekends are my only free time to get things done around the house!" Ewan Murphy berated Maya over the phone. She gripped the receiver and bit her tongue, suppressing a flash of anger. Ewan, annoyed, continued yelling, "If you have something to talk to me about, you can call my office and make an appointment like everybody else."

Maya glanced at Sandra, who was sitting across the desk from her in their office, looking on intently.

Maya paused, took a deep breath, and then said softly into the phone, "It's about Chloe Denning's scholarship."

Ewan's aggressive manner seemed to suddenly retreat. "Oh? What about it?"

"Chloe told my daughter, Vanessa, that you were the one who contacted her to let her know she had been awarded a full four-year scholarship and I just have a few questions I was hoping you might be able to clear up."

There was a long beat before he replied quietly, "What kind of questions?"

"I think it would be better if we spoke in person. Can Sandra and I swing by your house later?"

"No! Beverly will be back from grocery shopping by then. I'd rather discuss this privately. Can you come right now?"

Maya was taken aback by his sudden cooperation. She honestly had expected him to hang up on her, but she had somehow struck a nerve with this particular topic of Chloe's scholarship. Something he was apparently not anxious to share with his wife of fifteen years. "We can be there in twenty minutes."

"Fine. Hurry up!" Ewan snorted before ending the call.

Sandra quickly stood up. "What did he say?"

"He got very rattled the moment I brought up the scholarship money. He obviously knows something. He's willing to talk, but we have to go over to his house right now."

Without another word, the two women bolted out of the office and moments later were in Maya's car speeding across town to the historic West End neighborhood of Portland, where the Murphys resided. Their three-story house behind a rusty, wrought-iron gate was a New England–style Victorian home with a turret that was perfect for gazing out at sea. The house was in need of a facelift, having endured a lot of beatings from the rough Maine winters. Maya pulled up to the curb in front of the house, and she and Sandra got out of the car and ambled through the gate, heading up the walkway to the front porch.

Maya rang the bell.

They waited for a few moments, but there was no answer.

Maya pressed the doorbell button again.

Still no answer.

She banged on the door.

"Maybe he had to go out," Sandra suggested.

"No, he insisted we come over right away while Beverly is still out shopping."

Maya noticed a Volvo parked in the driveway. "That's his car. He must be around here somewhere."

Maya grabbed the door handle.

It was unlocked.

She poked her head inside the foyer. "Ewan? It's Maya Kendrick. Ewan?"

They cautiously entered the house and wandered down the hall to the kitchen. There were cereal bowls and spoons in the sink. The coffeepot was still warm. The Murphys had obviously eaten breakfast not too long before. As Sandra continued poking around the kitchen, Maya rambled into the living room, with its large bay window overlooking a vast lawn and gazebo and a peek of the ocean through a thicket of trees, a view probably better appreciated from upstairs. Suddenly, she narrowed her focus on something sprawled out in the grass close to the house. Maya gasped and covered her mouth with her hand.

It was a man's body.

"Sandra!" Maya yelled, running back to the

kitchen and out a side door that led to the backyard. With Sandra close on her heels, they rushed up to discover a man lying face down, wearing a plaid work shirt and rumpled jeans, his crumped body twisted and broken. His head was turned in an odd position, as if his neck had been snapped. His eyes were open, his face frozen with a look of shock.

It was Ewan Murphy.

Maya frantically grabbed his wrist to feel for a pulse.

Nothing.

He was definitely dead.

Sandra shook her head in disbelief. "You talked to him less than twenty minutes ago. What happened?"

Maya spied a ladder propped up against the side of the house. She popped up to her feet and raced over, climbing the rungs to the rooftop of the house, where she found a stack of cedar shake shingles, a nail gun, an air compressor, and a hatchet strewn about, everything you would need to repair a roof. Maya could only surmise that Ewan had been up on the roof working when he must have slipped or tripped on something and fell off, breaking his neck on impact.

Or perhaps that was the scenario someone wanted them to believe. Maya knew in her gut that Ewan Murphy was keeping a secret, one he was ready to share, only to conveniently wind up dead before he got the chance.

# Chapter 36

After immediately calling 911, Sandra remained on the back lawn near the body as Maya stayed up on top of the roof, surveying the potential crime scene while they waited for the police to arrive. Maya immediately noticed that the tools appeared as if they had been kicked around, perhaps during a scuffle. She bent down to inspect the tools and noticed a smear of blood on the sharp edge of the hatchet, as if it had been used as a weapon against someone.

Maya crawled back up to her feet and made her way to the edge of the roof, calling down to Sandra, "Check his body to see if he has any visible injuries."

She could hear sirens in the distance as Sandra circled the body, carefully examining it for any cuts or bruises or torn clothing. After a few moments, she shook her head, yelling up to Maya, "No! Not a scratch!"

It was obvious Ewan died from a broken neck, perhaps blunt force trauma, but not from a hatchet wound. Which meant that it was probably Ewan who had swung the weapon at someone else, causing them to bleed.

The sound of the sirens grew in volume.

They were getting closer.

Maya knew she only had a few more minutes before the police pulled up to the scene and ordered her down from the roof. She surveyed the area one last time, noticing the rain gutter along the roof had been torn loose and was dangling. There were also scuff marks on a couple of the shingles. It was becoming increasingly obvious that Ewan Murphy had not accidentally slipped and fallen off the roof on his own. Someone else had been up here, and there were telltale signs of a physical altercation. Either Ewan fell during a fight or he was intentionally pushed.

Maya could see from the roof several squad cars screeching to a stop in front of the house and a dozen officers suddenly swarming onto the property, circling to the back lawn to question Sandra, who stood over the still body of Ewan Murphy. Moments later, a black sedan pulled up and Detective Beth Hart got out of the passenger's side. Her eyes flicked upward, instantly zeroing in on Maya standing on the roof. She scowled and shook her head and called up to her, "I'm sure you're enjoying the view from up there, Maya, but maybe it's time you came down and let my officers take over."

Maya waved limply, then shuffled over to the ladder propped up against the side of the house and began climbing down until she reached the bottom and joined Hart, who was interviewing Sandra next to the body.

"He was already dead when we got here," Sandra said.

Hart glanced up at the roof and back down at the body, also noticing the dangling gutter. "So he was up there working and maybe tripped on something, lost his balance, and just tumbled off the roof, landing here and breaking his neck."

"No," Maya said flatly.

Hart cocked an eyebrow, curious. "No?"

"Definitely not. This is a homicide."

Hart sighed and folded her arms. "Okay. Do tell."

Maya recounted what she had found up on the roof. The signs of a struggle. The blood on the hatchet. "If you dust the handle for fingerprints, I will bet you anything they will be a match for Ewan. He was the one wielding it as a weapon. He was defending himself. That blood on the tip belongs to someone else, most likely the person who killed him."

Hart was not prepared to accept Maya's off-the-cuff theory. "Perhaps."

"No, this is not that hard to figure out. Murphy was murdered," Maya insisted.

Hart had heard enough. "You know what is hard to figure out? Why you and your friend here always seem to be around when a dead body turns up. I have given you two a lot of leeway in the past, mostly because you and I came up through the ranks together, but you're not a cop anymore,

Maya. You're just a private citizen with a PI license. We are not a team working this case together, capisce?"

Maya sighed. "Okay, got it, Beth."

"So my officers are going to put up some yellow police tape around the perimeter and I expect you both to stand *behind* it."

She then stormed off to confer with one of her junior detectives just as Ewan Murphy's wife, Beverly, came around the side of the house, dumbfounded as to why there were police cars parked out front and officers milling about her property. She had yet to see her husband's body sprawled out on the back lawn.

Her eyes flicked toward Sandra. "What's going on here? What happened?"

Sandra slowly moved toward her. "Beverly, I'm afraid I have some very bad news. . . ."

Before Sandra could get it out, Beverly finally spotted Ewan's body as Hart huddled with some other detectives a few feet away. She stared at it for a long time, stone-faced, before casually asking, "Is he dead?"

Sandra nodded, putting a comforting arm around her shoulder. "Yes. I'm so sorry, Beverly."

Beverly shook Sandra's arm away and gave a little shrug. "Did he fall off the roof? I told him it was too dangerous to go up there to try to fix the leak himself. I must have said a hundred times he should hire a professional to do the job, but does he ever listen to me? No. Never."

Her face was strangely devoid of emotion.

The sight of her husband's crumpled, lifeless

body splayed across the grass seemed to barely register. And the tone of her voice was almost robotic. "That man has always thought of himself as invincible. I'm surprised something like this didn't happen a whole lot sooner."

Maya tried suppressing a flash of anger. How could this woman be so cavalier? Her dead husband was right in front of her and she was acting as if the tragedy was a neighbor's dog defecating on her property.

Sensing Maya might snap at Beverly, Sandra squeezed her arm tightly and whispered in her ear, "People handle these types of situations differently. It doesn't mean she's not upset. She may be in shock."

"I suppose the police are going to want to talk to me." Beverly groaned. "Looks like I'm going to have to cancel my hair appointment later and live with these gray strands until they can fit me in again, Lord only knows when."

Maya stared at her, slack-jawed, astounded by the lack of empathy from this woman.

Hart had noticed Maya and Sandra talking to the victim's spouse and made a beeline for them. Beverly sniffed, "Well, she's just going to have to wait. I have some frozen vegetables in my trunk that are going to melt if I don't get them into the freezer."

She started heading back around the side of the house to the driveway where her car was parked with her groceries when Detective Hart intercepted her. "Mrs. Murphy, I'm so sorry for your loss. I know it's a very difficult time for you, but I really need to ask—"

Beverly rolled her eyes and cut her off. "Yes. Fine. But I'm not going to stand out here and let my frozen food go to ruin, so walk with me to the car." She blew past Hart, who was just as surprised by her indifferent attitude as Maya.

Sandra and Maya followed them to Beverly's GMC Yukon parked in the driveway out front, where she popped open the back door and grabbed a recyclable bag before heading into the house. Hart, losing patience, followed her. The grocery receipt flew out of the bag Beverly was carrying and floated to the grass, where Sandra scooped it up and studied it.

Sandra wrinkled her nose.

Maya instantly picked up on her concern. "What is it?"

"The time on the receipt. Here, take a look."

She handed it to Maya.

11:46 a.m.

"That was well over an hour ago," Sandra said. "It's only a ten-minute drive to here from the grocery store."

"So? Maybe she had to run some more errands before coming home," Maya suggested.

"Maybe. Or maybe she drove here, had a fight with her husband that resulted in him falling to his death, and then left again to drive around until she could double back and arrive home *after* the body already had been discovered."

It was certainly a plausible theory.

After all, the woman's reaction to her husband's

sudden death was borderline boredom. The odds of her donning a black veil and going into a period of mourning were practically nil. Sandra was correct. People did react to death in many different ways, but Beverly Murphy appeared, if not gleeful, almost relieved that Ewan was gone. And Maya strongly suspected that Beverly may have been the one to drive him to his early grave.

# Chapter 37

Beverly Murphy poked at her salad with a fork in a turquoise booth at a diner near her home as Maya and Sandra sat across from her, Maya with an untouched bowl of chili topped with onions and cheese and Sandra with just a cup of coffee.

The women had invited Beverly out for a bite to eat once Detective Hart finished questioning her, which took over two hours. With yellow police tape surrounding her property and rubbernecking neighbors constantly watching from their windows, not to mention the local news reporters shouting questions from the street, a disheveled Beverly, desperate to escape the unwanted glare of the spotlight, had appeared at her front door after Hart and two other detectives finally had left and her husband's body was driven off to the morgue, only to find Maya and Sandra still on the scene. She invited them inside, apparently making a decision to lean on the only two people who seemed to be at all interested in her well-being. Beverly had offered to make them some tea, but Maya feared they would be constantly harassed by a flurry of calls on the landline and reporters ringing her doorbell trying to get an interview. It was best if they left the premises and found refuge elsewhere, a place where they could talk in peace. So they piled into Maya's car and squealed away.

One intrepid reporter tried following them in his beat-up Volvo, but Maya managed to lose him with a couple of hairpin turns down some side streets. They settled in at a diner near Beverly's neighborhood that she often frequented. After the humorless waitress, who was as gloomy as a day in March, delivered their food and drinks, they were finally able to talk.

Beverly, with puffy eyes, a snotty nose, and hair like a rat's nest, threw down her fork in frustration. "It was awful. They think I did it. They think I killed Ewan."

Beverly noticed Maya and Sandra exchange a quick glance as she sipped her glass of ice water and frowned. Silence filled the space between them.

Sandra did not want Beverly to pick up on the fact that she and Maya were inclined to agree with the police. "What do they think happened?"

"They believe in some cockamamie woman-scorned story! Detective Hart actually thinks I discovered Ewan was having an affair with Ellie Duncan and I was out of my mind, wild with jealousy, so I climbed up that ladder and tried shoving him off the roof when his back was turned. I mean, that's just bonkers! I couldn't care less what Ewan was up to when I wasn't around."

"How do they explain the signs of a struggle?"

Beverly scoffed. "Oh, that's a good one. They said Ewan must have caught a glimpse of me as I was coming up behind him and spun around, and we fought and he tried defending himself with the hatchet but lost his balance at some point, allowing me the opportunity to give him that fatal shove. Have you ever heard of anything so patently ridiculous?"

Sandra did not think it sounded ridiculous at all.

It was a totally credible scenario.

Sandra studied Beverly.

She certainly appeared to be a strong woman. She was also taller than her husband. It was not impossible to assume she could have overpowered him with the element of surprise.

Beverly pushed her salad away. "Well, they swabbed the inside of my mouth so this will all be cleared up once the test results come back and they find out there is none of my DNA on that damn hatchet."

Maya swallowed a spoonful of chili. "What about the blood? It didn't belong to Ewan."

"And it didn't belong to me! I stripped down to my underwear to prove I had no cuts or gashes on my body, which was, as you can imagine, a grueling exercise in humiliation. But even that didn't convince her of my innocence. She just wants to arrest someone, anyone, so she can wrap up this case sooner rather than later. Trust me, I would *love* to confess."

Sandra's eyes widened in surprise.

"Ewan was a liar and a cheat and I must have daydreamed a hundred times about how much better my life would be if he was out of the picture."

"I hope you didn't tell Detective Hart how you feel," Maya cautioned.

"No, of course not. Why give her more ammunition to use against me? But it's the truth. I wish it had been me up on that roof. To see his shocked face when I sent him flying off that rooftop." She paused, staring off into space as if she was imagining the whole scene before redirecting her gaze back to Maya and Sandra. "But I didn't do it. It was someone else. Ewan would probably still be alive today if he didn't fancy himself as one of the Property Brothers, but he was always deluding himself. Those boys are much better-looking, and Ewan was just a clumsy oaf who had no business attempting his own home repairs. He never should have been up there in the first place. I told him so, but of course he always refused to listen. We were barely on speaking terms anyway."

"If you were so unhappy in the marriage, Beverly, why didn't you just leave him?" Sandra asked.

"I was waiting for the right moment. I was squirreling away cash into a private bank account that Ewan didn't know about, hoping to have enough of a nest egg one day to get me started somewhere else, far away from Ewan. But I wasn't quite there yet. I was still saving and biding my time. It didn't help that we've had some severe financial setbacks lately, all of which were completely Ewan's fault!"

Maya cocked an eyebrow. "How so?"

Beverly flagged down the waitress. "This salad is not cutting it. I want a burger, rare, with the seasoned crinkle fries."

The stone-faced waitress nodded and headed off to the kitchen.

Beverly turned back to Maya and Sandra. "I did extra ab work at Pilates today before I went shopping, so it's all good." She did not wait for them to reply. "In addition to Ewan thinking he was a competent handyman, he also foolishly thought he was a keen-eyed money guru, but he wound up frittering away most of our savings on a series of bad investments. I could have stopped him if he had bothered to tell me, but no, he kept it all a big secret. I only found out we were heavily in debt when the bank called to inform me our savings account was overdrawn. He basically wiped us out. Thank God he didn't know about my hush-hush account or he would have blown that money too. Now it's all I have left."

This was another motive Beverly was offering up as to why she would want to kill her husband. But if she was indeed guilty, Sandra surmised that Beverly would probably be acting far more evasively.

"The irony was, in the last few days, Ewan was crowing about how he had found a way to fix everything."

Sandra straightened up in the booth. "Fix everything? How?"

Beverly shrugged. "I have no idea. Like I said, we were living separate lives at this point and rarely talked. But he knew how upset I was over him draining our life savings and he was trying to make it up to me. Just how he was going to replace all that lost money, though, is anybody's guess. He always had one scheme or another going on."

"Did you tell this to the police?" Maya asked.

"No," Beverly replied abruptly before shrugging. "They didn't ask."

Sandra knew they had just learned a tantalizing new detail. The salary from Ewan's school board position would hardly be enough to cover their losses. So his financial windfall had to have come from another source. And if they could pinpoint this source, another player in this game, they might have the name of the person whose blood was on that hatchet and who most likely had sent Ewan Murphy plunging to his death.

# Chapter 38

Sandra and Ryan sat side by side on the white leather couch in the family den as Vanessa stood in front of the fireplace, reading from some papers she held in her hand.

"In closing, I want to thank the teachers and staff at SoPo High for their dedication, support, and mentorship. You have inspired us to pursue our dreams and reach for the stars. And to our parents and families, we thank you for your unwavering love, support, encouragement, and sacrifice. None of us would be here today without you. And so, fellow graduates, let us embrace the as yet unwritten future ahead with open hearts and open minds, knowing that we together have the power to create a better world." She lowered the pages and glanced up at Sandra and Ryan, who were perched on the edge of their seats with big, uplifting smiles. "That's it. You can clap now."

They both began applauding loudly.

Vanessa grimaced. "I don't know. It feels a bit by the numbers."

"No!" Ryan protested. "It's perfect!"

"You have to say that. You're my boyfriend."

"It's well-written, to the point, it's what a valedictory speech should be," Sandra assured her.

"You didn't think that whole part about standing on the cusp of a new chapter in our lives, using the tools we learned from our education to make a positive impact on the world, blah, blah, blah, wasn't too run-of-the-mill and boring?"

"No, I found it inspiring," Sandra said. "And you make it personal by talking about your own challenges."

"I went back and forth on whether or not to talk about Dad. Do you think he's going to be upset with me mentioning his time in prison?" Vanessa asked nervously.

Sandra shook her head. "I think your father is going to be very proud of you. It's a thoughtful, moving speech."

They heard the front door slam shut.

"Hey, where is everybody?"

"Speaking of fathers." Ryan grinned before calling out, "We're in here, Dad!"

Moments later, Sandra's ex-husband, Stephen, drifted in with a rolling suitcase and a cheerful smile.

Ryan jumped up to greet him, and Stephen enveloped him in a bear hug. "How was your flight?"

"Late as usual. I think there's some kind of rule that any flight in and out of the Portland Jetport is delayed by at least an hour and a half." Stephen winked at Vanessa. "Well, if it isn't Miss Valedictorian with the four point zero GPA. How's the speech coming along?"

"We just finished a dress rehearsal. I'm second guessing everything," Vanessa said.

"It's perfect," Sandra insisted, standing up from the couch. Ryan pulled away, allowing his father to move in and hug Sandra. She stiffened slightly in his embrace, her lips knitted together, still not fully adapted to their new normal as exes but trying hard to act casual. Stephen noticed her trepidation about physical contact and finally let go, mercifully not making an issue of it.

Ryan checked his Apple Watch. "You were supposed to get in around noon. It's after four. Was the flight up from DC really *that* late?"

"No, I had a couple of errands to run before I came here," Stephen explained.

Sandra relieved him of his suitcase. "Here, I'll take this to the guest room."

Stephen winced. He hated staying in the guest room and not upstairs in the main bedroom, where he had spent the twenty years of his marriage, but he was not about to argue. The divorce papers had been signed, after all, and were waiting to be filed with the state. "Wait, before you go, I have some news."

Sandra stopped and looked at him expectantly.

For a moment, she thought he was about to drop a bombshell like he was getting married again or not running for reelection. Stephen was always full of surprises.

"I went by the school after I landed and had a little talk with Principal Williams."

Sandra furrowed a brow. "About what?"

"I decided it was time she and I had a sit-down to review Ryan's papers and test scores in geography class to assess why his dear departed teacher was threatening to flunk him."

Sandra grimaced. She had no doubt Caroline Williams had dropped everything to meet with Stephen, a powerful US senator. Stephen had never been above using his vaulted position to twist an arm here or there to get his way. She was also annoyed that he had willfully ignored her when they last spoke. Sandra had filled him on Ryan's predicament, how unfair Ellie Duncan was treating him before her untimely death, and she had promised him that *she* was handling it and that it would be best if he did not get involved at this point. But as on so many other occasions, Stephen had not listened. He just charged ahead on his own, without consulting her, to take command of the situation.

Sandra folded her arms. "So what happened?"

Ryan held his breath.

"The moment she took a serious look at his records, it became obvious Ryan was being unfairly singled out. Ryan had better exam scores than a lot of kids to whom she gave higher grades. In the end, it was a pretty easy call."

Ryan took an eager step forward. "You mean I'm going to pass?"

"Not only are you going to pass, you're getting a B plus," Stephen announced. "It's the least they could do after all you went through with that unhinged harpy."

"Stephen, please, the woman died," Sandra scolded.

"I'm sorry, but nobody messes with my number one son."

"I thought Jack was your number one son," Ryan chirped.

"Jack's not here," Stephen replied with a wink.

Ryan took Vanessa by the hand. "Looks like I'm going to be in the front row at graduation cheering you on during your valedictory speech after all."

Vanessa threw her arms around his shoulders. "We have to call Chloe and Cooper and tell them!"

Stephen, who was standing next to Sandra, whispered under his breath, "Don't mention it to Ryan, but I had my lawyers contact the school right before the meeting just as a precaution."

Sandra gasped. "You threatened to sue the school?"

"No, I just wanted to shake Williams up a bit, to let her know we were not going to allow Ryan to be targeted simply because of who his father is. Turns out it didn't matter. The principal was already leaning toward resolving the issue in a way that was amenable to everybody."

Sandra did not appreciate his interference, his privileged white male strong-arming, but she wondered if Principal Williams would have been so agreeable if she had been the one advocating on behalf of her son. Still, she could not argue with the outcome. At least it was a fair and just result and Ryan would be marching down the aisle with the rest of the senior class. So she decided to let it go. For now. "I'd better get dinner started. I assume you don't have a fundraiser tonight?"

"I'm all yours," Stephen said, winking again.

"I'd better get online and order my cap and gown before they run out of my size. I thought I'd be here at home watching someone's live Instagram." Ryan started to head out of the den with Vanessa trailing him when Stephen intercepted him.

"Wait, there's one more thing before you go." Stephen produced from his pants pocket a small blue box with a gold ribbon wrapped around it, the SoPo High school colors. "I got you a little something for graduation."

Ryan's face lit up. "What is it?"

"A fifty-dollar Starbucks gift card. You're going to need a lot of caffeine, pulling those all-nighters to keep your grades up in college." He directed another wink toward Sandra as if she was in on this, but she was as clueless as everyone else. He had not consulted her about any gift.

Ryan tore off the ribbon, not believing his father for a second. Stephen Wallage would never give his son a gift card for graduation. It had to be something much better. As he ripped open the box top and peeked inside, his mouth dropped open in shock.

Sandra braced herself.

What had Stephen gone and done now?

Ryan, rendered speechless, slowly lifted a set of keys from the gift box. He held them up, dangling them in front of him for all to see. "Are these . . . ?"

Stephen, eyes twinkling and sporting a wide grin, gestured with his head toward the front door. "You might want to check outside."

Ryan and Vanessa, without hesitation, bolted out of the den, leaving behind a delighted Stephen, whose grin faded slightly at the sight of Sandra glowering. "Oh, come on, the kid deserves it. He's worked hard."

"Just tell me it's nothing too expensive."

"Okay."

"Okay what?"

"I won't tell you it's expensive."

Sandra let out a heavy sigh and marched past him as she heard whoops and hollers coming from outside. When she got to the front door, she saw Ryan behind the wheel of a brand-new, sleek, red pearl coat Dodge Charger as Vanessa gleefully jumped up and down on the edge of the sidewalk. Ryan, euphoric, was already revving the engine.

Stephen, sensing Sandra's discomfort over the expensive gift, rested a palm on her shoulder. "Look on the bright side. Now you won't have to ferry him back and forth to and from college. He can drive himself."

"Your other son is not going to be happy about this. You bought Jack a used 2018 Nissan Altima."

"Well, if he can get his grades up, maybe we can trade it in for something flashier," Stephen said with a chuckle.

Sandra decided not to press the issue any further. Now that they were divorced, she no longer had a say in any decision he made. If Stephen wanted to spoil his two sons, that was his prerogative. In a few weeks, Ryan would be turning eighteen and finally a legal adult. He could do as he pleased.

But it still rankled her.

She could feel her heartbeat knock against her rib cage.

Why did she feel like she always had to play the bad cop while Stephen, the fun one, could swoop in on a moment's notice and make everything a party?

It just did not seem fair.

# Chapter 39

"Wait, Ryan! Stop the car!" Sandra cried from the back seat of the Dodge Charger.

Ryan, who was behind the wheel, slammed his foot down on the brake, screeching the car to a sudden halt as they all fell forward, luckily fastened in by their seat belts. The Charger idled as Ryan twisted his head around to see why his mother felt the urgent need to stop.

"Not in the middle of the street! I meant pull over to the curb," Sandra commanded. Stephen snickered from the passenger seat as Vanessa clutched the sleeve of Sandra's shirt, holding on for dear life after the unexpected jolt.

Sandra had tried to politely bow out when Stephen had suggested they all pile into Ryan's new car for a joyride, but her ex had insisted she tag along in the back seat. She was going to argue some more, but then she remembered Ryan had inherited his need for speed from his father, so it would probably behoove her to join them to ensure he followed all of the traffic laws and did not wind up with a speeding ticket during his first ride in his new car.

Ryan had started out cautiously enough, but it was obvious he was dying to get out on the open road and test the sports car's horsepower, so Sandra strongly urged he stick to the residential neighborhoods. They found themselves in the West End of Portland, swerving down a street, which Sandra immediately recognized as the one she had just been the day before, the same street where Ewan and Beverly Murphy's house was located.

Sandra had decided not to call any attention to it, noticing that the yellow police tape had been removed after the forensics team concluded their preliminary work. Beverly did not appear to be home because her car was not parked in the driveway. As Ryan zipped past the house, Sandra shifted and took note of the house directly across the street. That was when she yelled at Ryan to stop.

And now they were parked in the middle of the street, holding up a mail truck that was idling behind them while Ryan spun around to see what had triggered his mother's reaction.

Stephen tapped the steering wheel. "Son, maybe you ought to pull over."

Ryan pivoted and flipped on his blinker as he carefully pulled the car over to the curb, as if he was in the middle of a driving test. Then he jammed the car in the Park position and swiveled back around. "Mom, what's gotten you so hysterical?"

"Don't call her that," Vanessa warned. "It's out-dated and misogynistic, calling a woman hysteri-cal."

"Okay, sorry," Ryan sighed heavily.

Stephen snickered again.

Not wanting to tick off his girlfriend, Ryan tried rephrasing, "Mom, why were you so . . . deter-mined that I stop the car?"

"That!" Sandra pointed out the back seat win-dow.

They all looked up to see a security camera set up above the garage door of the neighbor's house across the street from the Murphy home.

"The camera is aimed directly at the Murphys' yard, with a clear view of the house's rooftop. If it was on and working yesterday, it would have picked up anyone who might have shown up, maybe even the exact moment when Ewan fell off the roof."

"I can see a woman in the kitchen window," Stephen said. "Why don't we ask her if we can take a peek at the footage?"

Ryan excitedly pressed the engine Stop button and released his seat belt, about to spring out of the car, but Sandra reached forward and held him back. "I want you all to stay here. I will go talk to her."

"You sure you don't want me to come along?" Stephen asked with puppy dog eyes.

"Yes. I can handle this. It's what I do."

"The crack private eye," he replied with a twin-kle in his eye. "I'm so proud of you."

She suspected there was a note of condescen-

sion in his tone, but she chose to ignore it. Sandra
hurried up to the front porch of the Victorian-
style home, like so many others lining the street,
and rang the bell, hoping she might get lucky the
same way Maya had with the security camera across
the street from Ellie Duncan's house when they
identified Ewan Murphy leaving early in the morning.

A few moments later, a harried-looking woman
in her late sixties, drinking a fruit smoothie and
wearing a leotard and yoga pants, opened the
door. "Whatever you're selling, I'm not interested!" Her voice was raspy, her tone tinged with
utter annoyance.

"I'm not here to try to sell you anything. I just
want to talk to you," Sandra said sweetly.

"I don't have time. My restorative yoga class
starts in twenty minutes and sometimes there's terrible traffic this time of day." She reached behind
the door and grabbed her baby-blue yoga mat.

"Please, this will only take a moment—"

The woman's gaze drifted to the Dodge Charger
parked in front of her house. She could see
Stephen sitting in the passenger seat. "Wait, no! Is
that . . . ?"

Confused, Sandra wheeled around to see what
had suddenly diverted her attention. "Who?"

"Omigod, that *is* him. That's Senator Stephen
Wallage. What is he doing hanging out in front of
my house. This is so surreal!"

"He's my husband. I mean, my ex-husband,"
Sandra said, correcting herself.

There was a hint of vague recollection in the

woman's expression. She did not seem to care about Sandra's presence. She quickly started waving at Stephen, who politely waved back. "I voted for you!"

He mouthed, *Thank you.*

"He is so much more handsome in person than when I see him on the news. I mean, don't get me wrong, he's a gorgeous man, there's no two ways about it, but the television does *not* do him justice."

Sandra knew the only way she was going to get what she wanted was by dragging Stephen into her plan, so she gestured for him to come join them. Stephen instantly hopped out of the car and sauntered up the front lawn to the porch.

Sandra heard the woman emit an audible gasp.

"Stephen Wallage, how do you do?" he said, giving her a flirtatious wink and taking her hand.

She stared at him longingly, finally breaking away to address Sandra and gushing, "Those blue eyes. When they look at you, they make you feel like you're the only person in the whole wide world."

Stephen was still gripping her hand. "What's your name?"

It took her a moment to conjure it up, but then, with an embarrassed giggle, she blurted out, "Kathleen. Kathleen Conners."

Stephen noticed the yoga mat under her arm. "We don't want to keep you from your class."

She practically hurled the mat to the floor. "No, it's okay. I go four times a week. It's no big whoop if I miss one. I had a stroke last year and the doctor said yoga would be good for my balance issues, flexibility, muscle weakness, and depression."

"Your doctor's right. It helps with all sorts of physical and emotional challenges," Stephen agreed.

Sandra waited patiently.

This was Stephen's superpower.

Charming his constituents.

She just needed to allow him to do his thing and before long he would steer the topic of conversation toward the security camera.

"You've done so much for Maine," Kathleen cooed. "We're very grateful. I used to be a teacher, so I personally appreciate the increase in public education funding, not to mention the crime rate has come way down since the time you've been in office. . . ."

"That's not because of me, that's because of people like you being proactive, like having that security camera trained on the neighborhood."

Bingo.

"Yes! It takes a village!" Kathleen concurred, her eyes dancing as she drank in the handsome features of one of her US senators.

"That could come in quite handy to law enforcement after what happened across the street yesterday," Sandra interjected.

Kathleen could not tear her gaze away from Stephen, speaking to him as if Sandra was not even there. "That poor man. He was so much nicer than his wife, who has zero personality, if you ask me. Plus, she keeps a bird feeder in her backyard and all the dirty pigeons constantly show up and chow down like it's an all-you-can-eat buffet, and then they come flying over here and poop all over my roof. I told Beverly what was happening, but do you think she cared? No, of course not!"

Sandra subtly signaled Stephen to get his fawning admirer back on track.

"Say, Kathleen, would you mind if Sandra and I took a quick peek at your security cam footage from yesterday? You would be doing me a huge personal favor." He touched her arm and she swooned, her heart aflutter.

Sandra had to suppress an audible groan.

"I would like nothing more than to help you. But I can't."

Stephen tried his best to look wounded. "Why not?"

"Nothing's on it," Kathleen explained.

"Is it broken?" Stephen asked.

Kathleen shook her head. "No, it's working fine. But the police showed up at my door yesterday, asking me the same thing, and when I downloaded the footage to my computer, there was nothing on it; the screen was just black. We thought it might have somehow malfunctioned, but one of the officers got a stepladder from my garage and climbed up to inspect it and discovered someone had spray-painted the camera lens with black paint. Can you believe that? You can't trust anyone these days!"

Whoever shoved Ewan Murphy off his roof to his death must have spotted the security camera and vandalized it so it would not pick up the action on top of the roof across the street. Luck was not on their side this time.

"I'm sorry I couldn't be more help," Kathleen pouted.

Stephen gave her yet another wink. "No, you've been great, Kathleen. The next time you find yourself down in DC, give my office a call and I will give you a personal tour of the Capitol."

Kathleen appeared as if she was going to faint, or at least pretend to, so Stephen would have to catch her in his big, strong arms.

Sandra was already texting Maya with this latest information.

If the killer was clever enough to take out an electronic eyewitness before committing murder, most likely Ewan's death was not a crime of passion but premeditated. Someone had taken calculated steps to cover their tracks before that fatal shove off the roof.

But the burning question still remained.

Who and why?

# Chapter 40

"**I** thought we were all going to have dinner together tonight," Stephen whined, disappointed.

"I told you, I have plans. Why don't you take Ryan and Vanessa out to dinner?" Sandra said crisply as she stood in front of the mirror in her bathroom, snapping a Lizzie Fortunato twenty-four-karat, gold-plated wine hooped earring in her left lobe.

Stephen was loitering outside the bedroom. Sandra could tell he was slightly agitated. He gave her the once-over.

"Little dressy for a PTA meeting, don't you think?"

"Stephen, I told you, I haven't been president of the PTA for about three years now."

This was typical.

Stephen was so consumed with his own career,

he did not have time to follow Sandra's own responsibilities, even when they were still married.

Stephen was not about to give up and took another guess. "Are you and Maya going out on the town?"

He was not about to let this go.

So why not just be up front about it?

"I have a date," she said flatly, pursing her lips and applying some lipstick liner before folding.

Sandra could see Stephen's body stiffen. She knew he had suspected she was meeting her new boyfriend, but hearing it out loud made him cringe slightly. He quickly covered with a breezy tone. "Oh, right, the coach? What's his name, Lucky?"

"Lucas," Sandra shot back.

"That's right. Lucas. Is he picking you up here or are you meeting him someplace?"

"I don't see how that is any of your business," Sandra snapped.

Stephen chuckled to himself. "Is he old enough to have a driver's license?"

She had heard enough.

Sandra marched over to the bathroom door and said evenly, "I need to finish getting ready." And then she slammed the door in his face. She planted the palms of her hands on the basin and took a deep breath. She was not going to allow him to get to her. He was obviously jealous and feeling a little threatened, but that was his problem, not hers. Still, she wanted to remain civil and not start a fight, especially because Stephen would be with them until after Ryan's graduation before he headed back to DC. She just needed to get through the next couple of days.

One thing was for certain.

She was not going to put Lucas through the third degree from her often intimidating ex-husband when he showed up at the door, although she was sure Lucas could handle it. This was more for her not having to endure such an excruciating face-off. So she shot off a text telling Lucas that she would meet him at the high school instead, where he would be wrapping up baseball practice. She did not offer an explanation, but Lucas did not seem to care because he responded within seconds with a thumbs-up emoji followed by a kiss emoji.

After spraying some Chanel Coco Mademoiselle behind each ear, she took one last look in the mirror, walked back into the bedroom, grabbing her Yves Saint Laurent calfskin leather envelope clutch from the night table, and headed down the stairs. She could hear voices emanating from the kitchen as she retrieved her car keys from a glass bowl in the foyer.

"So you really like him?" Stephen inquired.

"Yeah, he's pretty cool. And he adores Mom," Ryan said.

There was a long pause.

"I'm happy for her, really I am. I just think he's a bit young for her. I mean, the guy is, what? In his early twenties? He's still a baby," Stephen said.

Sandra felt her cheeks flush with anger.

Fortunately, Vanessa was in the kitchen with them and was having none of that. "Why is it that if a man dates a younger woman, he gets high fives and back slaps, but when a woman is with a younger man, there is immediate cause for concern? It is such a double standard and *so* misogynistic!"

Sandra smiled to herself.

Maya had taught her daughter well.

Vanessa had knocked him back on his heels. She could picture Stephen, who prided himself on being a fierce feminist, which was a cornerstone of all his political campaigns, a champion of women's rights, throwing up his hands in surrender. "You're right, Vanessa. You make a good point. I'm sorry. I'm usually better than that."

Sandra knew Vanessa had her back, so she quietly slipped out the front door to meet Lucas.

When she arrived at SoPo High twenty minutes later, it was after six o'clock in the evening and the halls were deserted. She stopped by Lucas's office, adjacent to the gym, but he was not there. She assumed he was taking a shower in the boys' locker room before their dinner. Instead of waiting, she sent him another text requesting he meet her outside the administration offices where she could pop by and say hello to Principal Williams and also dig around a bit to see if she had heard any new information on either Ellie Duncan or Ewan Murphy. But upon her arrival at the office, she discovered the door locked and the lights off.

"You just missed her," a man's voice bellowed from down the hall.

Sandra whirled around to see Don Talbot, his phone clamped to his ear, leaning up against a row of lockers. His tie was loosened and his sleeves rolled up as he spoke to what sounded like his secretary on the phone.

"Email me the prospectus so I can go over it tonight before the meeting tomorrow morning. Oh, and cancel my lunch with the Harper Group tomorrow. I want to take Cooper out for a celebratory lunch. Okay, Sarah, have a good night." He ended the call and pocketed his phone before he strode purposefully toward Sandra. "Caroline and I had a meeting. She just left for the day, maybe five minutes ago. I was just calling my office before heading out myself."

His face was lit up with a broad grin.

"Good news?"

Don gave her a vigorous nod. "Caroline has decided that Cooper is going to receive a passing grade in geography class, which means he will graduate after all."

"Congratulations."

"It took some tough negotiations. We went back and forth on it, and things got pretty heated. Let's be honest. Cooper's situation was hardly the same as your son's. Ryan at least was squeaking by on his test scores and actually handing in his class assignments. Cooper, on the other hand, was goofing off most of the school year and was routinely blowing off his homework. Sometimes the kid didn't even bother showing up for class. But after a very stern lecture from both me and Caroline, he has agreed to do some extra credit work to bring him over the finish line."

"I'm sure you're quite relieved," Sandra observed.

"That is an understatement. My boy has so much potential and I hated seeing him fritter it all away.

Now, he has a second chance to create a successful future for himself and make me proud."

With his father's help paving the way, of course.

She had no doubt that Don was already making some substantial financial donations to a few select colleges to up the pressure on them to accept Cooper for the fall semester. But Sandra was not about to call him on it. She knew both of her own sons had distinct advantages because of their own father.

Still, she could not help but feel sorry for Cooper. Given his father's exceedingly high expectations, he must be feeling the weight of the world on his shoulders. Any eighteen-year-old would naturally be overwhelmed by the demands placed on him.

"I'm clearing my schedule on Sunday. I want to throw a barbecue at our weekend home in Kennebunkport to celebrate Cooper finally getting past all of this Ellie Duncan drama."

"And to celebrate Phoebe advancing to the state spelling bee?"

Don waved his hand dismissively. "Well, she hasn't won yet. It's still a long way to the nationals."

"She won the local and regional competitions. That's quite an accomplishment in itself," Sandra reminded him.

Cooper was not the only Talbot kid to be feeling the heat from their perfectionist father, with his exacting standards and rigid expectations.

Don could sense her consternation with him.

"But of course I'm proud of her," he mumbled half-heartedly before lightening his tone. "Will you come? Bring your husband."

"We're no longer together."

"Well, if he's in town, have him tag along anyway. I'm going to invite a few of my clients, and they'll be very impressed I snagged a US senator to attend my barbecue."

Don Talbot was nothing if not transparent.

But underneath his bubbly surface, Sandra could detect an enormous sense of relief, as if he had avoided a catastrophe.

Was it just because Cooper skirted the prospect of flunking out of high school his senior year? Or was there more at play? Were the stakes much higher than that?

Sandra knew in her gut that when it came to Don Talbot, there were still more questions than answers. Especially given the fact he no longer had an alibi for Ellie Duncan's murder. Still, she was not ready to confront him just yet. She needed to know more.

# Chapter 41

Nestled high atop a scenic knoll in Cape Arundel Woods in Kennebunkport, Don Talbot's five-bedroom, four-and-a-half-bath Maine shingle-style cottage, with its multiple expansive porches, decks, and patios, not to mention a heated three-car garage, did not strike any of his guests as a simple weekend getaway cabin as he had made it out to be. Don loved surprising people, and everyone was admittedly taken aback by this grand seaside home surrounded by meticulously maintained grounds of manicured woodlands.

Thirty invited guests milled about the property as Don, wearing a black apron that said, "Kiss the Cook But Don't Touch the Buns," stood at the massive, fifty-four-inch freestanding gas grill complete with a rotisserie and smoker box, flipping burgers and steaks and chicken breasts as one of his assistants snapped photos with his phone for the company's various social media accounts. Once the photo op was finished, Don quickly stepped away from the grill to allow one of the half-dozen hired help to take over and do the actual cooking.

Don grabbed a cocktail from the bar and mingled with his guests; mostly clients, but also a select few connected to his two children, Cooper and Phoebe, which explained Maya and Sandra's presence, along with their families. When Stephen had shown up, Don made a big display of welcoming him, figuring it would not hurt to have a powerful politician in his corner. Stephen had come with Ryan and Vanessa, while Sandra opted to arrive with her date, Lucas. Max had also been invited, but it took some doing to convince him to attend. Since his release from prison the year before, Max had been reticent to socialize, believing the community had yet to forgive him for his past transgressions.

"People have long memories," he warned Maya.

But Maya had more faith in people. He had paid for his crimes and deserved a fresh start. It took some strong-arming, but she had finally convinced him to tag along. Still, now that he was here, Max hung back, hovering behind her, not engaging anyone in conversation, expecting some kind of negative reaction from someone at some point. Sandra noticed a few guests eyeing him warily, not inclined to go over and say hello. But in her mind, that was their problem, not Max's.

Lucas approached Sandra and handed her an iced tea as he nursed a screwdriver. "I just ran into your husband at the bar. He told the bartender to check my ID to see if I was old enough to drink."

Sandra sighed. "Ignore him. He's just not used to seeing me dating. Especially someone younger and hotter than him."

Lucas perked up. "Really? You think I'm hotter than your ex?"

The corner of Sandra's lips curled up into a seductive smile. "Trust me. I know Stephen. Your six-pack abs are making him feel incredibly insecure right about now. Your age is the only weapon he's got."

She spied Stephen surreptitiously glancing over at them, trying to act casual but failing miserably. Sandra took the opportunity to buss Lucas on the cheek. He turned toward her, responding with a gentle kiss on her lips.

Sandra resisted the urge to steal a glimpse back at Stephen, but she guessed he was melting on the spot, like Margaret Hamilton at the end of *The Wizard of Oz*. If Stephen thought belittling Lucas about his age would sour Sandra on the handsome coach, he was dead wrong. In fact, it was having quite the opposite effect. Stephen's boorish and jealous behavior was only drawing her closer to him.

"You want something to eat? I was going to go get a burger," Lucas offered.

"No, stay here and keep Maya and Max company. I'll go get one for you. Medium rare, onion, lettuce, tomato, mustard, no ketchup."

Lucas turned to Maya and Max, beaming. "Wow. She's the first girlfriend to ever remember how I like my burger. She *sees* me!"

Maya and Max chuckled as Sandra made her way over to the giant grill to request two hamburgers. Don was kneeling down in front of Phoebe, who was frowning.

"Honey, you have no reason to be nervous. I know you're going to be great. Just keep practicing and don't lose focus. You can beat Annabelle, no sweat." His eyes flicked over to Annabelle, who was stuffing her face with ruffled potato chips as her two fathers chatted up Stephen. "I just don't understand why you wanted to invite her and her two dads. I find it's always best to keep your competition at a distance."

"She's my friend," Phoebe said softly.

"And that's fine. But have you ever thought that maybe by being your friend, she's trying to distract you, chip away at your confidence, throw you off your game?"

Phoebe stared at her father, dumbfounded. "She's really nice, Dad. She hasn't done any of that."

Don, the ruthless businessman, was finding it difficult to believe that there was no ulterior motive to this friendship. He was trained to be suspicious of the competition at all times. He planted his hands on Phoebe's arms and squeezed. "You girls can bond all you want . . . *after* the state spelling bee, okay?"

Phoebe stared at the ground, disappointed. "Yes, Daddy."

He gave her a hug. "That's my girl. Don't worry. You got this!" He then stood back up and made a beeline for one of his more important clients.

Sandra noticed a disappointed Phoebe staring longingly over at Annabelle, wanting to go say hello, but when Annabelle made eye contact with her, Phoebe got nervous and instantly looked away, pretending she hadn't seen her.

After the large, bald, barrel-chested cook manning the grill served Sandra her two burgers, she made her way back to Lucas, Maya, and Max, who had now been joined by Cooper and Chloe and Ryan and Vanessa, all chowing down on hot dogs and grilled chicken sandwiches.

Chloe had a dab of relish on her cheek, which Cooper lovingly wiped away with his finger before licking off the remnants with his tongue.

"Thank you, Coop," Chloe said with a forlorn smile. Deciding she had had enough, she tossed her half-eaten plate in a nearby trash can.

Sandra instantly picked up on Chloe's somber mood. "Everything all right, Chloe?"

"Yes, everything's fine. I just wish my dad would have come with us today. Cooper invited him, but he hasn't left the house since he got out of jail. He's been so withdrawn. I know something is wrong and I want to help, but I don't know how."

Sandra was stumped for an answer.

Burt Denning was obviously hiding something.

She had no doubt about that.

But he had stubbornly clammed up and was not talking, and as long as he remained silent, they were not going to get anywhere with finding out his secret.

"I asked him if he would at least come see me graduate, but he wouldn't even commit to that. He said he'll see how he feels when the day comes. I want him there so bad, but deep down, I know he's probably just going to bag it and stay home."

Cooper put a comforting arm around Chloe. "Do you want me or my dad to try to talk to him?"

Chloe shook her head. "I honestly don't think it will do any good. He can be pretty pigheaded. I know he's sick and doesn't have a lot of time left, but I was really hoping he would be there when I receive my diploma."

Sandra felt sorry for Chloe.

She was a good girl who did not deserve any of this. To have to deal with not only her father's failing health but also his bonkers, out-of-left-field murder confession was almost too much to bear. Vanessa had confided to Maya that Chloe tried getting her father to open up, to explain why he had confessed to a crime he did not commit, but Burt had refused to explain anything, just telling her she needed to put all that behind her and focus on her future at college and beyond.

Sandra noticed Max, chomping on a hot dog, staring off into space, lost in thought. She suspected what he was thinking and so did Maya, who pulled him aside and said sternly, "Stop it."

Max looked at her, confused. "What?"

"Stop spiraling. I know what you're thinking. Burt Denning doesn't want to go to Chloe's graduation out of fear of what people might say and you're going down that same road."

Max lowered his gaze, his face twisted in a scowl. "I'm a pariah in this town, Maya. Why risk embarrassing Vanessa on her big day? The last thing I want is to be a distraction."

"Vanessa wants you there just as much as Chloe wants her father there. Nothing else matters. So you're going. End of discussion."

Sandra could see Maya's absolute determination to keep her family moving forward, to put the unpleasant past that had dogged them for years firmly behind them. And she admired her for it. And for his part, Max knew that when Maya put her foot down, that was it. He was going to be in the audience for his daughter's graduation, his head held high, no matter how many haters did not want to see him there.

Maya prioritized her family above all else.

And that's why Sandra admired her so much.

# Chapter 42

"Where's Phoebe?" Don bellowed above the din of the crowd as he gathered with his son, Cooper, and a young and talented professional photographer holding an expensive-looking camera who Don had hired for the day. They were setting up a photo with a gorgeous view of the woodlands behind them. Everyone within earshot glanced around, trying to locate the girl, but she was nowhere to be found. Don stepped away and approached Sandra. "Have you seen Phoebe? I want a picture with the three of us that I can give to Nan Mulroney, who I've commissioned to paint a family portrait. I want to commemorate this moment with Cooper starting his adult life and Phoebe winning the National Spelling Bee. Their mother would be so proud."

"That's sweet, Don," Sandra remarked. She wanted to remind him that he had just said himself that Phoebe was a long way from winning nationals, but he obviously did not want to hear his words thrown back at him. "I haven't seen her. Hang on, I'll go see if I can find her."

"Thanks, Sandy," Don said.

Sandy.

That one almost stopped her in her tracks.

No one had called her Sandy since high school, and mostly because she used to bear a striking resemblance to the Sandy character Olivia Newton-John played in the classic movie *Grease*, especially with her blond hair in a ponytail and when she was wearing her cheerleading uniform.

Don clapped Cooper on the back. The kid was preoccupied, chomping down on another hot dog as Sandra walked away, her eyes scanning the property for any sign of Phoebe. She happened upon Ryan and Vanessa canoodling under a tree around the side of the house, stealing kisses and whispering in each other's ears. When Ryan caught sight of his mother approaching, he quickly took a step away, putting a little space between him and Vanessa. Sandra laughed to herself. It was not as if she did not have a clear picture of what those two were always up to when she was not around.

"Have either of you seen Phoebe?"

Ryan shook his head. "Nope."

"Wait," Vanessa said. "I think I saw her head into the house a little while ago."

"Okay, thanks. Carry on," she said as she kept walking before stopping and pivoting back toward them. "But not too much, do you hear me?"

Ryan sighed loudly as Vanessa giggled.

Sandra entered a door that led into the kitchen, where some of the staff were loading the dishwasher and cleaning up. There were still about twenty people left at the party who were outside in the backyard, eating and drinking. "Excuse me, did Phoebe come by here?"

"No, we haven't seen her," one of the staff answered with an apologetic look. Sandra continued out to the dining area and large living room before heading up the Colonial staircase to the second floor. She could hear a Taylor Swift song wafting from one of the bedrooms at the far end of the hall. She followed the sound of the music to a white door that was open just a crack.

Sanda knocked softly.

A girl's tiny voice answered. "Come in."

Sandra entered the bedroom and was overcome by pink. Pink walls. Pink décor. Pink bedspread. Even a pink princess phone on a white night table. Phoebe sat on the floor, playing with a Barbie doll wearing a pink feather boa. Next to her was, unsurprisingly, a Barbie Dreamhouse in pink, as well as a pile of assorted fashion accessories. Phoebe cast a quick look up at Sandra.

"Hi there," Sandra said brightly.

"Hi," Phoebe mumbled, eyes back on her Barbie, which she was still dressing.

"Did you get a little bored at the party?"

Phoebe gave a shrug but did not answer.

"Your dad is looking for you. He wants to take a family photo."

"Okay," she said sullenly.

Sandra knelt down to her level. "Is anything wrong, Phoebe?"

Another shrug.

"Trust me, I know what it's like having to be on

all the time at parties. I was married to a politician. It was my job to smile every minute and pretend I was having a good time."

Phoebe put the now fully dressed Barbie down on the floor. "Do I have to go back out there?"

"I think it would mean a lot to your father. He's hired a local artist to paint a family portrait. He's just so proud of you and Cooper."

"Why do I have to be in it? Cooper's the golden child who can do no wrong. He won't even miss me if I stay up here."

"That's not true, Phoebe. He loves you both very much and he has a great deal of pride in you. Do you know how hard it is to get to where you are in the spelling bee? You beat some serious competition."

"But now he expects me to go all the way and win nationals. He keeps saying I'm going to win and it just makes me more nervous. What if I get knocked out at state? He's going to be so disappointed."

"No, he won't," Sandra said.

But her words rang hollow.

Don Talbot expected only the best from his two children.

It was an incredible amount of pressure to put on such a young girl.

Phoebe gave Sandra a deeply skeptical look. "You don't know him like I do."

There was no arguing with that.

Sandra gently rubbed Phoebe's back with her hand. "You just do your best and it will all work out."

Phoebe scrunched up her face, which was full of doubt.

Sandra could see she was not making much headway with her pep talk.

Sandra debated with herself about whether she should speak to Don, give him a heads-up about how he was putting his daughter through the ringer, but she feared she would just be butting into another family's private affairs. Don might not appreciate her interference.

"At least Annabelle gets me."

"I didn't know you and Annabelle were friends."

"We've gotten to know each other better since we've both been competing in the spelling bee. She's supernice and she understands what I'm dealing with because she's going through the same thing."

"Her dads are putting a lot of pressure on her too, I suppose?"

Phoebe nodded. "In some ways, they're worse than my dad. They think they have to be the perfect family because they're not like a traditional family with a mom and a dad."

"That sounds tough."

"We started hanging out more at school, practicing our flash cards during recess, texting each other at night. She even wrote me the sweetest card, wishing me luck at the state competition." She gestured toward a card propped up on the dresser. Sandra stood back up and wandered over, picking it up. On the cover was a pink doughnut with eyes and a smile. Above the image, *Donut Be Afraid.* On the bottom, *You Got This. Good Luck.* Sandra flipped open the card. Inside, Annabelle wrote, *Whatever happens we'll always be friends. Love, Annabelle.*

Sandra stared at the handwriting.

And then it struck her suddenly, and she had to suppress a gasp. She took a moment to collect herself and then turned to Phoebe, who had resumed playing with her Barbie doll.

"Phoebe, would you mind if I hung on to this for a little while? I promise to return it."

Phoebe gave her a puzzled look. "Um, okay."

She did not ask why, which was a relief to Sandra. How would she ever explain the reason she needed to keep the card was because Annabelle's handwriting was exactly the same as the handwriting in the threatening note that Rocco Fanelli found in his school locker?

# Chapter 43

Sandra rushed out of the house, clutching the card in her hand, and made a beeline over to Maya, who was now standing with Max and Lucas near the bar. "Maya, do you have a screenshot of the note left in Rocco's locker?"

Maya reached into the back pocket of her jeans and pulled out her phone, tapping in her security code and then scrolling through her photos. She stopped, enlarged the photo, and handed the phone to Sandra.

Sandra held up the card next to the phone's screen and compared the two sets of handwriting.

They appeared to be an exact match.

Maya furrowed her brow, curious. "What is it?"

"I know who left the note in Rocco Fanelli's locker. Have you seen the Chastain-Wheelers?"

"I saw them leaving maybe two minutes ago," Lucas piped up.

Sandra dashed off as Maya chased after her. The two women rounded the side of the house to the long gravel driveway in the front, which was lined with cars. Down the road, Sandra spotted Doug, Noah, and Annabelle walking to their parked Lexus. She ran to catch up with them before they drove off as Maya tried keeping up with her. Hearing the scrunching sound of Sandra's slip-on sneakers in the gravel as she approached, the family turned and was somewhat startled by the sight of Sandra running toward them.

"Sandra, what is it? Did we forget something?" Doug asked.

She landed next to them, resting a hand on Doug's arm to take a moment and catch her breath as Maya came up behind her. They could tell from Sandra's dour expression that whatever was on her mind was something serious.

Maya hung back, allowing Sandra to take the lead on this one.

"Why are you leaving so early?"

Doug and Noah exchanged a somber glance with each other. Doug finally spoke. "We weren't even going to come today. We're not exactly close with Don Talbot. But Annabelle begged us. She and Phoebe have gotten pretty close, and she wanted to spend the day with her, but when we got here, Phoebe kind of ghosted her the whole afternoon, so we decided to just go home."

Annabelle sadly stared at her shoes.

"I'm sorry that happened to you, Annabelle," Sandra said.

Annabelle did not respond.

Noah instinctively knew something was amiss from the gravity etched on their faces. "What's going on? What's wrong?"

"We need to speak to you," Sandra said before flicking her eyes toward Annabelle. "Privately."

Doug picked up on the cue and put a hand on top of Annabelle's head. "Sweetheart, why don't you get in the car and watch a show on your phone? We'll leave once we've had a chance to chat with Mrs. Wallage and Mrs. Kendrick."

"Okay." Annabelle shrugged as Doug opened the door to the back seat. Annabelle popped in some earbuds and started playing a video as she climbed in. Doug slammed the door shut behind her and then whirled back around to face Maya and Sandra. "Would you explain what's happening now, because you're making us both very nervous?"

Sandra handed the card to Doug. "Annabelle gave this card to Phoebe, wishing her luck at the state spelling bee."

The two fathers opened the card and skimmed the note. "Well, that was very sweet of her. We raised her to be kind and thoughtful. Clearly, Don Talbot didn't raise his own kids to have the same admirable qualities," Noah snipped.

Sandra handed Doug Maya's phone. "This is a screenshot of the threatening note someone left in Rocco Fanelli's locker to get him to drop out of the spelling bee."

They both read it. Doug appeared oblivious, but Noah's mouth dropped open in shock.

"What?" Doug scoffed. "I don't understand the point of you showing us this."

"The handwriting," Noah mumbled. "It's exactly the same."

Doug's eyes widened in fury. "No, it's not!"

"Come on, Doug, look closer. It's obvious who wrote that note," Maya said.

Doug hurled the phone back at Maya. "How dare you accuse Annabelle? She would never do something like that! We raised her better than that."

"Maybe someone who might have been desperate for her to win somehow encouraged her, sent the wrong message . . ." Maya let the words trail off.

Doug's nostrils flared. "Are you accusing *us* of forcing our daughter to make threats against a classmate? That's preposterous! What kind of monsters do you think we are?"

Maya raised her hands. "We're not saying that."

"Well, you damn sure just implied it!" Doug roared.

Noah suddenly noticed the back-seat window was open halfway. "Please, Doug, keep your voice down. Annabelle might hear you."

"She's got her earbuds in. She can't hear us. Now get in the car. We're going home right now," Doug seethed.

"I really think we should have a talk with Annabelle before you go," Sandra whispered softly.

"I will not allow you to traumatize my daughter with wild accusations," Doug yelled. "Come on, Noah, I said get in the car."

Noah rubbed his chin, worried. "Now, wait, I don't see the harm in just asking her—"

Doug was apoplectic that his husband was not

holding a united front. "No! And if you two keep up this harassment, we will sue you for everything you've got."

"It was me," a child's tiny voice said from inside the car.

It brought the heated exchange between the adults to a screeching halt. Doug reached for the handle and opened the door to the back seat.

Annabelle, her eyes welling up with tears, sat there with the earbuds in her hand. She had not been watching a video after all. She had been listening to the entire conversation.

"I did it. I wrote the note. I'm sorry," she murmured.

Doug was struck dumb, but Noah knelt down and took his daughter by the hand. "Honey, why would you do something like that?"

Tears streamed down her cheeks. "I was so scared he was going to beat me in the spelling bee and I didn't want to disappoint you."

Noah gave her a light kiss on the forehead. "Why were you scared?"

Annabelle shrugged.

She did not want to explain why.

But it was obvious.

She had reacted to the pressure her two fathers had placed upon her to be the perfect daughter, the perfect family. Just like Phoebe had said.

Doug was not ready to concede just yet. "But I heard it was Hunter Hamlin who left the note. How did he get his hands on it?"

"I left it in one of his textbooks and paid him to put it in Rocco's locker."

"With what?" Doug demanded to know.

"I saved up my allowance."

"Dear God, this is a nightmare," Doug wailed.

Annabelle burst into more tears. "I'm sorry!"

Noah wrapped the shaking girl in a warm hug and gently patted her on the back. "It's okay, sweetheart. It's not your fault. We put too much pressure on you. Daddy Doug and I are the ones to blame."

Doug, finally absorbing the situation, turned to Maya and Sandra. "What happens now?"

Through a flood of tears, Annabelle cried, "Am I gonna get expelled?"

"No, June bug, trust me, I will *not* allow that to happen," Doug promised.

Although how he could promise something like that was a mystery to Sandra. Once Principal Munn learned what had happened, anything, including immediate expulsion, could be on the table. But Sandra secretly hoped that Annabelle would be spared and not get kicked out of school, because in her mind, the poor girl was just a victim of extreme helicopter parenting and should not have to pay the price for the untenable pressure put upon her to win at all costs.

But that was not Sandra's decision to make.

Even though they had finally solved the case, their clients, the Fanellis, no longer cared. They had already fired Maya and Sandra and moved on with their lives. And a child's misguided plan to knock out her spelling bee competition was not getting them any closer to finding out who cold-bloodedly murdered Ellie Duncan and Ewan Murphy.

# Chapter 44

Maya jumped out of her car and darted across the street to intercept Meredith McKinley, who had just emerged from a Starbucks carrying a coffee. She was just about to hop in her BMW and drive away when Maya intercepted her. "Meredith, do you have a minute?"

Meredith glanced up, surprised. "Maya, where did you come from?"

"I was just at your house. Ben, your lovely husband, told me that you usually stop here for coffee on your way to the office."

Meredith laughed uneasily. "Are you stalking me?"

"I tried calling and texting you."

She looked at her phone. "So you did. I was working out with my trainer earlier. He forbids me to leave my phone on." Meredith clutched her paper cup, a little apprehensive. "Is something wrong?"

"No, not really, I just have a couple of questions I'd like to ask you."

Meredith checked her watch. "Well, I have a meeting at the office in twenty minutes with some clients in Stockholm. I really can't be late."

"This won't take long, I promise. I want to know about the Fordham Group."

"Wow," Meredith exclaimed with a rueful smile. "I haven't heard that name mentioned in a long time."

"Can you tell me more about it?"

Meredith took a sip of her coffee and leaned against the side of her BMW. "Um, sure. The Fordham Group was a major life lesson in finding out just how inexperienced I was right out of college. A couple of business school friends and I decided we didn't want to go to work for a big, faceless corporation; we wanted to start our own investment firm, so we started an S Corp called the Fordham Group, which we named after our undergrad alma mater."

"How long were you associated with the Fordham Group?"

Meredith chuckled. "Six, maybe seven months. We were young and cocky and really had no idea what we were doing. We got our parents and some of their friends to invest with us and then we blew the money on a series of bad calls and went bust in less than a year. I left New York with my tail between my legs. That's when I moved back to Maine and got a dispatch job at the police department, where I met you."

"Was the company dissolved?"

"I honestly don't know. I myself got out, and so did my roommate, Jen, who wound up moving down to DC to become a congressional aide." She paused, remembering. "But Jonny, our third partner at the time, wanted to hold on to it, thinking maybe one day, when we all had more experience, we could somehow revive it. But that was a pipe dream, and I don't think he ever did. Besides, Jonny now works for a big-time accounting firm in New York. I'm sure he doesn't have the time."

"What's Jonny's last name?"

"Stanton. Jonny Stanton. Why? What's this all about?"

"My daughter, Vanessa, has a friend, Chloe Cooper, who was just awarded a full, four-year scholarship to college."

"Lucky her."

"Yes, very lucky because, to be honest, her grades were not all that impressive. Something felt off about the whole thing, so I did a little digging and discovered that the organization that's giving her the money is the Fordham Group."

Meredith dropped her cup to the ground and some coffee splashed out and landed on her shoe. "What? That's impossible."

"So you know nothing about this?"

"No! Of course not!"

"Because you are listed on the website as one of the co-founders and trustees."

"This has to be some kind of joke."

"The scholarship is worth over a quarter of a million dollars in total," Maya informed her.

Meredith stared at her, slack-jawed, eyes wide

with astonishment. "I don't understand. It's a dormant company. Where on earth could the money be coming from?"

"That's what I wanted to know, so I called Oscar Dunford. Remember him from your days as police dispatcher?"

Meredith nodded with a fond smile. "Oh, yes. The sometimes creepy, sometimes sweet IT guru. I remember he used to have a huge crush on you."

"He still does, which can come in handy on occasion, like today. I tried contacting the Fordham Group website to learn more about their criteria for the scholarship but never heard back, so I enlisted Oscar's help and he was able to trace the administrator of the website to a fake email account."

"Why would someone go to all that trouble to pay a random girl's college tuition?"

"That's what I wanted to know. Oscar was able to discover through a sophisticated algorithm process I don't even pretend to understand that the bogus email account was created using an IP address that belonged to Jonathan Stanton, separate from the one he uses at work."

"This makes no sense. Does Jonny even have a connection to this girl who received the scholarship?"

"No, none that we could find."

"Jonny's comfortable but hardly rich. There's no way he's some anonymous, wealthy benefactor showering kids in financial need with oodles of money."

"Exactly, which suggests he might have been paid by someone else to set this whole thing up."

"For what purpose?"

"I'm still trying to work that out. Maybe one of his clients at the accounting firm got him involved?"

"It's a very large firm. They must have hundreds of clients. I couldn't tell you who they are. Maybe you should ask Don."

Maya perked up. "Don?"

"My boss. Don Talbot."

"He's one of Jonny's clients?"

"Yes. I was the one who recommended Jonny to him. Don's been with him for about seven years now. They've become quite tight. I think they even go golfing together some weekends. Why? What does Don have to do with—"

"Thank you, Meredith," Maya cried as she hurried back across the street to her parked car to call Sandra.

The case had just blown wide open.

# Chapter 45

Don Talbot grimaced when he saw Maya and Sandra standing in front of his Tesla, which was parked in its assigned space in the structure adjacent to his office building in Downtown Portland. Maya's arms were folded across her chest in a confrontational manner and Sandra, as well, had an unexpectedly serious countenance. They could tell from his adverse reaction that he did not want to talk to them. He slowed his pace, pretending to check something on his phone but was probably just buying time before he had to deal with whatever they wanted to talk to him about, which, based on their body language, could not be good.

"Afternoon, ladies," Don said, eyes still glued to his phone, stopping a few inches from them. "How can I help you?"

He seemed completely disengaged.

Maya loudly cleared her throat, startling Don enough that he finally made eye contact.

"We wanted to ask you a few questions regarding Jonathan Stanton," Maya said.

"Jonathan? He's my accountant. One of about a dozen or so. Is he in some kind of trouble?"

"No, we're just interested in knowing more about his connection to the Fordham Group."

Don paused, his hand slowly rising to his heart, as if he was suddenly feeling a tightness in his chest. He averted his eyes like most people did when they are lying. "The Fordham Group?"

Sandra eyed him suspiciously. "You don't know it?"

"No, I'm afraid I don't," he insisted, his jaw now tightening. "Am I supposed to?"

"I would think so," Maya scoffed. "You used Jonny Stanton's phantom company, the Fordham Group, to funnel a large sum of money—a quarter of a million at least—that used the funds as college scholarship money."

Don opened his mouth to protest, but Maya cut him off. "Please don't insult us by denying your involvement. We have the receipts. Wire transfers, texts, emails, even a statement from Stanton himself. He told us everything."

Maya was fibbing. Although Oscar was working on gathering evidence, they had little they could take to the police just yet. And they had not even spoken to Stanton himself. But the bluff worked. She had scared Don enough to get him talking.

"So what?" The blood drained from Don's face, but he fought to maintain his cool. "Talk to any lawyer. It's not a crime to anonymously establish a college scholarship fund."

"We never suggested it was." Maya shrugged. "But why Chloe Denning? If you look at her academic record, she was barely an average student. Of all the deserving recipients at SoPo High, why *her*?"

Don took a moment before responding. He was acting extremely carefully now, afraid he might say the wrong thing.

Maya and Sandra, both of them scrutinizing him intensely, which made him even more nervous, waited patiently.

Finally, letting out a heavy sigh, Don admitted, "Yes, it was me. I was the one who put up the money for Chloe's college tuition. Go ahead. Arrest me. Arrest me for having a kind heart. The poor girl's father is dying. He's got four, maybe five months to live, and no means to help his daughter when he's gone. I just felt bad. She's a nice girl; she means a lot to Cooper. I just wanted her to have a fair shot in life."

Maya smirked. She was not buying any of this altruistic hogwash. And Don knew it. "So why not just be up front about it? Why all the subterfuge with the fake organization?"

"That was Burt's idea. When I came to him with my offer to pay for Chloe's education, Burt was afraid she wouldn't accept that it was coming from me. She would think that she owed me, or feel obligated to pay me back, like a student loan, and Burt really wanted her to finish college with a clean slate, have a fresh start with no debts, so we came up with the scholarship scheme together. Jonathan very kindly offered to use his moribund

S Corp, the Fordham Group, to keep my name out of it. I know, we probably should have been honest and up front about where the money was coming from, but it was very important to Burt to keep Chloe in the dark, to make her feel like she earned the money and was not just some charity case I took pity on. It made perfect sense to me, so I went along with it."

Maya and Sandra exchanged dubious glances.

His explanation did make sense. But Don's heroic story, portraying himself as the selfless knight in shining armor to the rescue, a kind and generous and benevolent benefactor, qualities he had never shown a trace of in the past, was almost laughable. And that made his heartwarming tale all the harder to swallow.

"Is that all? It's been a long day and I'd really like to go home and spend some time with my kids," Don growled, pushing past them and jumping in his Tesla.

The taillights illuminated and the car soundlessly began backing out of the parking space, forcing Maya and Sandra to step aside. They could not see Don at the wheel behind the dark, tinted windows, but they could only assume he was inside his car, shouting and cursing at them.

Don kept backing out as a Honda Civic sped through the garage toward them. Maya and Sandra waved their arms at the Tesla to stop, but Don was obviously discombobulated by their encounter and was not paying attention, and the Honda smashed into the back end of the Tesla with a loud crunch. The door to the Tesla flew open. There was loud beeping and flashing lights, lots of warning signals that failed to stop the collision, no doubt because Don was so rattled and upset.

A young woman of Korean descent in her early to mid-twenties, with a slight build, got out of the Honda. She was pale and shaken from the accident but lucid enough to know the accident was not her fault.

"How could you not see me coming?"

Don threw up his hands in the air. "You're right. I wasn't paying attention. This was my fault." He looked apprehensively over in Maya and Sandra's direction. "I will pay for all the damage to your car. Let's just exchange information and be on our way." He handed her a business card.

She studied it with suspicion. "How do I know this is real?"

Don sighed and then pointed to Maya and Sandra. "These ladies know who I am. They'll vouch for me."

Maya sauntered over to the young woman and glanced at the card. "Yeah, that's him. But make sure you take a photo of his driver's license, just in case."

Don glared at her. He did not appreciate how much Maya was enjoying this.

"We should probably call the police and report this," the young woman suggested.

"No!" Don shouted, panic rising in his voice. "There is no need to involve the police. Please don't drag them into this."

The rear door of the Tesla, crushed during impact, began to slowly open, revealing the back boot. Don, alarmed, raced over and slammed it shut.

"My insurance company requires a police report for any accident claim," the other driver said flatly.

Sandra was happy to pipe in, "That's true. My insurance company has the same rule; otherwise they reject the claim as incomplete."

Don threw her an annoyed look.

"But you don't have to even file a claim. I already said this was my fault. I will pay you whatever you want out of my own pocket. I won't even go through my own insurance company. I can write you a check for any amount right now. What's your name?"

"Anna Choi."

"Nice to meet you, Anna. I'm Don Talbot," he said, popping open his briefcase and frantically searching for his checkbook and a pen.

She appraised him with lingering doubt. "How do I know it won't bounce?"

Don began losing it. "Because I'm rich. I drive a Tesla, for God's sake! Trust me. It won't bounce. If it makes you feel better, I can Venmo you the money right now. Just give me your email address."

The rear door began rising again.

Don darted over and tried slamming it shut. He whipped his head around to see the young, dark-haired woman with deep-set eyes crowned with long eyelashes surveying the damage to her car. "I'd feel better leaving the scene of an accident with a police report."

She started tapping her phone.

"No!" Don bellowed, running toward her, as if he was going to wrestle the phone from her, determined to keep the cops away.

The warped rear door of the Tesla popped open again, but this time Don was not close enough to slam it shut, allowing Maya and Sandra to get a peek inside the boot.

There, in plain sight, was a can of black spray paint.

And suddenly they had all the evidence they required.

# Chapter 46

Maya and Sandra waited for Don to exchange all the pertinent information they needed to file claims with their individual insurance companies. Maya and Sandra assured Anna Choi that they would serve as witnesses and back up her version of events in the event of a lawsuit or trial. Knowing what they were now dealing with, they were most focused on getting Anna away from the scene, out of possible harm's way once they confronted Don.

Anna hemmed and hawed, making more noises about calling the police, but when Maya flashed her PI badge, promising her she had pull at the police department as a former cop, Anna finally relented, got back behind the wheel of her car, and drove off, secure in the knowledge that Maya and Sandra had her back.

When Sandra reached into the trunk and picked up the can of black spray paint, Don suddenly got fidgety and started to sweat, shakily loosening his tie and unbuttoning his shirt collar.

"Is this what you used to black out the security camera across the street from Ewan Murphy's house?" Sandra asked.

"You can't prove that!" Don scoffed.

"Two people. You killed two people in cold blood," Sandra spat out, disgusted.

"That's a damn lie!" he growled.

Maya noticed something sticking out of the side of Don's collar. It appeared to be some kind of bandage. She calmly reached out and tugged at his shirt collar, pulling it back just enough for her to confirm it was exactly what she had thought.

Don recoiled, taking a step back. "What are you doing? Stop touching me!"

"How did you hurt your left shoulder, Don? Did you somehow get injured when you recently came in contact with a hatchet maybe?" Maya said calmly, exchanging a knowing look with Sandra.

"I will bet if he takes off his shirt, we'll also see some scratches from Ellie Duncan's fingernails when she was desperately trying to defend herself," Sandra surmised.

"You two have no idea what you're talking about. This is outrageous! How dare you come here and try to—"

Maya raised a hand in front of his face. "Stop, Don. Just stop. You're not going to be able to use your money or privileged position to wiggle your way out of this one. We know what happened."

"Ellie Duncan was being extra-tough on your treasured son, just like she was with my Ryan. If she flunked him, his bright and successful future would be at risk," Sandra said, noticing Don's face twitch a little. "Of course your first plan of action was to charm her. Don Talbot, God's gift to women. How could she resist? But somehow she did, so then you threatened to get her fired if she didn't bump up Cooper's grade. When that didn't work, you tried bribing her, all to no avail. You were getting desperate. There was no way you were going to allow a sourpuss geography teacher to mess up your grand plans for your screwup, party animal son. So that's when you decided to take it to a whole new level."

"You prerecorded your work presentation to use as an alibi, only providing live audio that you could do from anywhere. You showed up at the middle school in disguise, knowing Ellie would be there, in charge of the spelling bee," Maya added, eyes fixed on an increasingly anxious Don. "You strangled her when she was alone and stuffed her body inside the supply closet, then slipped out as if you had never been there, which explained why Phoebe thought her dad was a no-show."

Despite his desperate attempts to maintain an impassive, unimpressed expression, there was more than a flicker of fear on Don's face.

"Still, you didn't want to leave anything to chance with the cops sniffing around, so you came up with a foolproof plan," Sandra accused. "You knew Burt Denning was dying and facing severe financial difficulties, so you arranged a secret, out-of-the-way meeting with him to propose a hypothetical situation. How far would Burt be willing to go to ensure his daughter received a college education and a shot at a good life after Burt was gone? It turned out he would do anything, even go down for a murder he did not commit. He loved Chloe so much and wanted to provide for her, so you two struck a deal. Burt would take the fall for Ellie's murder and live what little time he had left behind bars so Chloe could go to college for free with your bogus scholarship."

"There was just one complication," Maya interjected. "There *was* a witness. Ewan Murphy must have seen you slipping out of the supply closet after strangling Ellie. When Sandra and Lucas stumbled across the body and raised the alarm, Ewan knew immediately it was you who had killed her. But instead of going to the police, he came directly to you because you were his ticket out of his own financial hardships. Ewan was willing to forget what he saw if you paid up. Ewan's wife, Beverly, told us he had been crowing about a financial windfall he was going to get very soon. But you had no intention of ever paying him off. He was too much of a loose end. He could always come back demanding more and more money; it would be an endless cycle, one you had to avoid. So you surveyed Ewan's house, spotted the security camera across the street, and blacked out the lens with this paint. You waited for Beverly to go shopping so Ewan was alone working up on the roof. You climbed the ladder, probably tried sneaking up behind him to give him a good shove, but he must have seen you coming and a struggle ensued, which would explain your injured shoulder. But in the end, you got him. He probably slipped and fell off the roof to his death. He was finally out of the picture and could never expose you."

"Now all you had to worry about was Burt Denning holding up his end of the bargain and keeping his mouth shut until he passed away from his cancer," Sandra said solemnly.

"Which he would have, if you two didn't stick your noses where they don't belong!" Don belted out, eyes wide with fury. There was no point denying it any longer. They had him dead to rights. The shoulder injury, the scratches, the prerecorded Zoom meeting. The can of paint. The evidence was insurmountable.

Maya pulled out her phone. "I'm going to call Detective Hart."

Cornered, Don dropped his hand into the trunk where the first aid kit was stored and yanked out a semiautomatic pistol.

Sandra, spotting the weapon gripped in his hand, threw herself into Maya to push her out of the way. "Maya, watch out!"

Don fired, and a bullet whizzed past Sandra's ear as the two women dove for cover. Don fired again and again, a hail of bullets flying all over the parking garage. Ducking behind a gray Nissan, Maya was on with 911 as Sandra peeked out from behind the fender to see Don stomping around, desperately searching for them. Within seconds, he would be right on top of them.

Sandra popped out one of her earrings and hurled it across the parking garage, where it smacked against the taillight of a Volkswagen, distracting Don, who wildly fired another round in that direction. They heard a clicking sound. Don was pulling the trigger, but he was out of bullets. Maya cupped a hand over her mouth as she whispered their location to the 911 dispatcher.

Suddenly, they heard a whirring sound. Don had returned to his damaged Tesla and was now trying to get away. He zipped past their hiding place and turned a corner. Assuming the coast was clear, Sandra emerged only to be surprised by the Tesla spinning back around, speeding right at her. Don was hell-bent on running her down.

Sandra whipped around and started running as the Tesla bore down on her. Maya hurled her phone like a Red Sox pitcher and it cracked against the windshield of the Tesla, startling Don, who lost control of the vehicle and plowed into a cement post, deploying the airbags and trapping him inside, his nose bloodied from the impact.

Maya ran over to Sandra, who was bent over, out of breath. "Are you okay?"

Sandra nodded, finally catching her breath. "At least I got my steps in today."

Maya erupted in laughter, and the two women hugged as they heard the faint sound of police sirens approaching from a distance.

# Chapter 47

$M$aya and Sandra anxiously gripped each other's hands as they sat in the fourth row left of center in the Hannaford Hall at the University of Southern Maine campus, watching the exciting conclusion of the State Spelling Bee Competition, the winner of which would represent the great state of Maine in the national competition.

It was down to the wire. There were only two students left standing and both of them were from the same school.

Annabelle Chastain-Wheeler and Rocco Fanelli.

Both had been last-minute additions to the roster of contestants. After Don Talbot's arrest, his daughter, Phoebe, had dropped out of the competition, so the runner-up, Rocco, was selected to take her place. As for Annabelle, she had been unceremoniously disqualified after it was revealed she had left the threatening note in Rocco's locker. There was a flurry of apologies and requests for a second chance. Both her fathers, Doug and Noah, had gone to the school board to make one last-ditch effort to get their daughter reinstated, explaining they had put undue pressure on her to perform well, and what had happened was all their fault, Annabelle was just trying to make them proud and did not think through the ramifications of her actions.

When the majority of the board members remained unmoved, Doug and Noah wrote a big check for a new, Olympic-size swimming pool at the school. Principal Munn at first refused, claiming it was a blatant attempt at a bribe, but the school board desperately wanted a middle school swim team, so they were more inclined to cave and allow Annabelle back into the spelling bee, satisfied she had learned a very valuable lesson. Munn had stood her ground, but Rocco and the whole Fanelli family showed up at the next school board meeting and announced they had no ill will toward Annabelle or her family, and had no problem with her competing. So, much to Doug and Noah's elation, Annabelle was allowed back in the spelling bee.

One positive development was the friendship that had developed between the two spellers. They had clearly bonded, and when Sandra went backstage to wish them both luck before the competition, she found them practicing together with their flash cards. Rocco gave Annabelle the word "chrysanthemum" and she rolled her eyes. That was an easy one. She told Rocco they planted them every spring in her dad Noah's garden when the weather got warmer.

"C-h-r-y-s-a-n-t-h-e-m-u-m," Annabelle rattled off confidently.

Rocco aced all of the words that Annabelle threw at him as well. Vivacious. Pneumonia. Flamboyant. He was on a roll. Spelling them perfectly one right after another.

So now it was down to the two of them, and there was a palpable tension in the air. Both families, the Fanellis and the Chastain-Wheelers, were on the edge of their seats in the front row, focused squarely on the two kids onstage. One of the judges at the table set up downstage right picked up a card with the next word.

This one was for Rocco.

"Equilibrium," the judge read from the card.

Rocco squeezed his eyes shut, bit his bottom lip, and concentrated, spelling the word in his head.

There was absolute silence in the auditorium.

Then, Rocco popped his eyes back open. "E-q-u-i-l-i-b-r-i-u-m. Equilibrium."

"That is correct," the judge crowed.

There was thunderous applause from the enthusiastic audience, especially Maya and Sandra and the whole Fanelli family.

It was up to Annabelle now.

If she spelled her next word correctly, the competition would go into a lightning round. If she misspelled it, Rocco would be the state champion.

It was a nail-biter.

The next judge picked up her card and said the next word. "Chrysanthemum."

Sandra exhaled.

Annabelle had this one in the bag. She had just practiced it minutes before the competition.

Annabelle tapped her foot nervously on the floor of the stage, flicking her eyes over to her two fathers, who smiled and nodded encouragingly.

Then, she looked at Rocco, who gave her a look that said, *Don't worry, you got this.*

Annabelle leaned into the microphone. "C-h-r-y-s-a-n-t-h-e-m . . ." She paused before quickly adding, "e-m. Chrysanthemum."

The judge frowned. "I am afraid that is incorrect. Rocco, you are the new Maine State Spelling Bee Champion."

Doug and Noah both deflated.

Annabelle turned and marched off into the wings as a triumphant Rocco ran to the edge of the stage, where his whole family was jumping up and down with joy and the entire audience cheered his victory.

Twenty minutes later, Maya and Sandra made their way backstage to congratulate Rocco. The Fanelli family was still excitedly buzzing about Rocco's big win. Sandra noticed a more subdued Annabelle with her two fathers. When Doug and Noah were suddenly distracted by some school board members, no doubt wanting to talk about the new swimming pool, Sandra seized the opportunity to approach Annabelle.

"You did great out there, Annabelle," Sandra said. "Coming in second in the whole state is not too shabby."

"I got nervous. I lost focus. I messed up. Those are the breaks."

"Don't beat yourself up. Chrysanthemum is a difficult word to spell," Sandra said before adding,

"For most people. But it should've been easy for you."

Annabelle gave her a puzzled look.

Sandra folded her arms. "I saw you practicing with your flash cards backstage with Rocco. He gave you the word 'chrysanthemum' and you spelled it perfectly. And then, remarkably, that was the word you got during the competition and you spelled it wrong."

"Like I said, I was nervous. All those people watching, the lights in my eyes, it just got to me and I blew it. It happens."

"Not to you. I have never seen you suffer from stage fright. You are a tough competitor. You misspelled that word on purpose so Rocco would win. Why?"

Annabelle shrugged, staring at the floor.

"Was it because of the pressure your dads put on you to win? Did it just get to be too much?"

Sandra did not expect Annabelle to answer her. But she knew she had nailed it on the head.

Annabelle finally looked up at Sandra, tears in her eyes, and whispered, "Please don't tell them what I did. They're already so disappointed I lost."

"They will never hear it from me. I promise you, Annabelle," Sandra reassured her.

Doug and Noah ambled over.

"Want to go out for pizza, sweetheart? We need to celebrate," Doug said, putting his arm around her and squeezing her tight.

"But I didn't win," Annabelle muttered.

"You came in second. That's quite an accomplishment and we could not be prouder," Noah said, winking at Sandra. "Daddy Doug and I feel as if we won too because we hit the jackpot and got ourselves an incredibly smart and kind and beautiful daughter."

Sandra beamed as she watched Doug and Noah each take one of Annabelle's hands and lead her down the hall toward the exit as she happily skipped along.

They had no idea just how smart and kind their daughter Annabelle was. She turned to see Rocco's parents thanking Maya profusely for solving the case so they could enjoy this wonderful moment. Sandra got emotional, observing the euphoria on Rocco's face, and she knew deep down, despite the fact that Annabelle had intentionally misspelled a word, if the competition had continued, given the fire in his eyes, the determination to make his family proud, Rocco Fanelli still would have come out on top.

Of that she had no doubt.

# Chapter 48

The weather gods were kind to the SoPo High School Class of 2024 for their graduation ceremony, held outdoors on a beautiful June afternoon. The sun was shining and there was a cool breeze in the air as the students, decked out in their blue and gold caps and gowns marched single file past friends, family, and faculty, all applauding warmly, to take their seats down front. Principal Caroline Williams stepped up to the podium on the stage that had been set up to welcome everyone and make some introductory remarks.

In the fifth row behind the students, a beaming and excited Burt Denning sat on the end, next to Maya and Max. Burt had nearly clogged up the procession of graduates when he jumped out in the middle of it to snap photos of Chloe as she passed by. At the sight of her relentlessly proud shutterbug father's disruption, Chloe turned a deep shade of red as Ryan and Vanessa, who were marching behind Chloe, erupted into a fit of giggles. She frantically gestured for Burt to sit back down and stop embarrassing her.

On the other side of Burt was Lucas Cavill, who sat next to Sandra. Stephen sat on the opposite side of his ex-wife and their older son, Jack, up from Boston.

Max noticed in the row opposite them sat Phoebe Talbot, there to support her older brother, sitting next to an attractive blond woman in her midforties with a sun-kissed face and a smart white suit. He leaned over to Maya. "Who's that?"

Maya casually glanced over. "Don Talbot's sister. From what I heard, after Don's wife died, she tried to become more of a part of Cooper and Phoebe's lives—they've always adored her—but Don wasn't interested. He was afraid she'd spoil them and make them soft, so she finally gave up and moved to California. But she came back to Maine the minute Don's arrest hit the news to look after the kids while their father deals with his mountain of legal woes and upcoming murder trials."

They watched as Cooper cranked his head around and waved at his aunt and sister.

Both of them happily smiled and waved back.

Cooper had been given a reprieve after a make-up test and some extra credit work and would now be allowed to receive his diploma.

Burt turned to Maya and Max. "So Chloe's going to be in the first group called to receive their diplomas, right? Denning is a 'D,' pretty much near the front of the alphabet. I just want to make sure I don't miss the moment."

Maya patted his knee. "Don't worry. It's a long walk across the stage. You'll have plenty of time to capture it for posterity."

Burt was practically bursting with pride. He could barely contain himself. Maya had delivered the promising news to him when they had arrived for the ceremony that she had spoken to Detective Hart just that morning. Hart was not yet fully willing to commit, but she did hint that after all the facts came to light, she might decline pursuing charges against Burt for his false confession. It was hardly a done deal, but Maya remained hopeful. Burt had already returned all the money he had received in his bank account from Don Talbot and was back to being broke. Chloe's future college plans were in doubt again, but he was adamant that he would work double shifts, pick up a nighttime job, and scrape together the necessary funds so Chloe could attend a state university; maybe not in the fall, but with any luck, the following semester, in January.

As for Rudy Holmes, he had been welcomed back with open arms by the school board, which issued a very heartfelt apology. This was due to a stern rebuke from Sandra, who punctuated that everyone is innocent until proven guilty, and that the board would be wise to remember that constitutional right in the future lest they find themselves embroiled in an expensive lawsuit. Whatever the politics involved, Rudy was ecstatic to be able to finally return to his old job.

Principal Williams was just wrapping up her opening remarks. "And now, although this is not in your program, I would like to take this opportunity to introduce Sandra Wallage, our former PTA president, to award a very special scholarship. I know this is a bit unusual, but we did not have time to include this honor at our awards banquet last week because it had not fully come together yet. So, if you will indulge us, ladies and gentlemen, please welcome Sandra Wallage."

Maya arched an eyebrow, confused.

Sandra had not given her a heads-up that she would be speaking. The audience clapped their hands, with Ryan hooting and hollering as Sandra took to the stage, stepped behind the podium, and spoke into the microphone.

"Thank you," Sandra said, waiting for the applause to subside. "While academic excellence is undoubtedly important, we cannot forget the significance of a student's potential and moral character. After all, grades only measure a narrow aspect of a person's abilities and talents and do not always accurately reflect their potential for success. Academic scholarships based solely on grades can create a biased system that often favors those who have access to better resources and support rather than those who have the potential and drive to succeed but may have faced certain challenges or obstacles in their lives, who possess character qualities such as determination and resilience. By recognizing these traits, we can provide financial support to students who have excellent potential but may not have a perfect academic record. With this award, we can encourage and promote positive values and behaviors among our students and perhaps have a profound impact on our community and society as a whole. We need leaders who are not only academically talented but who also possess strong values, such as honesty, integrity, and compassion. So thanks to the generous contributions of some like-minded donors, I am thrilled to announce today, the recipient of the very first South Portland High School Character Excellence Scholarship . . . Chloe Denning!"

Her fellow students went wild as a tearful Chloe made her way to the stage to hug Sandra and accept her award trophy, which had been bought at the last minute and had not yet been engraved with her name. It did not seem to matter. The real prize was tuition for a four-year college education. Burt, caught off guard, fumbled for his camera. Max was quicker and managed to snap a slew of shots with his own camera that he could later text to Burt.

After a few more speeches, it was time for the valedictory speech. As Principal Williams introduced Vanessa, Maya and Max gripped hands. This was it. This was the big moment Vanessa had been working so hard for. Vanessa, a foot shorter than Principal Williams, adjusted the microphone downward and got some feedback. Maya took a deep breath and closed her eyes, waiting for Vanessa to begin.

"Fellow graduates, distinguished faculty, honored guests, and classmates . . ." She paused and looked down at her note cards. Almost as if she had already lost her place.

Silence filled the air.

Vanessa bowed her head and then looked up again to speak. "As I stand here today, I can't help but feel an overwhelming sense of gratitude and appreciation for those who have helped me reach this point. But there is one person in particular who I want to honor and acknowledge today . . . my father, Max Kendrick."

Maya shot a look over to Max, whose mouth dropped open.

"As many of you know, my father has been through a lot, including a stint in prison. I know this is a difficult topic to discuss, but it's an important one. When my father went to prison, he could easily have given up. He could have allowed his mistakes to define him and his future. But he didn't. He took responsibility for his actions and worked hard to better himself. He attended classes and workshops, learned new skills, and focused on his personal growth. When he was released last year, he was a changed man, with a newfound sense of purpose and direction. He was determined to be a better father, a better husband, and a better person, to work hard every day, to provide for his family and to be a positive influence in our lives."

Max squeezed Maya's hand harder as tears streamed down his cheeks.

"But he couldn't have done it alone," Vanessa continued. "My mother was there every step of the way. She was his rock, encouraging him, believing in him, even when he didn't believe in himself. She held our family together during the toughest of times and I am forever grateful for her love and strength."

Now it was Maya's turn to cry. Sandra handed some tissues down the row so she could dab her eyes.

"My parents have taught me that no matter how

difficult life can be, we all have the power to choose how we respond to it. With hard work, dedication, and a strong support system, anything is possible. So to my father and mother, to all the other parents and guardians here today who have faced their own challenges and come out stronger on the other side, thank you! Thank you for being the role models and inspirations that we so desperately need in our lives."

Max and Maya were completely overcome, hanging on to each other. Maya turned her head in Sandra's direction, and the two women exchanged a knowing smile. Life was about to change. They were going to be empty nesters; all their children would be out in the world, on their own. It would take time to adapt to this new normal.

After Vanessa finished her speech and rejoined her classmates, Maya noticed Stephen resting a hand on Sandra's knee while he proudly watched Ryan lining up with his fellow students to receive their diplomas, waiting for his name to be called. Sandra's eyes flicked down at Stephen's hand squeezing her kneecap, and she very casually removed it. Then she reached out and took Lucas's hand in hers, and they playfully leaned into each other, bumping shoulders.

A warm feeling washed over Sandra.

Life was changing in so many different ways.

And she found herself suddenly excited about all the possibilities that lay ahead.